W9-AVW-848

---- ★ ----

I placed my feet and took another few steps upwards off the ledge, but stopped when I heard Marmalade above me, hissing and spitting and shrieking. I'd never heard her do that before. I couldn't see her anymore. Instead, I saw something very big and very dark against the bright sky, something that appeared to jump out over the edge of the cliff and then hurtle toward me. I saw a blur of green. Instinctively, and that instinct probably saved my life, I threw myself flat against the rock, banging my nose in the process. The harness pulled me up tight and then dropped me a sickening foot or two back toward the ledge.

Scott must have been scrambling to get out of the way himself.

Something heavy slammed against my shoulder, and the afternoon went into slow motion. I will have a bruise there tomorrow, I thought. Then I thought, I'm glad I saw it coming so I could get mostly out of the way. Then I wondered where the awful screaming was coming from. It sounded very close.

It was me.

---- ----

Previously published Worldwide Mystery titles by
FRAN STEWART

ORANGE AS MARMALADE
YELLOW AS LEGAL PADS

My Gratitude List

Patty Glenny and Cindy Pitts own The Singin' Bean Coffee House & Eatery in downtown Lawrenceville, Georgia. Surrounded by happy groups of people, I often sit there sipping coffee and writing about murders.

My sister, Diana Alishouse, serves as my main resource for information about bipolar disorders. Glaze is a better person because of Diana. Diana is also one of my group of early readers who routinely put up with my chaotic approach to writing a book. Darlene Carter and Millie Woollen are the other members of that elite coterie. I owe all three of them profound gratitude.

Father Brendan Doyle and Ginny Pope at St. Marguerite d'Youville Catholic Church in Lawrenceville most generously gave of their time to help a non-Catholic understand the details necessary to create a living character. You'll have to imagine the brogue as Father Doyle reviewed what I had written and told me, "Now, now, Fran. You simply must capitalize the Mass."

Brandon Davis, my contact at Vision Paper, a company that manufactures kenaf paper, fielded a barrage of emailed questions. He informed me that he was very sorry, but I would not be able to hide a murderer in a kenaf field in early May, since the plants wouldn't be tall enough yet. Ah well, rewrite again....

This is a work of fiction, but there is one character in this book (the short man) whose description I lifted as closely as I could from Bill Coolidge, a dear friend of mine. His face was just too memorable to pass up. The major difference between my character and Bill is that Bill had one of the sweetest dispositions I have ever known, coupled with a wry and self-deprecating sense of humor. Two weeks before he died, he emailed me that he was "so pleased to be immortalized, and in a murder mystery, no less."

Dan Barber, philosopher and master mechanic at AutoStop in Buford keeps my car running smoothly. He took me seriously when I asked him about the car stuff that ended up in *Green*.

Judy Edens, one of the delightful women in my tap and jazz class, gave me the best line in the dance class scene. And Anne Hammer told me about falcons and reindeer.

The wonderful staff of holistic healers at Loving Touch Animal Center in Stone Mountain confirmed that the ending as I wrote it was possible.

Librarians are often on my gratitude lists. My library experts, particularly Liz Forster, Vicki Parsons, and Joe Sewell, work at the Forsyth County Libraries. Vicki and Joe gave me invaluable advice about how librarians processed books before computers became the norm.

Pam Ledbetter, co-publisher of *Accent Gwinnett Magazine,* agreed to let me use information from a delightful article by Alec Young in the September/October 2004 issue. Mr. Young interviewed Tom McGee, a longtime resident of Lawrenceville, in a piece called "A Walk with McGee." I adapted his story about parallel parking and put it into the mouths of Rebecca Jo and Sadie.

My editor, Nanette Littlestone, deserves a standing ovation at least. Her stringent attention to detail has never kept her from seeing my vision for these characters, for this series. She knows how to be exacting and still be kind. No wonder her business is called The *Right* Word.

And to the wonderful crew at Doggie in the Window Publications, how can I thank you enough for your patience and encouragement? You are frequently on my daily gratitude list.

Naturally I take full responsibility for any errors in fact or judgment that may have crept into this book. I was probably sitting out by the creek when that happened, if indeed it did.

I wish you good reading always and all ways,

Fran Stewart
from my house on the back side
of Hog Mountain in Georgia
April 2005

Part I
The Fall
Mid-June

ONE

THERE WERE THREE Diane Marie's in Martinsville. One of them I liked. One of them I hardly knew. One of them I hated. And now one of them was dead.

Today started off in such an ordinary way. But now I, Bisque McKee (Biscuit to most people), Martinsville's librarian, was clinging to a cliff, staring at Diane Marie Ames's body forty feet below me. I married Bob Sheffield, the town cop, six weeks ago. I thought I was going to live a quiet life. For someone who likes gardening and staying home with her cat…

My name is Marmalade.

…I'd had more than enough of my fill of excitement.

Just before noon, my twenty-two-year-old son, Scott, who had flown in from Alaska to attend my wedding and who had extended his visit indefinitely, drove down the valley from his grandmother's house and walked in my front door. "Hey, Mom," he said, "do you want to go on an adventure?"

I like adventures.

"An adventure?" I asked. Marmalade pranced around my ankles, rumbling her loud purr. Sometimes I almost think she understands what I'm saying…

Mouse droppings!

…because she purrs so endearingly at all the right times, as if we were talking to each other. It's very comforting.

"Yeah," Scott said. "An adventure. It'll be lots of fun."

"Like the time when you were nine and we went up into the high meadow and looked for snakes?"

"Oh, Mom, they weren't poisonous." He grinned. "You learned a lot of new stuff."

Scott really believes in learning. In large part, I had to admit, because I'd taught him that people need to keep expanding their knowledge all their lives. Stretches those brain cells. Keeps them active and vibrant. Me and my big mouth.

Scott escorted me up the hill to the base of the cliff that overlooks Martinsville. Eventually I asked him, "Are you sure this thing will hold me? What if I fall?" I put my hands up against what, from a distance, had looked like a solid rock wall. This close, though, I could see the knobs and fissures and cracks and dents. Surely a cliff that had been standing here for thousands of years wouldn't collapse on me or break apart in my hands.

"Mom, just trust it, okay?" Scott leaned back against his end of the rope. "You're not even off the ground yet."

"That's easy for you to say. This is scary, Scott."

"Of course it is. So what?"

So what, indeed. I was, after all, the one who had agreed to try rock climbing. I just had not envisioned such a steep first attempt. Tightening my hold on a projection at about shoulder height, I looked down so I could place my feet, shod in an extra pair of Scott's climbing shoes, on a likely bump. As I pulled myself up a good three inches, Scott leaned back so the harness I was wearing snugged up, ready to support my weight.

"Great, Mom. Now try a real step, and don't try to pull yourself up with your arms like that. You'll get exhausted. Use your feet. Those shoes grip the rocks. Make them work for you."

Right.

"Go on, Mom. It'll be fun. You'll see."

Fun. Right.

"Mom?" He didn't sound worried as much as puzzled. Even as a baby he'd had no fear. He would climb up anything, over anything, into anything, and always came up laughing. Maybe laughter would help in this case.

"Tell me a joke, Scott, so I'll relax."

"Okay, why *did* the chicken cross the road?"

"I don't know. Why *did* the chicken cross the road?"

"To get to the other side."

"Scott, that's not even funny." But I laughed as I said it.

"See, Mom, it worked. A corny old joke and you laughed, anyway. Here's one more. What did the prosecuting attorney ask the defendant in Fairbanks?"

"I give up."

"Where were you on the night of October to April?"

Before I had a chance to register that as an Alaska joke, Scott ordered me again. "Take a big step."

I found a spot for my right foot. There was a crack, and if I wedged my foot into it sideways, I could… No, I couldn't.

"Quit thinking about it, Mom, and just do it. Push with your left foot, and as you do that, shift your weight onto the right foot."

"Oh! Hey, this works!"

"Sure does. Now you're up about two feet. Only fifty or sixty to go."

"Thank you for your encouragement, kind sir." I looked for another foothold, moved my hands higher, grabbed a likely rock that jutted out from the cliff face and pushed with my right foot. Yes! What fun! I was forty-nine years old and I was rock climbing!

Before he strapped me into the harness, Scott had free climbed—without any rope holding him from above—and tested the bolts already in this section of cliff. He knew the cliff well. He'd learned his craft here, starting when he was eleven, when we gave him rock-climbing lessons.

We weren't very far out of town, since the huge L-shaped cliff paralleled Martinsville on the west and shut off the bottom of the little dead-end valley. The Metoochie River ran from north to south through a narrow gap in the short arm of the L, and our small town nestled between the river and the L's long arm. Martinsville was at the bottom of what we called the Upper Valley of the Metoochie. That part of the valley contained six little towns, one of which was the county seat for Keagan County, the smallest county in the state of Georgia. In fact, it was so small, most Georgians didn't even know it was here.

There was another town called Enders, just a short way

down the river from Martinsville, but a good seventy miles away by road, at the top of what we call the Lower Valley of the Metoochie, tucked into the side of another one of these cliff-enclosed hills. The cliffs that surrounded it were even steeper and higher than the one here in Martinsville, and the only way to reach Enders was the long way around. As my Grandma Martelson always used to say, you can't get there from here. These cliffs extended the whole length of the valley, so anyone who wanted to go anywhere had to drive twenty-five miles up-river to Russell Gap (where there was a big breach in the cliffs) before they could turn west, away from the river.

There were a few places in this Upper Valley, between here and Russell Gap, where the cliffs gave way to gentle uplands with lovely meadows. Some of the families along the river maintained small farming fields there, mostly for growing kenaf, an annual crop used for making paper. Saved trees. I kind of liked the idea of saving forests, and using fewer chemicals in the paper production process. The kenaf stalks had glorious bright yellow flowers on them, but I had to give up on the idea of planting any in my garden. Those plants grew fifteen feet in a single season. When all the talk about growing kenaf first started a dozen or so years before, most of us in the Upper Valley were afraid it would turn out to be the newest version of kudzu. It took a lot of meetings and a lot of convincing before we came to see that the growing season simply wasn't long enough for it to set seed. So our land was safe. Gradually the local farmers planted one field, then two, then more in kenaf. And within six years, Keagan County was one of the top producers of kenaf in the southeast. A great deal of the land above the valley-long cliff was dedicated to kenaf growing. The fields, tucked into the hollows of the land, stretched back a mile from the cliff edge. Surprisingly, though, there was no terrain up there near the cliffs that would allow for regular paved roads. The one road that meandered through the county giving access to the fields was more than a mile back from the cliffs. There were lots of places for hikers in these hills, since paths criss-crossed the forests that filled the uplands between the kenaf fields.

Rock-climbing clubs from the area claimed their regular spots all along the cliffs of the Upper Valley, but this particular cliff was gentler than the others. It looked plenty steep to my novice eyes, though. And so quiet today. We hadn't seen another soul. Just the two of us and Marmalade, who had walked here with us. She was prowling around at the base of the cliff. Her orange-and-white fur stood out against the gray of the cliff and the green of the weedy grass.

I am investigating the smells.

The bolts in the rock wall had been in place for years but were still holding strong. As Scott inched his way upward, he hooked his rope onto the rings of the bolts using little doohickeys called carabiners. This meant his rope was always connected to a spot no more than eight or ten feet below him, which he seemed to think was safe. The logical part of me knew he was well-trained. He'd been doing this for years and had always been safety-conscious, but it still looked pretty scary to me. If he slipped, he could fall as much as twenty feet before the rope would grab. Of course, he had me strapped into a harness below him, paying out the rope. Fat chance I could stop him if he fell. He weighed a lot more than I did. Eventually, however, he attached the line all the way to the top of the cliff. Scott was lithe and muscular. He made it look easy.

I stepped back far enough from the cliff that I could watch his ascent without putting too much of a crick in my neck. I heard a "whoopee!" from my ever-enthusiastic son and saw him haul himself over the rim of the cliff onto the flat rocks at the top. He stood up and looked around. I knew he could see all the way west across the kenaf field and north along the path that winds around it. The plants were still pretty short that time of year, maybe twelve inches or so. Kenaf reminded me of bamboo, but without bamboo's invasive habits. That meant that by July they would be twice my height. Scott turned and waved down at me. After a moment he started back down—an act of sheer guts as far as his mother was concerned. He was letting out the rope somehow or other so that he had control over the rate of his descent. He obviously didn't trust me to know what I was doing. He was being smart. His instructions had made sense when we were both standing on firm ground, but once he was up there, I hadn't a clue. His descent looked terrifying and terrific at the same time. How I longed to do that. Heck, I wanted to learn how to skydive, too, but I knew it would take me a long time to get my courage up to try that. It was one thing to think of jumping out of an airplane. Another thing to *do* it.

Now, I DANGLED from the rope he'd threaded through the rings, and he was attached to the other end, counterbalancing my weight. I was medium-weight, and at five-foot-ten Scott was a good three inches taller than I, so I knew I shouldn't worry. I worried, anyway.

"Mom, you're thinking again. Stop it and climb."

"Scott, what if…"

"Mom, let go of the rock right now and lean backward."

"What?"

"I mean it. Let go and lean out and see what happens."

So I did. To my surprise, the harness supported me. It felt kind of like flying, so I spread my wings.

Your arms.

As I leaned back in enjoyment, I glanced up toward the top of the cliff. I could see Marmalade peering over the edge at me. How had she gotten up there?

There is a steep trail nearby. It is not often traveled.

…Just a few minutes ago she was down here with us, watching me get harnessed up. I knew she was a remarkable cat, at least *I* thought so, but I didn't know cliff-climbing was in her repertoire.

I have many talents of which you are not aware. One of them is that I do things the easy way.

AFTER I PASSED the halfway mark, I saw a little ledge off to my right. It was two or three feet deep and five or six feet long. I edged over that way and stepped onto the end of it. I briefly considered lying down and taking a nap, but Scott would never have understood. Instead, I paused for a long breath and looked over my shoulder, across the trees that lined Fifth Street and hid the houses there from my sight. The scenery was a spectacular view of the steep cave-riddled hillside across the Metoochie River. I looked upward once more. Marmalade was still there. I could see her little head craning over the edge. I felt exhilarated. Energized. Exhausted. It seemed a shame not to keep going, though.

It had been quite a while since I'd hollered anything to Scott. I needed my breath for the climbing. These legs and shoulders of mine would be pooped tomorrow. To say nothing of my butt muscles. After the first twenty feet or so, Scott had stopped calling up encouragement to me since he seemed to understand that I'd gotten the hang of it, although I was climbing very slowly. I had to look at my feet to guide them to the available fissures and bumps, and I still had to watch my hands. But I was beginning to rely more on touch than sight, beginning to feel the rock.

I placed my feet and took another few steps upward off the ledge, but stopped when I heard Marmalade above me, hissing and spitting and shrieking. I'd never heard her do that before. I couldn't see her anymore. Instead, I saw something very big and very dark against the bright sky, something that appeared to jump out over the edge of the cliff and then hurtle toward me. I saw a blur of green. Instinctively, and that instinct probably saved my life, I threw myself flat against the rock, banging my nose in the process. The harness pulled me up tight and then dropped me a sickening foot or two back toward the ledge. Scott must have been scrambling to get out of the way himself. Something heavy slammed against my shoulder, and the afternoon went into slow motion. I will have a bruise there tomorrow, I thought. Then I thought, I'm glad I saw it coming so I could get mostly out of the way. Then I wondered where the awful screaming was coming from. It sounded very close.

It was me.

TWO

ONCE I QUIETED DOWN, I began to hear Scott calling me.

"Mom? Mom? Are you alright? Can you hear me?"

I nodded. I couldn't trust my voice.

"Mom, you need to climb down now. I can't help you, but I can talk you down. Mom, you have to let go with your hands. You're safe. Let go of the rock. Lean backward in the harness, away from the cliff face. Just feel with your feet. I'll lower you down very slowly. Just keep putting your feet against the cliff, each time a little lower. Start with your left foot. Your other left foot, Mom. You have to get off that ledge. Don't look down here. Whatever you do, Mom, don't look down."

Of course, I looked. From forty feet up in the air, a dead body looks somewhat unreal, but I recognized her lime-green shirt. It was Diane Marie. Diane Marie Ames. She was blonde. Several times over the past few weeks, I had seen her wearing that almost-fluorescent green shirt. The color stood out against the low-growing ground cover and the gray stones littered around the small lawn at the base of the cliff. Scott had moved off to one side. I guess he realized there was nothing he could do for her. There was a lot of blood. I could see it even from this far up.

When I got down, finally, Scott helped me remove the harness. We just stood there looking at each other for a moment.

"Are you okay, Mom?"

I took a quick inventory. My nose hurt. My shoulder ached. I felt light-headed and lead-footed. My head felt hot and my hands felt cold. "Yes," I said. "Yes, I am."

"What do we do now?"

As if I knew. I took a deep breath to try to calm myself. "What time is it, Scott?"

He looked at his super-duper impact-resistant waterproof climber's watch that told the time all over the world. "It's 2:38 p.m.," he said. "Why?"

"Because we'll have to tell what time this happened."

"Your nose is bleeding."

"Is it? Maybe that's why it hurts so much." I swiped carefully at my nose with the back of my hand. It came away red. I stared at my hand and couldn't quite figure out what to do with it now that it was bloody. Neither one of us wanted to turn around and look at the woman on the ground, but we did. And then we did what every mother/son duo probably does when faced with the sight of someone who has fallen to her death down a sixty-foot cliff face. We both gagged at the same time.

I STAYED WITH Diane Marie's body for an eternity while Scott ran to call for help. My teeth were chattering, so I turned aside to Scott's duffel bag where I had folded my blue plaid flannel shirt before I started climbing. Despite the early summer, this valley had much more moderate temperatures than a lot of Georgia, so I generally carried something long-sleeved with me anytime I left the house. That day its soft warmth was comforting. I stood there, not too close to the body since the ground was splattered with her blood, thinking that I was glad we weren't far from the houses on Fifth Street. Martinsville was built on a hillside, with five numbered tree-lined streets that paralleled the river. First Street wound right along the river, and the business district, if you can call it that, was the collection of buildings that lined the upper side of that street. There weren't any buildings between First Street and the river. In 1802 a serious flood washed away the houses there, and the decision was made to turn the land right beside the Metoochie into a town park. Naturally, there hadn't been a major flood since then.

There were connecting streets, named for various trees, that joined the five parallel streets. My husband, Bob, and I lived on

Beechnut Lane. The police station where Bob worked was in the town hall on Juniper, but Bob wasn't there that day. He was in Atlanta, meeting with his brother, Barkley. He was due back soon, but I didn't know exactly when. I hoped he would hurry.

I looked over at the body. She must not have known that Scott and I were climbing there. What I had seen looked like she took a running jump and leaped over the edge. I wondered who was going to tell her son that his mother was dead.

Scott will call the doctor, I thought. The doctor's office was on Magnolia Way, so it wouldn't take him long to get here. Just a few blocks. I kept up my mental inventory of the streets in the town. It was something to do. It kept me from looking back at Diane Marie. I couldn't stand the woman, but somehow...now... all her obnoxious bossiness seemed irrelevant.

Scott finally came back at a run, followed by Sharon Armitage who owned the Beauty Shop & Gift Store on First Street. She was carrying one of her crocheted afghans and some water and even her first-aid kit, but it was pretty obvious that those were superfluous. She took one brief look at the body, then turned to me and held out her arms. "Scott used my phone to leave a message for Bob," she said, "and he called Doc, too. Doc will take care of your poor nose when he gets here." That sounded good, but I figured he'd have more important things to consider than my bloody nose. Sharon was still holding me when Dr. Nathan Young pulled up in his old green Chevy. He took a quick look at Diane Marie's body before he walked in my direction.

Green shirt, green grass, green car, I thought. Green shirt, green grass, green car. Green shirt...

"Mom, you don't look too good."

The next thing I knew, Nathan and Scott turned me away from the body and sat me down with my head between my knees, a cold pack on my nose and a few drops of Rescue Remedy under my tongue.

BOB SHOWED UP not five minutes later. He took one quick look at me and made sure I was okay, and then he and Nathan turned all official, asking us what had happened.

Bob finally insisted that Scott and Sharon and I move far back from the body. That was fine with me. I was trying to ignore the whole situation, but the cliff behind them seemed to magnify the men's voices. Although they were speaking quietly, we could hear every word they said.

Nathan pointed to the ghastly-looking gash on the back of her head. "This injury doesn't fit with the way she landed."

"Assuming she fell without hitting anything other than Biscuit on the way down, but that would be hard with the way the cliff angles." Bob ran his hand over his jaw as if he could wring some answer out of it, and walked over to our little group. "Scott," he said, "tell me again exactly what you saw."

"I was watching Mom pretty carefully. She stops climbing, and I can't tell if she needs some advice about which angle to head up, but before I can say anything I hear Marmalade screeching like a banshee." Scott looked upward as if he expected to hear the sound again.

I hadn't seen Marmalade in all the furor, but it hadn't occurred to me until now to be worried about her. The scream had sounded angry to me, but what if she were hurt up there?

Scott echoed my thought. "Where is she, anyway?"

"We'll find her. Go on with what you saw," Bob prompted.

"When I look up, I see her, the woman that is, jump off the cliff. It all sort of went into slow motion."

Even though I still felt raw and shaky, I noticed that Scott kept bouncing back and forth between past tense and present tense. It seemed to reflect the state of his nerves.

He was silent for a moment. Bob's voice was very gentle when he asked, "Did you see her land? Did she fall straight down?"

"Yes. I mean no. Yes, I saw her land, and no, she didn't fall straight." Scott pointed upward, and we all followed his gaze. "She fell close to Mom and then hit that ledge just below where Mom was…and then I saw her sort of flip and topple over. I can tell she's headed straight for me, so I jump out of the way. It's hard because—" he pointed to the pile of climbing gear "—I was holding the ropes for Mom, and I'm trying to watch where I'm headed and keep my eye on that woman, all at the same time."

"Scott, can you remember how she hit the ledge?"

"What do you mean?"

"What position was she in when she hit?"

"Oh." I could see Scott's eyes go slightly out of focus. He looked like he was trying to call the picture of it to mind. "She was falling almost straight down. I don't know. She just sort of slammed into it. It was like for a split-second she was going to stay there. But she sort of crumpled and rolled and…and…" We all waited for him to continue.

"What happened then?"

I loved Bob's gentle voice.

"She—she bounced the rest of the way and…and landed face down…right where she is now."

Nathan shook his head and looked up at Bob, who motioned the doctor back toward the body. Of course, we could still hear what they were saying. Nathan shook his head again. "I'm no medical examiner, Bob, but I'd be willing to swear that she died immediately when she hit her head here in back. I'd say she hit it on the way down, and was dead before she reached the ground."

I watched Bob rub his hand back and forth across his five-o'clock shadow. He looked up at the cliff face, then down at the body.

Nathan kept talking. "The path up there is pretty solid. Also, it's well back next to the kenaf field. Nobody could trip and fall that far out over the edge."

"Yeah. It's fairly flat up there. She would have had to walk right to the edge to begin with."

Nathan nodded. "She may have fallen accidentally, or she might have jumped on purpose. If she wanted to kill herself, this is a pretty sure way of doing it."

I wondered idly if people who jumped like this ever had second thoughts on the way down. What a ghastly idea.

SITTING ON THE GRASS overlooking two men discussing a dead body was not my idea of a good time. Some of the people from the nearby houses had formed a small clump a little beyond where Nathan's car was parked. Bob seemed to be keeping an eye on them. Every once in a while they'd begin to edge closer, and he'd motion them back. I didn't want to see anyone or talk to anyone, so I turned away from them. I hoped they couldn't hear Bob and Nathan's conversation. I didn't think they could because they were talking among themselves.

I drank some water from Scott's canteen and then noticed a little anthill near my feet. Ants are amazing creatures, I thought. I watched one of them lugging a dead bug of some sort. The dead guy was easily three times as big as the ant. Each one of the other ants heading out from the hill paused and checked out the newcomer. I wondered if they used smell or some sort of chemical password to identify hill-mates? Did all ants look alike?

They were all the same color. They seemed about the same size, but surely their buddies could tell the difference? The food-bearer must have passed the test because the other ants continued on their way. I felt strangely aggrieved on that ant's behalf. They could have turned around and helped him.

Sharon leaned a little closer to me and whispered, "Father Ames is going to be pretty broken up about this. I wonder what his mother was doing up there in the first place?"

"Maybe she just wanted to take a walk," I said.

"Walk? Her? Ha! She doesn't walk anywhere. I've seen her all over town the past few days. You know how she visits all the shops when she's here? Just wants to give everyone a hard time, I suspect. But she always has her daughter drive her from one block to the next. She was down at the Beauty Shop just a little while ago, before I went home for a late lunch. Yep. I thought she wanted to make an appointment for herself—she could use a good trim if you ask me. Those fancy, schmantzy hairdos are a waste of time—"

"Sharon," I interrupted, "the woman's dead. Her hairdo hardly matters now."

"That's what I mean—look at her. She's a mess. What good

was it to have an expensive hairdo when she could have died just as well with one of *my* haircuts?"

Because there didn't seem to be a logical answer to that, I asked, "If she didn't want an appointment, what was she doing in your shop?"

"She wanted an appointment for Madeleine, that sweet daughter of hers. Well, Madeleine said she didn't want a haircut, but Diane Marie insisted. Told her that her hair was ugly and said she didn't like being embarrassed by a plain-Jane daughter. Yep. That's what she said, right out loud so everybody in the shop could hear. Can you believe it? If I'd been Madeleine, I would have killed her."

"Madeleine wouldn't do that."

"Well, honey, she looked like she wanted to. She turned around and stormed out of the shop. Like that was the last straw or something. I saw her run up the street. She left her mother high and dry." Sharon took in a deep breath and held it. "You don't suppose…" she said, "that she…could Madeleine have pushed her off?"

"Sharon! You're talking murder. Madeleine? Nonsense."

"I guess you're right," she admitted, "but you didn't see her face when she ran out of my shop."

"What did you do?"

"I quite happily told that woman that I didn't have any openings at all, even though that wasn't true. Ida cancelled her two o'clock perm and I didn't have anybody else on the docket, so I would have had plenty of time, but I didn't want to give that overbearing dictator the satisfaction. I came home for a late lunch instead. Her daughter must live through hell all the time." Sharon's face took on a rosy hue. "Here I am talking ill of the dead. I should know better. But it's exceedingly hard to think of anything nice to say about that woman."

We both glanced back toward the body. It *was* hard to think of anything nice to say about Diane Marie. Why, I wondered, was there such an injunction against saying anything negative about people who've just died? Were we afraid at some elemental level that they'd come back to haunt us? We *think* ill of the dead all the time; surely there wasn't that much difference. Wait—yes, there was a difference. Spoken words were stronger somehow. I made a mental note to start reading my gratitude list out loud every night. If I did, though, Bob might think I'd gone nuts. No, he'd understand.

He was shaking his head and gesturing up toward the cliff. It looked much more intimidating now than it had an hour ago. Taller and more formidable. Like it was brooding.

Sharon touched my arm. "Biscuit? Do you want me to get some more ice for your nose? You're looking a little peaked."

Peaked? I could imagine what I looked like, and peaked was a very kind word compared to how I felt. "No, thanks. I'll be fine." For want of anything better to do, we both looked back toward the body. "Maybe her son will think of something nice to say about her," I said. "Priests can always think of something nice to say, can't they?"

"That's funny," Sharon said.

"What's funny?"

"Not funny, just odd. When she came into my shop a little after one o'clock, she was wearing that horrible lime-green blouse—" Sharon pointed toward the body "—but her slacks were beige linen. Yep. I remember noticing them and wondering how she'd managed to buy something that was in good taste for a change."

Diane Marie's outfits instilled a fair amount of hilarity into the gossip circuit in Martinsville every time she visited. She was always drastically overdressed, with an excess of gold jewelry. Rings, bracelets, brooches, necklaces. Usually all at the same time. And the colors she wore were of the electric variety. I looked a bit closer at the body. Her legs and one arm stuck out from under the afghan—Sharon's afghan—that Nathan had draped over her. Legs encased in blue jeans, and no jewelry on that one arm.

Sharon grabbed my arm. "Do you think she was robbed? And then they threw her over the cliff to her death, the poor dear?"

I wondered if I should remind her that just a moment before

she had castigated the poor dear as an overbearing dictator, but decided against it.

Sharon called to Bob and Nathan and explained her robbery theory.

"How do you know who it is?" Bob asked her.

"Every woman in town would recognize that lime-green blouse," Sharon told him. "Yep. It stands out a mile away."

Bob glanced at me, and I nodded in confirmation. "We'll check around up top," he assured her. Of course, I knew darn well he'd been planning to do that, anyway.

At Bob's insistence, we left before the ambulance got there. That suited me just fine. The last thing I wanted to do was watch them turn that woman over. Nathan told me my nose was broken. He insisted I go straight to his office so he could X-ray it. "Why?" I asked. We already knew it was broken.

"I need to be sure the bones around your eye socket weren't cracked."

Oh, that was just dandy. "I'll call Polly and set a time later this afternoon. Right now I just want to go home and lie down." I wanted to find my cat before I did that.

"I'm going to walk up top to look for Marmalade," I told Bob.

"No," he said. "Don't do that. I need to get up there first. I'll look around for her."

Scott, who had been uncharacteristically silent for a long time, spoke up. "I could climb up and take a peek. See if I can spot her."

"No," Bob said again. "You two stay away from the cliff, the path, the kenaf field, the whole place." He didn't leave us much room for misinterpreting his instructions. "I promise you I will look for Marmalade. Now go on to Nathan's office, and I'll call you if I find her."

Nathan drove Scott and me to his office, X-rayed my head, found a hairline crack below my right eye. Taped it and told me not to bump it for a couple of weeks. Bump it? All I wanted to do was lie down and not move for a month or two.

THREE

EVEN THOUGH BOB had promised to call as soon as he found Marmy, Scott and I sat around staring at the phone and making sparse comments. When I couldn't stand it any longer, we went out looking for Marmalade, anyway. I carried my ice pack along with me and applied it to my nose at judicious intervals. We didn't go anywhere near the kenaf field. But we did walk up to the path at the top of Beechnut Lane that heads up into the woods. The trail wound its way past some lovely meadows with little copses of river birch and huge old tulip poplar trees. We searched the ground on either side of the path, and called out her name constantly. Well, maybe we got a little bit close to the kenaf field at the top of the cliff. Close enough to see Bob and Nathan far ahead of us on the path. Nathan must have gone back to help Bob search the area. Before they could turn around and see us, we scooted home.

I was almost frantic with worry about Marmalade. Scott tried to reassure me. "She's been in other scrapes before and always come out okay. She probably just ran off and now she's exploring or doing whatever cats do. She'll be home soon, and worrying about her won't help one bit."

My son sounded insufferably preachy, but I tried to listen to the reasonableness of it. He was right. Marmalade would be fine. I sat down at the kitchen table and looked out the bay window. I was feeling pretty rocky. I thought that I'd gotten over it, sitting there at the foot of the cliff for such a long time with Sharon, but now the horror of what I had seen came flooding back and my hands started shaking. I felt cold and stiff. I was glad I still had on that flannel shirt, but this cold was deeper than anything a comfy shirt could remedy.

"Mom, I don't want to leave you alone if you're not doing well."

"How about you? You saw it, too."

"Yeah, but I'm a man."

Before I could gather the words to tell him what I thought of that comment, he went on, "And I'm luckier than you. I didn't know her."

He was right. Maybe that was the difference. Even when Marmalade and I had found the body last year in the library, it was a stranger, and already quite dead by the time I got there. This was different. This was immediate. This was a woman I knew, even if I didn't like her.

"Here, Mom." Scott set a glass of water in front of me. All his life I'd been teaching him about the value of drinking plenty of water. I guess some of those lectures sank in. He had his own glass of water in hand.

"Thanks, hon. I'll be okay."

"If you're sure, I'd really like to get home." Home for him was my mother's house in Braetonburg. He'd been staying there ever since the wedding. I did wonder when he was going to make a decision about whether to go back to Alaska or stay here in the valley. Oh, well, he had tickets to some of the Olympic events in Atlanta, so he'd be around for another couple of months at least.

I watched him drain his glass. "I'll be fine, honey. I'm feeling particularly sticky and dirty. I want to take a long hot shower and get into some clean clothes." I stood up and hugged my son. My legs did a good imitation of rubber as I walked to the front door with him. He loped down to the curb where he had parked his grandma's car. She was spoiling him rotten, letting him use her car the whole time he was here. Of course, that's what a grandma was for, I thought as I had a fleeting vision of myself letting four-year-old Verity Marie draw with her markers all over the floor of the laundry room. I couldn't see anything wrong with that.

UPSTAIRS I TOOK OFF the blue flannel shirt and started to peel off my green polo shirt. It seemed to be stuck to my back. I knew I'd gotten a bit sweaty while tromping around looking for Marmalade, but this was ridiculous. I gave a tug, and the shirt came loose. Yuch! There was a wide streak of dark stuff down the back of the shirt from my shoulder almost to the waist. It had gone all dried and stiff and crusty. It wasn't bright red anymore, but I could tell it was blood. I swung the bathroom mirror back and forth so I could inspect my whole back. There didn't seem to be any cuts or scrapes. So how did I get all that blood on me?

I ran a sink full of cold water and dunked the back of the shirt in it as I thought. It took a while to scrub and dunk, scrub and dunk, but I got it mostly clean. Until I'd sent it through the washer, I wouldn't know if the stain was set in there permanently. Oh, well, I could always wear it for gardening if it was ruined. Too bad, though. This was the shirt I'd bought as part of a pair at Mable's. "His and Hers" shirts. But Bob wasn't all that enthusiastic about his shirt. I think he would have liked blue better. Maybe it was just as well since this half of the duo was ruined.

Everything I'd been wearing needed to go into the laundry, anyway, so I piled it all, including the sopping wet shirt, into the almost-full laundry hamper and jumped in the shower. Well, I didn't jump exactly. It was more like a slow crawl. My body was beginning to sprout an amazing collection of bruises here and there where I slammed into the cliff face. I'd seen the start of at least one black eye, maybe two, in the mirror over the sink. I felt an irrational anger at Diane Marie for having hurt me on her way down, but it lasted only a moment or so until it dawned on me that I was alive, and she wasn't.

Somewhat chastened, I let the water soak into me. I *loved* hot water when I was feeling grungy. I washed my hair, carefully avoiding any contact with my nose, and let the water course over me, rinsing all the aches and the horror away. No. Not quite all the horror. I could still see that poor woman's body sailing through the air toward me as a black outline against the white sky. Of course. That was where the blood down the back of my shirt had come from. It was hers.

As I TOWELED my hair dry, I wondered why on earth Diane Marie Ames, who was rich as the dickens and astonishingly self-assured, would want to kill herself? Every time I'd seen her she'd been pushy and abrasive, but from what I'd read in the paper, she was fairly well-known in Atlanta for her social gatherings and fundraising committees. Maybe she badgered people into donating money. Maybe she was nicer to people who weren't what she considered *inferior,* as I'm sure she had tagged me and probably everybody else in this little podunk town. Well, I liked this podunk place, and we had a lot of good people here. People like Diane Marie's son, the priest at St. Theresa's. I'm not Catholic, so I didn't know him well, but I'd seen him in the library many times, and he was always polite. More than polite. Father Ames was interested in other people and seemed to have a sense of humor reflected in his twinkly eyes. Anyway, Bob liked him a lot, so he had to be a good guy.

I thought back to the first time I'd seen his mother, Diane Marie. It must have been six or seven months ago. Sharon Armitage and I were talking outside the Beauty Shop, and we saw Diane Marie parading up the street, followed from store to store by a pleasant-looking young woman.

"That's Father Ames's mother," Sharon had whispered to me. "The one in the fluorescent colors. The shadow behind her is her daughter." Sharon crossed her arms and sighed. "Madeleine, the daughter, must live the life of a peon. Her mother is never nice to her."

"Oh, she can't be that bad," I whispered back.

"You haven't met her yet," Sharon said. "Just you wait."

My turn came too soon. A few days later I was in the library. I had just finished putting the final touches on a new sign for the reference area, and I looked up to see Diane Marie Ames walk in the front door. That day she was wearing a blazing outfit, a cross between a caftan and a tent. She looked like a ship in full sail. Wasn't there a culture that used to have red sails like that on all their boats? Hmm. I would have to look that up. Diane Marie stalked up to where I was sitting at the rolltop desk, pulling the quiet, rather mousy-looking Madeleine in her wake.

"Do you know anything about architecture?" she asked without preamble.

"Good morning, Mrs. Ames," I said, unwilling to give up the niceties. "I know a little. What can I help you with?"

"We need to settle a difference of opinion. I need a book about windows."

I glanced at her daughter, who shrugged her shoulders slightly. If Diane Marie hadn't turned to follow my gaze, Madeleine might have rolled her eyes. I could like Madeleine, I thought, but her mother was an obnoxious nitwit. "Windows?" I asked.

"Windows. The glass things," she enunciated. "Lucerne windows."

Fortunately, I recalled looking through a big coffee-table book of architectural photos only the week before, so I led the two women straight upstairs and right to the heavy volume. If Diane Marie was impressed with my efficiency, she gave no indication of it whatsoever.

"It's well-indexed," I told her. "You should be able to find what you need."

"You're the librarian. You find it," she said, inspecting my cotton blouse and calf-length skirt as she spoke. I felt like a bug under a microscope. "What I want," she went on, "is a picture of a lucerne window. I saw some in that town up the way as we were driving here, and I said they were lucerne windows, and my daughter, Madeleine, here…" She sounded so clinical, as if Madeleine were one of those bugs, too. I didn't feel quite so alone, then. "…said they were eyebrow windows."

I knew exactly which windows she was talking about. When I

first moved here, I walked around town and saw the funny little windows on the house that turned out to be the one I moved into just a couple of months ago. Elizabeth Hoskins' old house. I did some research on windows and found out that Bob and I were the only people in town with Queen Anne eyebrow windows. They lit the attic. I noticed the other day, though, that they were awfully dirty. It was going to take a long ladder to go up what amounts to three stories. Maybe they didn't need to be washed quite yet.

As I was thinking about that house, I leafed through the index to find the relevant photos. "Here they are," I said. "Madeleine is half right. The ones you saw—I assume you mean on the county courthouse building in Garner Creek—are called eyebrow *dormers*." I went on to explain to them that eyebrow *windows* were set into the wall, usually tucked up under the eaves. They were flat along the bottom and rounded on the top. The *dormers,* on the other hand, were on the roof. "The difference," I told them, "is that with *lucerne* dormers, the arched top of them is finished with a different material than the rest of the roof. With an *eyebrow* dormer—" I pointed to a different illustration in the book "—the roofing shingles form a wave that carries the same material over the arch above the window."

If you asked me, those eyebrow dormers looked more like eyelids than eyebrows. As if the roof was the head of a giant multi-eyed carnivorous dinosaur gazing down on the taxpayers going in and out of the courthouse. Downright creepy. Glad they went out of style. Dormers, not dinosaurs. Of course, *they* went out of style, too.

Before I could broach the topic of eyelids versus eyebrows, Diane Marie stuck out her chin, narrowed her eyes at me and ended up looking rather like one of those dormers herself. "How would you know?" she pouted. "You're only a librarian." She stalked down the stairs and out the front door. If she were a football player, she'd be an offensive tackle. If there had been an open window right there, I might have pushed her through it. Oh, nonsense! I wasn't like that. But the thought was still there.

That woman tweaked every button I had. I couldn't quite read the expression on Madeleine's face as she watched her mother descend the staircase.

Once her mother was out of sight, she turned to me. "I'm so sorry," she said. "Mother gets in a bit of a huff when she's contradicted."

"If that's a bit of a huff, I'd hate to see her when she's really angry."

Madeleine nodded her head and started down the stairs. "You've got *that* right," she said in a low voice. I didn't think she meant for me to hear her.

But my point was that I couldn't imagine why a woman as pushy as that would ever kill herself. She'd drive other people to drink, or maybe she'd make people think about murdering her, the way I had thought about it there in the library and every time I've seen her since. She simply *invited* rancor. Yes, she'd invite murder, but she'd never jump off a cliff. If she *did* want to kill herself, she'd use pills. She wouldn't want to mess up her neon outfits and her fancy hairdo. So—I wondered who killed her?

By this time my hair was almost dry and I was tired of thinking. I wrapped up in my fuzzy bathrobe and lay down across the forest green bedspread. Such a soothing color. I wondered idly if I would ever know what had led up to Diane Marie's death, but then, before I knew what was happening, I was sound asleep.

Part II
The Month Before The Fall

FOUR

Diane Marie's journal—Sunday, May 12th
*...I tried writing to my sister today, but it made no sense. I
wanted to tell her things I can't seem to say on the phone.
Nobody sees the real me, not even her. There is an undercurrent of anger in this old house. I can't even begin
to say what I want to say. So I threw the letter away. I'll
just have to keep going, one day at a time, but I don't know
how long I can stand this.*

Wednesday, May 15—Atlanta

MADELEINE HOUSTON AMES jerked the wheel ever so slightly to
the left as she maneuvered down the steep driveway, barely reg-
istering her passenger's words. "I don't know why they rebuilt
the house on this side of the hill," Diane Marie complained in a
noxious whine. "It's such an inconvenience to have to deal with
this slope every day."

Her daughter barely glanced at her. "I'm the one who has
to drive it, Mother, and you know perfectly well why they rebuilt it over here. It's because the rubble from the fires would
have taken too long to clear out." It was *not*, she thought, just
for your inconvenience, either. Madeleine always said some
variation of that theme in answer to her mother's almost daily
complaint. She was getting tired of hearing her carp about it.
Couldn't Mother just let bygones be good-bye and gone? Madeleine knew her father had been lucky to find this old treasure
of a house years ago. She loved the house. But she hated what
her mother was doing to it now, taking out walls and changing

bath fixtures. Adding lights everywhere. What was wrong with quiet, muted evenings? Why did everything have to be bright, bright, bright all the time? It gave her a headache. No wonder her father went on so many business trips and spent so many nights at his office. He'd had a cot installed in one of the back rooms. Madeleine envied him.

DIANE MARIE HEARD ONE of those quiet sighs from the driver's seat. Now Madeleine would be uncommunicative for the rest of the day. Having her around all the time was just like living alone. No company whatsoever. Diane Marie had to do all the talking herself. A slight smile played for a half second on her carmine-caked lips. Before she slipped on her sunglasses she glanced up into the mirror built into the car visor, and the smile faded. That color was wrong in the sunlight. It had looked perfect in the vanity mirror. She'd paid a minor fortune for light bulbs that were supposed to reproduce the exact effect of sunlight. Couldn't you depend on anybody nowadays? Remodeling the inside of the old brick house had been a nightmare. Contractors were so difficult. Even though they acted like they were listening to her suggestions, they'd go ahead and do it their own way. Then she'd have to fire them and find somebody else and go through it all over again. Conrad was no help whatsoever. She asked him to help, but he'd just sit there at the dinner table grinding his teeth. That's what she got for marrying a Yankee.

Madeleine said something, but Diane Marie interrupted with, "I have a right to be upset with General Sherman and his nasty fires. He's giving me a headache."

"Mother! It was one hundred and twenty years ago!"

"You don't understand me! All I'm saying—"

"All you're saying is what you've said every time I drive you up or down this hill, and I, for one, wish you would drop it."

Diane Marie peered into the mirror again and patted an unruly blond wave back off her forehead. Maybe after her roots were retouched she'd have the hairdresser take off another half inch. "You don't have to be so nasty when we're having a nice conversation. And when are you going to let Patrick color your hair? You know that mousy brown is an embarrassment. We Houston women have always been praised for our lovely locks. I don't know how I ever managed to raise a child who didn't seem to care. You probably got it from your father."

Diane Marie was used to her daughter's silence, so the lack of response didn't surprise her. It did annoy her, though. She stared at Madeleine, who looked to her left, to her right and back to her left again, then pulled out onto the broad avenue that wound through a still-quiet back street in Atlanta's Buckhead District.

"PATRICK, DARLING, YOU'VE worked your miracles again," Diane Marie gushed with just the right amount of emphasis on the second word. He was, after all, the only hairdresser she'd ever found who could tame her two cowlicks. Disgusting name for the way hair grew in swirls. Madeleine had inherited the same cowlicks, only hers made her limp hair bump up on the top of her head. Diane Marie glared briefly into the large, tastefully-lighted mirror where she could see Madeleine's reflection between two of the potted palms in the waiting area. Diane Marie felt her blood pressure mounting. She once had such high hopes for her daughter. Madeleine, though, wasn't pretty enough to catch a husband with her looks. She wasn't bright enough to snare one with any sort of feminine mystique. She certainly wasn't powerful enough to make her own way as a hostess of distinction. She hadn't even done well at college. Just enough to get by.

There was nothing, absolutely nothing, to be said for that child, except that at thirty-three, she was a convenient housekeeper and driver for her mother. Diane Marie and her husband had agreed to hire Madeleine to run the house. It was a way to finance her and still keep her at home. There was no telling what the child might do if she was out on her own. Probably starve to death. What could she do to support herself? This way, since she couldn't get a husband, she could at least have a job.

"She's completely hopeless," Diane Marie murmured, shifting her gaze back to her own reflection.

Patrick leaned a shade closer. "What was that, dear?"

"I was simply admiring your artistry, you darling man. Now I'm going to have to go buy some new outfits to do justice to this hairdo." Diane Marie tilted her head forward slightly and looked up at her hairdresser. She parted her lips and allowed the ends of them to curve ever so slightly upward as she pressed the usual large tip into his well-shaped hand. How many times, she wondered, did I have to practice this smile before it became automatic? Wide enough to look warm and inviting. Not wide enough to cause any wrinkles. Madeleine, on the other hand, used to smile in a broad, face-splitting, wrinkle-inducing grin. Diane Marie was proud that she had put a stop to that. If I can do anything for my daughter, she thought, I can be sure she survives her thirties with a face worth saving. Unfortunately, Madeleine refused plastic surgery. Stubborn child.

MADELEINE STUFFED HER notebook into her purse and stood up as her mother glided past the potted palm. The haircut was perfect, she noticed. At these prices, it should be. Madeleine resisted the impulse to reach up and smooth back her own wayward hair. Short of teasing it and coating it with hair spray, there was no way to coax her fine-textured mop into any semblance of style. It was so much easier just to let her hair hang its own way, but she felt vaguely threatened on these monthly excursions when she waited for Mother, surrounded by reminders that hair must be controlled, tamed, coaxed, bullied into behaving as the dictates of fashion prescribed. No, it wasn't worth it.

Madeleine was convinced that no matter how much her mother said otherwise, Mother would have been devastated if her daughter had been beautiful or witty or bright. Diane Marie Houston Ames was not one to brook competition in any form. She'd made Madeleine get rid of every pet she'd ever tried to bring home.

Mother's aversion to competition took many different forms, as Madeleine had learned years ago. She felt the beginning of a rueful grimace, but stuffed it. She couldn't stuff the memory, though. Madeleine had been in love once when she was in eleventh grade. His name was Geoffrey and he used to hang out at their huge old brick house after school, getting himself invited to dinner, unless Madeleine's parents had one of their important parties. He was funny and happy. He kissed her behind the carriage house when he was walking her home through the dogwood grove. That evening, as Madeleine took leave of her parents and their important dinner guests, she heard her mother say, "You know, Madeleine has a boyfriend now who always seems to be underfoot, just so I'll invite him to dinner. I think he likes my cooking much more than he likes Madeleine." She could have killed her mother in that instant. Remembering it now in the beauty salon, Madeleine had to tell her hands to relax, had to ask her breath to begin again.

MADELEINE HAD BEEN sitting all day, it seemed. Her rear end was beginning to object. First at the hair salon, and now here at yet another fashion boutique. She squinted at her mother's back, wondering how on earth the woman could bear to dress in such colors. That royal blue completely overpowered her. No wonder she wears so much makeup, Madeleine thought.

Other people's mothers were more muted, less ostentatious. How did they arrange that? Some quirk of fate to give Madeleine this particular parent. She watched her mother turn a few more times in front of the three-paneled mirror before stepping back into the dressing room. The next outfit was bright red, fire engine red, atomic explosion red. Ridiculous. That was followed by a purple monstrosity that could have stood up under its own power. Then came, wonder of wonders, a relatively tasteful pair of beige linen pants with a matching vest. Madeleine put her glasses on to take a closer look. Yes, the linen was fine. Unfortunately, it was paired with the most outrageous fluorescent blouse, an ugly yellowish-green that nobody sane would have pulled off the display. Madeleine removed her glasses which improved the sight a bit by blurring the edges. She wouldn't need them until she was ready to drive away from here.

The next time Mother came out, she was in orange—heinous orange, orangutan orange. It was a cross between a muumuu and a caftan. Mother, in concert with an adoring sycophant disguised as a sales clerk, had wound a fringed silk scarf around her neck. It did nothing more than emphasize the turkeylike wattle beginning to hang below her mother's aging chin. Yesterday that flap of skin had been the subject of a prolonged telephone discussion about the virtues of more cosmetic surgery.

Aging, my foot, Madeleine reminded herself as she picked a minuscule bit of lint off the lap of her beige cotton skirt. She'll probably live another thirty years. She pulled her notebook out of her purse and penned a sentence or two. That means I'll be sixty-seven before I'm free.

Madeleine didn't consider killing her mother more than five or six times a week, usually. Maybe a nice hanging this time, she wrote, with that orange scarf? Or cannibals on a South Pacific island? Bent low over her notebook so she could see what she was writing, she forgot to keep an eye on the dressing room door.

Mother's voice cut across her reverie. "I *said,* what do you think of this one?"

Revolting, obnoxious, of dubious parentage, appalling, offensive... "It's right in line with your usual taste, Mother."

"Thank you, dear. I thought so, too." She turned to the hovering saleswoman. "I'll take the orange caftan and the tan-and-green set." She paused a moment. "Maybe I should take the red, too. Or the purple? What do you think, Madeleine?"

Her mother didn't really want to know. "It's up to you, Mother."

"Well, of course it's up to me. You wouldn't know fashion if it bowled you over. Would you please sit up straight? What are you writing, anyway?" She turned away once again. "I simply cannot make up my mind. I'll take all of them."

Madeleine refrained from rolling her eyes. She didn't even clench her teeth. She watched with little emotion as the saleswoman scurried to wrap up the clothing in white tissue paper with tiny purple stripes—the store's signature design. It was a blessing that Madeleine's glasses were perched on top of her head. This way, the colors of the outfits, bright enough to be plastered on billboards—and wouldn't Mother look like a walking billboard when she was wearing them?—blended with the off-whites of the counter and the tan chairs, while the details and the precise expression of her mother's face were blessedly indistinct.

Madeleine had worn glasses ever since fourth grade. Looking back, she knew now that she needed them much earlier than that. She had a vivid memory of being in the bathtub on Halloween evening when she was seven years old. Someone had burst into the bathroom, cackling in a high-pitched voice. There was a swirl of a black cape, and as Madeleine began to scream, she lost her hold on the side of the tub and slipped under the water.

Why was she thinking of that now, she wondered, as she continued to watch her mother and the sales clerk. It must have been the colors that reminded her. She remembered being pulled from the water and scolded by her mother for getting her hair wet and for splashing Mother's black cape. Her mother was on her way to a grown-up costume party at Aunt Martha's house. Madeleine had cringed at the sight of her mother's face above the black witch's costume. Behind Mother, she could see the fuzzy outlines of the brightly colored towels against the fuzzy fern pattern of the bathroom wallpaper. She knew that when she stood close to the wall she could see the ferns distinctly, but from the tub they were simply a comforting blur. She needed comfort. She'd been so frightened by the sudden unidentifiable apparition that she had peed in the bath water. But she was afraid to tell her mother that.

She glanced at her notes. Maybe a nice axe murder would be better this time around. Or drowning. That would be poetic justice indeed. Madeleine stuffed her notebook back into her purse and stood up to take the packages. She halfway expected a conspiratorial look of sympathy from the sales clerk, but the woman was too well-trained to jeopardize her commission.

"I asked you what you're writing," Mother harped as they approached the car.

"Just some lists."

"Well, pay attention to your posture while you're doing it. I don't want to be embarrassed by a daughter who slumps. You'll get a dowager's hump if you're not careful, just like my sister, Martha. Put on your glasses. You're squinting."

"Thank you, Mother," Madeleine said as she opened the trunk and put the packages inside. Maybe she could stuff her mother in there, too. Now, wouldn't that be satisfying?

MADELEINE AMES HAD BEEN writing horror stories for years. She refused to use her middle name. She hated her middle name. Mother had saddled both her children with her own maiden name, as if she were stamping them, branding them "MINE." But Mother couldn't own what she didn't know about. Madeleine had a post office box in downtown Atlanta. That's where all the rejection letters came. She rented a storage space in an anonymous-looking facility where she stashed her boxed manuscripts and computer backups. Fifteen full-length novels, none of which had been accepted by publishers. But she'd hired a new agent last month. There was hope.

Her latest book, the one the agent was pushing now, was set in an old brick mansion in Atlanta at Christmas time. It was called *A Slaying Song Tonight*.

Her novels generally included a short blonde middle-aged female who suffered the most horrifying death imaginable. It was always painful. Sometimes she changed the woman's age or hair color just so she wouldn't feel she was in a rut with her writing. But the victim was always Mother. Always. The perpetrators tended to be young women, crazed into homicidal urges by the vicious actions of the victim. The murderers did the world a service by eliminating the vile blonde. The murderer was the *good* one. Always.

Madeleine hummed a few bars of *Jingle Bells* as she pulled out of the parking lot.

FIVE

Thursday, May 16—Martinsville

IT WAS SOMETHING as simple as the garden hose that gave me a great idea. Since I had mostly native species of plants in my yard, I didn't have to worry about irrigating and pruning and fertilizing, but I did make a point of watering the baby plants for the first year. So there I stood near the edge of the woods in my backyard, sprinkling the little *Pieris* that I'd transplanted just a few days before my wedding, and listening to the riot of birdsong in the trees. The idea sprang up like green ferns on a creek bank.

Bob was inside reading the paper. He still wasn't moving too fast after his close call in Savannah. He'd been in the hospital during much of our honeymoon, but he was doing much better, thank goodness.

Marmalade was snuffling around nearby.

Snuffling? I am not a pig. I am delicately sniffing the leaf mold.

Her purr-box began to resonate, and I wondered what she found so fascinating about the dead leaves.

The forest floor is very healthy and contains deep, pungent smells which you humans miss. You miss my conversation, too.

I remembered reading once about some scientist who was watching his dog sniff around one day and decided to see if people could track things, too. He had surprisingly good results, but the problem was that he had to get on his hands and knees and put his nose right down to the ground.

That makes a great deal of sense.

If I tried that I'd probably end up in a back brace, I thought, and that was when my great idea started. I wasn't nearly as flexible as I used to be, the thought said. Like a garden hose that's been coiled up all winter, I couldn't unwind easily. Cancel that, I thought. I didn't want to think about what I couldn't do. I wanted to think about my new idea. It wasn't like I had a lot of extra hours that needed to be filled. I kept busy three and a half days a week with my job as librarian, and then there was the new house—well, an old house, but new to me—to be arranged and painted and tidied and loved. And someday I'd have to clean out that attic—but not this year. And there were the gardens to be cared for.

You have me to feed, too. Some chicken would be a good idea. We can go inside now.

And, of course, time to spend with Bob.

Marmalade left what she was doing, looked in my direction and started back toward the kitchen door. I watched her idly. The idea wouldn't go away. It kept popping up and sat there waiting for recognition, waiting for the germ of it to be watered and lovingly tended. I'd probably look funny doing it. It was a dumb idea. Listen to me! I was already throwing weed-killer on my little green hope.

Doggone it! This was something I'd always wanted, ever since I was a little girl. So, why not just go ahead and do it?

I did finish watering the *Pieris* first. But then I wound the fat flexible green hose onto its reel and walked into the kitchen, leaving my shoes right inside the back door. I had to step over Marmalade. While I was at it, I figured I might as well give her a little snack. There was some leftover chicken in the fridge. I kept a little blue-ringed dish handy for just such occasions.

Thank you. I am glad you finally got my message.

Tank, the green-eyed gray-and-white kitten who had found me last week as I was leaving Savannah, woke up as soon as the fridge door opened, and by the time I put Marmalade's snack in the bowl, Tank was eyeing the dish. He knew better than to pounce on Marmy's food. She'd given him a couple of good-size swats the first day or two.

He needed the training.

At least he learned fast.

The faster he learns, the sooner he can leave.

He probably thought Marmalade was his mother.

I am not his mother.

I was still not exactly sure how or why he ended up in the car as I was driving Bob home from our disastrous honeymoon.

You would be surprised.

One minute I was pulling the car out of the hospital parking lot, and the next minute there was a gray-and-white blob sprinting across in front of my Buick. I threw on the brakes and stopped to be sure the little thing was okay. He was lying on his side and mewing softly. I carefully picked him up, and as soon as I did, he planted his wide fuzzy feet on my chest and began to knead and purr. It did cross my mind that he might have been play-acting at being hurt, since he bounced up so fast, but cats didn't do that, did they?

Yes, we do, when it is necessary.

Well, I asked myself, whether he was acting or not, what could I do? He didn't have a collar, and there wasn't anyone around who looked like they were missing a kitten. What was I supposed to do—leave him there to get run over?

He knew you would not.

So I plopped him on Bob's lap. He (Bob, that is) still didn't have his full coordination back. He had a whole list of rehab exercises to do every day. But I figured he could manage one sleepy-eyed little kitten. "Just what do you expect me to do with this?" he asked me.

"Just hold him. He'll take your mind off your aches and pains."

"Maybe it's a *she*."

As I started the engine I glanced over at the fuzzy kitten. Dark gray-and-black tiger stripes ran along his back and sides. His tummy was white and so was his head and all four feet. He had big splotches of gray behind his ears. Cute little guy. He had settled into Bob's lap as if he belonged there.

"Of course he's a boy," I said. "Look at those enormous feet. He's going to be as big as a tank."

Once we got him home, we isolated him from Marmalade until we could drive him up to the vet in Russell Gap and have him checked out for all the usual things. We brought him home with a clean bill of health.

Introducing him to Marmalade involved some hissing and swatting until Marmy got him trained the way she wanted him to be. The funny thing about Tank, though, was that he didn't want to sleep with us, he wasn't a lap cat and he didn't want to go outside. But he sure did want to eat. We just let him be the way he wanted to be. He was surprisingly well-mannered right from the start.

He will have to be, considering where he is going.

No matter where he was in the house, he could hear the food coming out. So, I put down another little dish and put a few bites of the chicken on it. Then I just had to smile as he rumbled and snorted.

He is a noisy eater.

That done, I went back to my great idea. I whipped out our phone book. Even though it covered the whole county, it still wasn't thick enough to sit my four-year-old granddaughter on so she could reach the table easily. Once I located the listing, I took a deep breath. The number matched my birthday. A good omen. I dialed it.

"Miss Mary's School of Dance, Miss Mary speaking." The voice was high-pitched. Nice timbre to it, though. Didn't sound at all breathy. Of course it wouldn't. The woman probably had the breathing control of a fine-tuned athlete.

"This is Miss Mary," she repeated. "May I help you?"

One more gulp for courage. "Miss Mary? This is Biscuit McKee, the librarian? I saw that sign you put in your front window? I'd like to sign up, if it's not too late?" My voice sounded nervous even to me. My tight throat raised my voice and made questions out of everything.

"Too late?" She laughed. "Of course not. You're the first one to call. I did wonder if I'd be able to get enough students together for a class, especially for one that's going to be meeting over the summer. Do you have any friends you'd like to talk into taking lessons with you?"

Visions of my three elderly library volunteers flicked through my mind. From the moment I met them, the day they came as a group and volunteered to help me set up the new library, I started calling them my Three Petunias since they looked like a little row of flowers in their old-fashioned house dresses. But now the thought of Esther, Rebecca Jo and Sadie in leotards— hmm. "Well," I said, "I can't think of anyone right offhand, but I'd be glad to ask around."

"We need at least six to make up a class," she told me, "but the lessons don't start until June 4th, so there's time yet."

Two and a half weeks didn't sound like much time to me. We discussed class times (Tuesday evenings) and monthly fees (reasonable) and payment schedules (first class of each month) and required dress (leotard) and where to get the shoes (Atlanta or Athens). "I'll stop by tomorrow morning," I told her. "I can fill out the registration form then."

It was settled. "Honey," I called as I stepped over Marmalade again and walked into the living room where Bob was reading the *Keagan County Record,* "do you think you could stand to be married to Ginger Rogers?"

He tilted his head to the left around the newspaper and peered at me over the top of his glasses. "What on earth are you talking about, woman?"

"I want to be as flexible as my garden hose, so I'm going to take tap dance lessons. At Miss Mary's School of Dance."

My gratitude list for Thursday, May 16th
Five things for which I'm grateful:

1. These gratitude lists that I write each night. They keep me concentrating on what is good in my life.
2. Tap dancing, which I hope I can do without tripping over myself
3. Bob
4. Marmalade, who is purring and walking across my notebook right now
5. My wonderful yard

my gratitude list for today
chicken
cool breezes
Widelap and Softfoot
bird songs
the forest floor

SIX

Friday, May 17

I TWIRLED THE PHONE CORD around my hand and untwirled it as I waited for my sister to answer. Five rings. Six. What happened to her answering machine?

"Hello?"

It always surprises me, I thought, that someone that far away, in Philadelphia in this case, can sound as if she's no farther than next door. The miracles of electronic communication. I love telephones. They're so convenient. So helpful. So handy. So...

"Hello?" she repeated.

"Glaze, it's me. Biscuit."

Her big yawn came clearly over the phone line. "Why did you call?"

"I did it!"

"Did what?"

"I signed up for tap dance lessons!"

There was a dreadful silence. "Tap dance lessons? You didn't."

"Yes, I did. You're supposed to be cheering, not grumping at me."

"You just caught me by surprise. Of course I'm happy about it, but I didn't know quite what to say. When do you start?"

"Not for two more weeks. In the meantime I have to rope five other women into taking lessons."

"Why is it up to you?"

Good question. Why did I think it was up to me? "Well," I said, "because we have to have six in order to start the classes, and I was the first one to sign up. The sign's been there for three days already, and nobody else has called."

"So you figure you need to lead the way?"

I moved the receiver away from my ear for a moment and stared at it. "Are you being snide?"

"No, I'm just wondering why everything always has to be up to you."

"What's wrong with you? Did you forget to eat breakfast? Or forget your medication?" Glaze was bipolar. As long as she took her medication, she was a reasonable, even happy person. But if she forgot for a couple of days, she was gloom personified.

"Biscuit, it is seven-thirty in the morning and you woke me up, and you expect me to be all hip-hip-hooray about your stupid dancing lessons. How about asking me what's going on here?"

"Why aren't you up already? Are you sick?"

"No, I'm not sick, but I haven't found a job yet and I'm tired of getting no's, and I don't appreciate hearing about your stupid hobbies when I don't know when or if I'll have a paycheck coming in."

Oh, shoot. "Glaze, I'm..." What was I? Sorry? Pissed off? Apologetic? Angry? It was no fun being grumped at before eight in the morning. But she was my sister, after all, and I guess I did forget that she'd lost her job the day before she drove all the way from Philly to Martinsville for my wedding. Okay, so I told her I was sorry. By the time I said it, I really meant it.

The rest of the conversation was better, and after we hung up, I patted Marmalade who had crawled into my lap as I sat there at the kitchen table with my second cup of tea.

Marmy stood up and nuzzled my face...

You are unhappy, Widelap.

...and her whiskers tickled my nose. I rubbed my nose briskly to stop the tickling, and I thought about whiskers. They always amaze me. Every once in a while I find one that Marmy has shed. It might be lying on the floor, or on a tabletop, or on a chair. I always pick them up and drop them into a tiny green vase I have in my sitting room upstairs. It's brimming with a little spray of whiskers. I can't bear to throw them out. They impart so much information to a cat. Wouldn't it be enlightening if we humans had emotional whiskers to help us understand what was going on around us? Would they help me understand my sister?

You would look funny with whiskers.

It's awful when people you love are far away and you can't help them, and then you go and piss them off. I hate telephones.

BY THE TIME I GOT to the library, about 10:30 a.m., Sadie and Rebecca Jo (my mother-in-law) were already there. I could hear them laughing upstairs. They were all the way up in the third floor office. Must have been quite a joke. I headed upstairs to find out what was going on, and I found them sorting some of the books that had been donated to the new library when it opened last year. We still had dozens of boxes piled up around the sides of the office and out in the hallway.

"What's so funny?" I asked as I walked in.

They looked at each other and went into another round of guffaws. I've found that a lot of times, funny stories between women are of the *you-had-to-be-there-to-get-it* variety. But I still wanted to know what was going on.

Sadie, clad in bright yellow slacks and a soft yellow short-sleeved shirt, held up her hands about two feet apart and kept laughing. Was I supposed to understand that? "Okay, Rebecca Jo, tell me what's up."

"It really isn't very funny, I suppose, but Sadie and I were talking about all the changes in town in the last seventy years or so. We both can remember before the roads were paved, and before there were many cars. Just horses. I said something about remember the squabbles they had on the town council about painting the parking spaces, and Sadie said…" Here she started laughing again.

I gave her a moment to compose herself. "Yes?" I prompted. "Parking spaces?"

Sadie held up her hands again, about two feet apart. At the same time, they both spluttered, "Parallel parking!"

"What?" Were they insane? What was funny about parallel parking?

"When there were horses in town, dear," Sadie finally managed to explain, "that's all the room they needed for a parking space." And she and Rebecca Jo were off on another round of hee-hawing. You had to be there to appreciate it.

Once they toned down a bit, Sadie told me, "Rebecca Jo and I have decided to get at least two of these boxes emptied today."

That was a bigger task than it seemed. Simply emptying the boxes was the least of the effort, since each book had to be checked thoroughly to be sure there were no missing pages. Any papers left tucked in the book had to be set aside to be returned to the donor. Then there was the cataloging and the covering with clear plastic and the typing up of the various labels. Then all the information needed to be put on cards. Finally we had to find a place for each book on the shelves. Not a speedy job. Someday we would have a computerized system. I hoped it would hurry.

"Well," I said, "if you get two more boxes done, there'll be only forty or fifty left to go."

Sadie had the good grace to laugh at my poor joke. Rebecca Jo smiled, too. I loved having cheerful volunteers. Knowing the office was in good hands, I went downstairs to open the doors and be sure the lights were turned on.

Promptly at 11:00 a.m., the first patron of the day walked in. Sharon Armitage. Hmm. Her husband, Carl, owned the gas station and ran the Chief Movie House, and did some kenaf farming, too. He could probably watch their kids on Tuesday nights. "Sharon? Have you ever thought of taking tap dance lessons?"

MY SECOND NO CAME from Elaine Montgomery who stopped in to pick up another four or five romance novels. We had dozens and dozens of them, willed to us by old Mrs. Millicent. Somebody had introduced her to that genre on her 86th birthday.

She always said, or so the story went, that they kept her warm on winter evenings. After she and her daughter both died, the house and all the books in it were willed to the town for use as a library. The town council didn't know how to set up a library, which was why I was hired. I loved the work. But we still had all those books to sort out. Anyway, Elaine gave me a resounding negative. But she did wish me luck, and suggested that I ask Polly Lattimore. Good idea. Polly was the nurse in Dr. Nathan Young's office.

I called Polly and got my third no. Phooey.

SEVEN

THE NEXT MORNING, Bob went over to his old house on Upper Sweetgum Street to spend a few hours in his workshop.

He likes to spend time there.

We were going to have to sell his house soon. Where on earth would we put his workshop, though? There simply wasn't any extra space here, unless we built an addition onto the shed in the backyard. I went through a mental inventory of our Beechnut Lane house. Downstairs was the living room, big kitchen, office, laundry room and a small half bath. No basement. Upstairs there was a bedroom, a sewing and craft area, bathroom, my little sitting room and the stairs up to the attic. The attic was crammed with the detritus of many generations. There were domed trunks, hobby horses, lamps, hatboxes. Each generation who'd lived in this old house had left behind a legacy of mess, and each succeeding generation had added to it rather than weeding it out.

Maybe the shed idea would be the best solution. That would have to wait, though. I was upstairs in my sitting room, trying to deal with a space problem I'd encountered at the library. I was trying to figure out how I was going to fit all the gardening books Elizabeth had given us into the limited number of bookshelves we had in the Green Room at the library. The Millicents had a penchant for unusual wall paints, and each room was a different color. I'd brought home the measurements for each shelf and had a general idea of just how much room the nine boxes of books would take up. We'd gotten more garden books from other people, too, so there was a huge assortment of them. It seemed appropriate to put all the books dealing with growing things into the Green Room.

No matter how many times I redrew the shelf arrangement, I couldn't make it all fit. It sure was easier doing the rearranging on graph paper as I sat at home than it would have been if I'd lugged all the books into the Green Room itself. The graph paper definitely showed me it couldn't be done, simply because the Green Room, unfortunately, was the one truly small room in the whole Millicent Mansion. Nestled under the staircase to the third floor, part of the room had a sloping ceiling. It would have made a lovely children's tuck-away area, but we wanted the children's section to be down on the main floor where we could always keep an eye on them.

Maybe, I thought as I looked at yet another unworkable sketch, I should just turn the Green Room into something else. Then I could paint the Beige Room green and put the gardening books there. There was a lot of lovely sunshine in that room, anyway, so it made more sense for gardening books. Yes, that looked much more practical. I could put the astronomy books in the small tuck-away room, and there'd be plenty of space for them, because we had so few. Maybe geology, too. I knew I wanted to increase the science section, and I could paint the room an inviting light blue. Like the sky.

I took a moment to stretch my back and brought my attention back from the library to my little sitting room. This was where my sister and I had spent a lot of time while she recovered from her sprained ankle. I glanced at the wide coffee table and could almost see our Scrabble game spread out. I loved this room. It was so peaceful. It was so *me*.

It is me, too.

Right then I decided that I didn't want to remodel the upstairs. Bob and I had talked about making our bedroom bigger, but that was only so we could put in more closet space. It would be a lot easier if I just moved my clothes into the sitting room closet. I wouldn't mind keeping this as my dressing room, I thought, and then laughed at myself. I sounded so hoity-toity with all this talk about a dressing room. Next I'd be wanting a conservatory.

What is that?

Marmalade sat on the little love seat next to me, grooming her back legs and cleaning out between her toes. That would tickle the daylights out of me....

You could not reach your toes like this.

...Glad I wasn't a cat. I could see Tank through the open door of the sitting room. He was stretched out on the floor in the sewing area. He was simply not a lap cat. A big puddle of sunlight streamed over him from the front window. A patch of sunshine wasn't complete unless it had a cat plopped right smack dab in the middle of it. I could see the sun glinting on Tank's green eyes. I wished he were more affectionate, but I needed to let him be what he wanted to be.

He will be that regardless of what you do. He is a cat.

I saw his ears prick up. He stood, stretched his front feet far forward, yawned and walked his back feet up to meet the front ones. Then he headed downstairs. Sure enough, a few moments later I heard the front door open, and Bob came in calling, "Marmalade! Marmalade! Guess what I made for you?"

At the sound of her name, Marmalade sat up straight and cocked her head to one side. She and I listened as Bob made a tour of the kitchen, office, laundry room (we heard the door squeak open). He walked around the circle into the living room, and then headed up the stairs. "Marmalade, where are you?"

I am waiting for you.

Marmy just sat there, as if she were waiting for him to find her. I wasn't any help at all. I thought it was pretty funny. By the time Bob toured the bedroom, glanced into the sewing room and finally stepped through the door into the little sitting room, he was in much less of a buoyant mood.

"What are you doing just sitting here, you ungrateful varmint? Why couldn't you meet me at the front door the way Tank did?"

That is his job, not mine.

Bob had his hands tucked behind his back.

"What have you got there?" I asked him.

"Ta-daaa!" he proclaimed and revealed a long thin pole with what looked like a fishing line attached to it. At the end dangled...

There was an orange streak of fur as Marmalade pounced at the feathery bit of fluff at the end of the line. Bob jerked it away just in time, then spent several minutes flipping it through the air as Marmy leaped and cavorted, batting at it and pouncing. Eventually even Tank joined in, and Bob and I laughed at their contortions as they darted and jumped and swiveled around.

"Bob! It's wonderful! Did you make it?"

"Sure did," he said. "Just felt like taking some time out. It's a larger version of the Bisque Whisk." He was referring to a special fishing lure he made recently and named after me. I seem to remember having said it would make a great cat toy if it were larger, and didn't have a hook in it, of course. He must have remembered my chance comment. I sure do love that man.

"I think it's an unmitigated success," I told him as Marmalade made a flying leap. Bob whipped the pole back. It struck my little green vase on the second shelf of the bookcase, knocked it over and scattered my collection of cat whiskers all over the floor. Bob promptly folded up the toy and put it on top of the bookshelf, out of sight.

"Woman, I can't for the life of me see why you keep saving these cat hairs."

"They aren't hairs, they're whiskers."

"Whatever." He bent to help me pick them up, but I could tell he was just being polite. "What good are they to anybody?" he asked.

I use them all the time.

"What good are bird songs to anybody? What good are beautiful landscapes?" I was just getting warmed up. "What good are waterfalls or those fish you like to catch?"

"Whoa, lady! I just asked a simple question."

You asked the wrong question.

"You did *not* ask a simple question. You asked a loaded question. There's a big difference. A *simple* question would have been 'why do you like collecting cat whiskers?'" I didn't exactly glower, but I came close.

Bob was saved from a reply. As he bent to retrieve one more whisker, Marmalade used his back as a trampoline and launched herself onto the top of the bookcase. By the time we could stand up, she had the Bisque Whisk in her mouth.

"You're right about the cat toy," Bob said, laughing, as he reached up to lift Marmy off her perch and extract the toy from her mouth. "It's a success." He pushed his glasses back up onto his rather crooked nose, scratched Marmalade behind her ears and set her down on the carpet.

Thank you, Softfoot.

As I watched the two of them I thought how glad I was that my cat seemed to like the man I married. Bob had his moments, like most men, but he always treated Marmy with respect. He was such a tall man, it would be easy for him to step on her accidentally, but he was careful where he put his feet when she was around. Which was most of the time. I was through being ticked off at him. I put the vase back on the shelf and reached out to straighten the collar of his shirt.

Several minutes later I looked around for Tank and found he had retreated to his patch of sunshine.

EIGHT

Diane Marie's journal—Sunday, May 19th

9:05 a.m. From now on I need to start hiding this journal. I left it on my dressing table yesterday. I remember setting it down on top of my calendar. I'd left the corner of the journal pointing to the square for last Thursday because I wanted to remind myself to go back and stick in a note about my sister's phone call. But this morning I noticed it was pointing to Friday. If we had a cat, I'd figure the cat had bumped it or something. But we don't have cats anymore. I think my husband is reading my journal. I've never written anything in here that would upset him, just things like, "He's gone for a couple of days. I need to be sure the grass is mowed before he gets back, because it'll be too long if I wait for him to do it." I've never poured out what I'm thinking in here, and now I'm glad I didn't. I don't know what he'd do if he ever read anything like that. Yes, I do know what he'd do. Maybe that's why I don't write what I'm thinking. But now I'm going to tell him I lost my journal, left it at the diner in Garner Creek when I was eating lunch. I'll need to call the diner and ask if they've found it. That way, if he checks, he'll think I'm telling the truth. I hate this. I hate this.

I hate this. Why can't I just leave? It would be better than living like this, always wondering when he's going to blow up. He's nice enough in between those times, and I keep hoping so much that he'll just love me like he used to. Maybe he never did love me. Maybe all he loves is how I make him feel when I act the way he wants me to. I'm tired of feeling like everything is my fault.

Monday, May 20

REVEREND PURSEY WATCHED OUT the church office window as
Roger Winston Johnson IV snapped the last letter in place. He
was glad the young man was taking this job seriously. It had
been a hard sell getting the elders of the church to agree to hire
Roger to maintain the signboard that stood sentinel on the Old
Church lawn. Reverend Pursey believed that Roger had backbone, regardless of the fact that he was such a happy-go-lucky
soul, and something of a scoundrel, too. Roger's mother, Mary
Parkman Johnson, was fond of saying that Roger had been born
laughing. Always the class clown in Sunday school as he was
growing up, Roger generally had been surrounded by a large
group of other students who expected to be entertained every
time he opened his mouth. The young Roger had delivered.

Which was to be expected of a youngster, perhaps, Reverend
Pursey thought. But Roger was a grown man now. At twenty-
two, he should have known better than to lead Bob Sheffield
a chase with painting Mrs. Hoskins' mailbox all those bilious
colors. Now, as a crowning touch, it was Bob's mailbox that he
was painting, since Bob had moved into the old Hoskins house.

Reverend Pursey turned back to his sermon. It wasn't going
well, which was why he'd come into his office on his day off.
"Honor thy father and thy mother" was his topic, and he was
stuck with it now, since each week the church sign out front told
the whole world the title of his next sermon. That small part of
the world, that is, that walks or drives past Third and Juniper, he
corrected himself. Last week he had preached about humility.

ROGER HUMMED AS HE snapped the final R onto the church signboard. His latest song was going well. He wanted it to be a real
winner, this one. He must have written thousands of songs. Well,
hundreds, maybe. But why didn't they sell? He made all his tapes
and CDs in his recording studio, but most of them still sat there
on the shelves he'd built under the stairs.

That woman from Ireland or wherever made all her own recordings, and look at how they were selling. Millions. World-wide. That's what Roger wanted. He wanted to walk down the street and hear somebody humming one of his tunes. He wanted to turn on the radio and hear himself. He wanted to be invited to the big TV shows. It could still happen. Maybe this new song. He already had a great chorus and half the verses. Just needed a little…a little…well, something or other. He'd think about it.

He stepped back a couple of paces to admire his work. "Nobody ever calls it the Martinsville Community Church," he muttered. They should have put *The Old Church* at the top of the sign. Right below that, it always said the same thing.

REVEREND HENRY PURSEY
SUNDAY SERVICE—11:00 A.M.
WEDNESDAY PRAYER MEETING—7:00 P.M.
CHOIR PRACTICE—THURSDAY 7:30 P.M.

Boring. Predictable. Roger wondered if anyone ever bothered to read it. Probably not. But they did read the bottom half of the sign. The important part. His part.

NEXT SUNDAY'S SERMON:
HONOR THY FATHER AND THY MOTHER

Lower case letters would look better, he thought. It would be easier to read.

MARMALADE WALKED ALONG beside me as I headed up the hill. The day was mild with a few clouds and a slight welcomed breeze as I turned from the uphill slope of Beechnut Lane onto the relative flat of Third Street. I waved at Roger who headed toward me. As often as that kid had painted our mailbox, I still couldn't be upset with him. It was a long-standing joke, I guess, between him and Bob. At least he always painted it lavender again, the way I liked it. Last week it had been olive green. Funny how Bob could never catch him at it. But he always knew who'd done it.

He'd track Roger down and make him repaint the thing, and then three days later it'd be another color. It all seemed fairly juvenile to me. Maybe that was why I always thought of Roger as a kid.

"Hey, Miss Biscuit, how you doing?" Roger asked.

"Just fine, Roger. How are you?"

I am doing well also.

"Fine. Be sure you check out the sign, Miss Biscuit."

"The sign?" I asked. I knew perfectly well which sign he meant. Every time I saw him, he managed to mention it in casual conversation.

"The church sign. I just changed it."

You are proud of that.

Roger was gangly as a toothpick, with a shock of red hair that waved across his forehead.

His hair matches the Irish setters up the street.

He still lived with his parents in what he called his "studio," a little two-story addition to their big place on Fourth Street kitty-cornered from Bob's old house. Bless Roger's heart. He'd been trying since he was twelve to write some decent music, but from what Bob said, it had never turned out. Roger's mother, Tom Parkman's sister, Mary, told me a few weeks ago that she was so glad she was tone-deaf. Otherwise she couldn't have listened to his caterwauling all these years.

Roger stooped down to scratch Marmalade's head. "Do you think anybody reads it?" he asked.

I couldn't bear to disappoint him, but it occurred to me that he truly needed something more than a church sign to prop up his sadly bent ego. Who was I, though, to analyze him? "Of course they read it, Roger. This way everybody knows what's coming up each week." Why didn't he go out and get a real job?

"I'm glad this job doesn't take me too long each week," he said as he straightened up....

Thank you for the scratch.

"...This way I still have lots of time for writing my music."

My dad, the school band teacher, might have argued that description. I'd passed by Roger's "studio" on numerous evenings and heard his bizarre collection of notes wafting down the street. Of course, he was twenty-ish and I was almost fifty. Maybe it was just a generational thing. I needed a musical translator.

I would be happy to oblige, but I do not understand it, either. It reminds me of two tomcats fighting.

"Speaking of which," he continued, "I'd better get going. I've got a good one I'm working on right now." He hummed a few bars and drifted on down Third.

"Marmalade," I asked, for want of any other conversationalist, "do *you* like his music?" She might even have been answering me, because she leaped into my arms and carried on with her loud purr for the rest of the block.

NINE

Tuesday, May 21

THE PHONE WOKE ME much too quickly. My calves were still aching from the gardening I'd done over the weekend. All I wanted was to stay in bed on my day off. I loved working only three and a half days a week.

The phone was entirely too loud for its own good. Or for my ears. Why hadn't we put it in the other room? I thought about letting it ring, but knew that would probably bring Bob, dripping wet, out of the shower to see what was wrong. He didn't have the day off. So I answered it.

"Biscuit? How you doing? This is Myrtle."

Myrtle was Martinsville's own septuagenarian reporter for the *Keagan County Record.* She'd been there forever. "Fine, Myrtle, and you?"

"Fine. Where's Bob?"

I am fine, too.

"He's in the shower, Myrtle." I paused to yawn. "Can I give him a message?"

"Yes. I want to know what he thinks about the vandalism last night."

I shifted Marmy off my hip and reached over to turn on the light. While I was at it, I picked up a notepad. Where was the pen? "Vandalism?"

"You mean you haven't heard? I got a call this morning about it."

"Who called? What happened?"

"The Old Church."

I woke up rather fast at that. "Somebody broke into the church?"

"No," she said. "It's the sign out front. My caller said it had been vandalized."

Poor Roger. If somebody tore his sign down, he'd be pretty upset. I'd even seen him dusting it off one afternoon last week. Not just upset. He'd be heartbroken.

"Who called you?"

"I don't know. It sounded all fuzzy. The person refused to identify herself."

"Her? Was it a woman? A girl?"

"I couldn't tell for sure. The voice was definitely disguised. But I'm pretty sure it was either a girl or a young woman." Myrtle paused and I could sense her reporter's nose twitching. "It might have been a young man with a high voice."

The pen was under Bob's journal. I told Myrtle I'd have Bob call her right away. After I hung up I wrote, "Old Church. Female (?) informant. Call Myrtle." I left it sitting on the bed, threw on a robe and trooped downstairs to feed the cats and start breakfast.

BOB SMELLED SO GOOD when he walked up behind me and wrapped me in one of his warm, delicious hugs. "What was Myrtle in a huff about?"

"Somebody tore down the church signboard or something. I don't know exactly. Myrtle said it was vandalism." I turned around in his arms and gave him his second good morning hug. He smelled spicier during this one. "She wanted your opinion."

"She must have a deadline to meet. I'd better go check it out. Can you hold breakfast?"

I looked at the eggs I hadn't cracked yet, and the big iron skillet that held some leeks, onions and green peppers that I'd chopped. They were still sautéing in olive oil. "I'll turn the heat off and finish it when you get back." Frittatas were almost as easy as soup.

NOT FIVE MINUTES LATER, Tank walked out of the kitchen toward the front hall. I peeked around the corner and saw him sit down facing the front door. Bob walked in smiling. "That was fast," I said. "What happened?"

He reached down to scratch Tank behind the ears. "The signboard's okay." Following me back into the kitchen, he took his big blue police mug off the rack and walked to the coffeepot. "All they did was mess with the letters."

"Quit chuckling and tell me what happened."

"They switched a couple of letters around so it reads Penry Hursey instead of Henry Pursey. I just switched them back. It was a prank."

"Poor Roger. I hope he doesn't hear about this." I stood up and headed toward the stove. "He'd be so hurt to think that somebody had messed with his precious signboard."

"Serves him right for messing up the mailbox so many times. It'll be good for him to be on the other end of it."

"Bob! That's downright hard-hearted of you."

"But I'm right, don't you think?"

It did have a certain symmetry to it. I laughed. So did Bob. His eyes crinkled up at the corners in that cute way of his. "I'm going to have to call Myrtle," he said, "and she'll probably put it in her…"

The phone rang. Bob grinned. "What do you want to bet that's Myrtle now?"

"You pick it up, then. And be quick about it. I'm cooking this frittata."

"Bob Sheffield…. Hey, Myrtle. Yes, I'm fine. How about you…? Good…."

I tuned out at that point and paid attention to finishing breakfast. I had it on the table by the time Bob hung up the phone.

Wednesday, May 22

REVEREND PURSEY LOOKED OUT over the pulpit. There were almost a dozen more people than usual at the Wednesday Evening Prayer Service. He felt gratified, until it occurred to him that they probably came out of curiosity. After all, Myrtle's column that morning told the whole county about the vandalism. She'd called him yesterday to ask if she could get a picture of him standing next to the sign, but that struck him as undignified, so he had declined.

Maybe this was an example of good overcoming evil. He checked that thought. Changing the sign letters was hardly an evil act. It was a simple prank, like painting the Hoskins' mailbox.

It crossed the Reverend's mind that Roger might have done it himself to generate publicity for his sign. No, for the church. Reverend Pursey shook his head. Roger? No. No, he wouldn't do that—would he?

TEN

I DEFINITELY NEEDED some good sister-talk…

You can talk to me.

…so I called Glaze, hoping she'd be home. "I called for some sympathy, Sis."

"Nope, I'm fresh out of sympathy, but you can have both my ears."

What would you do with them?

"What do you mean, you're out of sympathy? What else are sisters for?"

Her merry chuckle filtered through the phone line. "Oh, all right, sympathy you can have. I'm really sorry for all that's going wrong. What, by the way, *is* going wrong?"

"I don't know. I just feel kind of blue, like something is wrong, but I don't know what," I told her as I stroked Marmalade's ears. Dr. Nathan had told me that animals' ears have dozens of acupressure points on them, so stroking them is quite beneficial for the animal….

It feels good when it is done gently.

…That was why it was such a shame when people docked a dog's ears. It took away a natural healing channel. "I just feel blue," I repeated.

Maybe you need your ears scratched.

"Is that all?"

"You're in a rare mood, Sis." Marmalade stood up and pawed gently at the side of my head. "What's gotten into you?" I asked my sister, but I could have been asking the same of Marmalade.

"Can't I just be happy?"

"Sure you can. But what are you so happy *about?*"

"Oh. Nothing much." Her voice was pointedly nonchalant. "Tom called yesterday, that's all."

"Oh?"

"What do you mean by that?"

"Nothing."

"Yes, you do." She drew the words out, long and slow.

"No, I don't."

This conversation is not making sense.

"All right, I give in," she said. "Tom called, and I think we have everything figured out."

Tom Parkman, Bob's best friend, had obviously been quite smitten with Glaze when he met her the week before my wedding. At least, it was obvious to me. But they'd had a major argument, mostly related to my sister's emotional unavailability. That wasn't surprising, I thought. Her last "gentleman friend" wasn't a gentleman and certainly wasn't a friend. He was a creep. Thank goodness he was in jail. Glaze had very little faith in her ability to pick a good man. Logical, I supposed, but frustrating for me. I had wanted to shake her and tell her to wake up. But this conversation was sounding promising. "So what happens next?"

Glaze took a deep breath. "He's coming for a visit in a couple of weeks so I can show him around Philadelphia."

For that he could take a bus tour, I thought.

What is a bus?

"Where's he going to stay?" I asked, knowing that her townhouse, shared with a roommate, had only two bedrooms. Not that it was any business of mine.

Then why are you asking her?

There was silence on the other end of the line. What was with my sister? She was forty-four years old, for heaven's sake. Did she really think anyone would care what she did with her private arrangements? This was the end of the twentieth century. There weren't any morality police running around. Well, come to think of it, there were quite a few people in this country who thought they could stick their noses into everybody else's private life. As if it was any concern of theirs. One of the problems of a small town is that some of those people were neighbors....

I know. That stink man who cuts human hair thinks he can tell me what to do.

...Wait a minute. She lived in Philadelphia. A city. People there probably wouldn't even know their neighbors. Nonsense. There was always somebody peeking out a window, keeping tabs on the comings and goings of... Oh, well, that train of thought wouldn't get me anywhere. I hoped Tom would propose soon. I could see him as my brother-in-law. Of course, I'd want to be the matron of honor. Glaze would look beautiful in white. Maybe I could wear a nice green dress that would match her eyes....

"Biscuit? Did we lose the connection? Can you send it up with Tom?"

"Send what up with Tom?"

"Oh, honestly, what have you been daydreaming about this time? I asked you to give Tom a couple of jars of Mom's mint jelly."

"Why do you need mint jelly?" What did that have to do with which bedroom he was going to sleep in?

"As a thank-you gift for Mr. Thurley."

"Who's Mr. Thurley?"

"Biscuit McKee, would you please tune in and listen to me?" She didn't sound nearly as jolly as she had a few minutes ago. "Tom's staying with old Mr. Thurley next door. He has an extra bedroom. The mint jelly is a thank-you gift for him."

Did I miss something here? By the time I hung up the phone, I still hadn't told Glaze about the vandalism at the church.

Dear Ida,
I'm sorry it's taken me so long to thank you for the gift card to Mable's. I can sure use it. Now I just need to figure out a time to get over there. Why on earth did I ever agree to move to Enders? Surreytown was so much closer to

you—not as the crow flies, maybe, but just a hop, skip and
a jump down the valley rather than all the way around.
Why am I explaining? You know all this.

> *It's not like he has to be close to his job—working from*
> *home has its advantages, I suppose, although there are*
> *times, like today, when I'm grateful that he has business*
> *trips so often. I'm still not sure why Kelvin wanted to move*
> *back here, except that, with his dad in prison, the house*
> *was empty. Maybe that's why. I hope they keep that man*
> *in jail forever. I know they won't, but the man's an ogre if*
> *you...*

Ida Peterson set the first page aside. She kept asking her sister to write on both sides of the paper. Save a piece of paper,
save a tree. Conservation and all that. But Diane Marie would
have none of it. At least her notes were seldom more than two
or three pages long

> *...asked me to go back to the grocery store a THIRD time.*
> *You'd think she could remember something as simple as*
> *celery seed...*

What? Ida glanced back at the first page. Then she looked
ahead to the third page. That was it; they weren't in the right
order. She chuckled to herself. They weren't in the *write* order,
either, she thought. Why didn't the woman ever use page numbers? Page two carried on about Bill Murchison, Diane Marie's
father-in-law, for two paragraphs, recounting the alcoholism and
the vehicular homicide. Ida knew all of that and didn't particularly want to be reminded of it. Thank goodness they'd caught
him.

She went back to reading her sister's letter, all about how
she was trying to help the somewhat frail but downright feisty
woman who lived next door. After the grocery store incident,
Diane Marie finally got to what Ida assumed was the real reason for the note.

Kelvin is going on another business trip for a few days, maybe even a couple of weeks. Is there a chance I could come stay with you while he's gone? Please say yes. I'll help with the cooking and housework as payment for my room and board.
Diane Marie
P.S. I'll call you in a couple of days for an answer.

"Let me guess." Ida heard her husband say from the doorway. "Green notepaper and you with a puzzled look on your face. Must be a letter from your sister."

"How'd you figure that out?"

"Heck, Ida, she always writes on green paper, and you told me a couple of months ago that she never writes unless she wants something." He sank into his recliner. "So, what does she want?"

"Nice to know you've been listening to me." Ida laughed. "You're right. Kelvin's going to be out of town for a while, and she wants to come for a visit."

Ralph's eyes narrowed. "How long?"

"She doesn't say exactly. Maybe two weeks."

"Two weeks? I can't do without you at the store for that long."

"You know I wouldn't desert you like that. I'll maybe take off the first day she's here, but that's all." Ida knew their grocery store, as successful as it was, still needed the two of them there almost every day. She enjoyed the work, whether she was filling in on the register, negotiating with the bank about the ATM machine, or training a new high-schooler to stock the shelves. "Maybe I'll get her to clean out our storage shed while she's here."

Ralph scratched his bald head and peered at her over the rim of his glasses. "Not if you ever want her to come back again, you won't."

ELEVEN

Saturday, May 25

"YOU WILL NEVER, ever in a million years guess what I'm going to do," I told my dear friend Melissa Tarkington when she walked into the library a little before two o'clock. We were beginning the straightening-up process which always took a good half-hour. Esther was picking up children's books and re-shelving them, while I was checking the reserve lists.

"You're taking up skydiving?" she asked. Melissa was great. She always had a quick reply. I was the kind who had to think about an answer first. I frequently came up with a snappy retort, but usually only after the conversation had already ended.

"No, silly. Have you seen the sign down at Miss Mary's?"

"You're NOT!"

"Yes, I am."

"Biscuit, that's amazing. I'm sure you'll really enjoy it."

"Do you want to join me? If you hadn't been out of town, I would have asked you last week."

She made a face, screwing her mouth into a tilde. "Not a chance."

I didn't want another no. "Why not?" I asked her. "It'll be fun."

"Fun? Nonsense." She shook her head to get her curly black hair out of her eyes. It was getting awfully long. "It's too much work," she went on, "and I should think it would hurt my toes."

"Your toes? What are you talking about?"

"Anyway, it's way too serious," she added.

"Melissa! Think about Debbie Reynolds and Gene Kelly...

and what about Fred Astaire and Ginger Rogers? There wasn't a serious bone in their bodies."

"What," she asked me, "do they have to do with ballet?"

"Ballet? Who said anything about ballet?"

"You did. You said you were signing up for ballet lessons."

"I did not! Where'd you get that idea?"

Melissa waved her hands in the air. Thank goodness the library was pretty much empty. Otherwise I'd have had to reprimand us. "You just told me you were going to the ballet class."

"Tap dance classes, Melissa. The sign says tap dance!"

"It says ballet," she insisted. "I saw it yesterday on the way to Ralph and Ida's." She was referring to the grocery store a block or so beyond Miss Mary's on First Street. All the stores along First Street looked out across the road and the riverbank to the Metoochie River. Everything we needed was easy to get to in this town.

The year I moved to Martinsville to become the librarian, I stayed at *Azalea House,* Melissa's bed-and-breakfast. We became good friends during that time. Thank goodness we'd grown close enough to argue like this without taking it too personally.

"Melissa, you're out of your blinkin' gourd."

"How dare you? I am not!"

"Yes, you are, and we're going to call Miss Mary right now and settle this so you can see how wrong you are." I turned away to my desk, the one with all the pigeonholes that I still hadn't cleaned out, and dialed the easy-to-remember phone number. All the numbers in this end of the valley started with the same first three digits, and this one ended in 0111. My birthday was January 11th. Simple.

"Miss Mary's School of Dance, Miss Mary speaking."

"Miss Mary, this is Biscuit McKee. Could you settle a little argument?"

"That's not my usual role, Biscuit," she said, "but I'll try. What's going on?"

Melissa crowded up close, trying to hear both sides of the conversation. Since I knew she was wrong, I graciously held the receiver a bit away from my ear. "I signed up for tap dance lessons, didn't I?"

"Well, of course you did."

I cocked my head and raised my eyebrows in Melissa's direction. She grabbed the phone. "Miss Mary, this is Melissa. Yesterday I saw the sign in your window, and it distinctly says adult ballet lessons."

"Yes," came the voice over the line. I could hear the high-pitched tones quite clearly. "There are *two* signs. I'm advertising tap *and* ballet lessons. It's the first year I've opened classes to adults, and whether they continue will depend entirely on how many…"

She kept talking, but neither Melissa nor I listened. Melissa said, "Oh. Well. Thank you for clearing that up." As she hung up the phone, she started wiggling her eyebrows in that funny way she has when she doesn't quite know what to say.

"Whoops," she said.

"Did we really do this?" I asked.

She looked at me, I looked at her and we burst out laughing.

"Quick," she said. "Hurry up and close the library and let's walk down to the Delicious to celebrate how silly we are over a piece of pecan pie."

THE DELISCHUSS—but everybody calls it the Delicious—was the local eatery, open Monday through Saturday, from seven to five. People from here and all the way up the Metoochie River valley made their way there for Margot Schuss' Norwegian desserts and Hans Schuss' German breads and pastries, to say nothing of the great sandwiches and soups. One of my favorite places in town.

As we walked in, I nodded at Cory. It looked like he was working on a large sandwich order. "Ariel will be with you in a minute, Ms. McKee. There's a free booth over there," he added, pointing with his nose. Melissa and I headed that way. She'd lived in Martinsville all her life, so she knew everybody. Since I'd lived here for a whole year, I knew practically everybody.

Not a bad track record. We smiled and nodded and chatted our way across the room, then settled in next to the window.

Once Ariel brought our sweet tea, we toasted ourselves. "Here's to stupidity," Melissa said, rolling her eyes as she lifted her glass to clink against mine.

"Here's to friendship," I countered. Setting the cold glass down on its paper coaster, I looked Melissa square in the eye. "So," I said, "are you going to sign up for tap?"

"I don't know," she said.

"How can you *not?* You love *Singin' in the Rain* as much as I do. Can't you just see us tapping our way down First Street, hopping on and off the curb?"

"With our umbrellas in hand?"

"Sure! We could do it!"

"Okay. When do we start?"

Yes! Now we had two in the class. Only four to go.

THE BELL OVER the deli's front door jangled as Henry Pursey walked in. He smiled at Ariel Montgomery and she smiled back. "Take a seat anywhere, Reverend P. I'll be right with you."

Henry glanced around the room. It was busy this time of day. He saw Roger Johnson slurping a cup of coffee, talking with a young fellow that Henry couldn't quite place. High school age. Local kid. Lots of young men crowding the place now that school was out. From Roger's gestures, it looked like he was telling his companion about how he had to fix the sign letters. Roger sure got a lot of mileage out of that sign job. Biscuit McKee and Melissa Tarkington were laughing at one of the booths by the window. Henry enjoyed stopping in a couple of times a week for a late afternoon cup of coffee. Across the room Father John Ames raised his hand and waved him over. Henry threaded his way between the tables, saying hello to parishioners as he went and slid into the booth across from the priest. "Afternoon, John. How's it going?"

"Great. You?"

"Same."

Ariel sashayed up to the table. Couldn't that young woman walk straight? Henry wondered. He must be getting old. Time when he would have enjoyed the hip-wiggling. Now it just seemed faintly silly. Behind her he could see Roger's companion watching her appreciatively as Roger kept up his monologue. Every other young fellow in the place was watching her, too. No wonder she was sashaying. Biscuit and Melissa didn't seem to have noticed anything.

Henry turned the heavy white mug upright. "I'll take coffee," he said.

"Lots of cream, right?"

"You're right, Ariel. Thanks for remembering."

"Why wouldn't I remember, Reverend P? You always get the same thing." She giggled and walked away. Wiggled away.

Wiggles and giggles, he thought. She couldn't be more than sixteen. He looked up and saw that John was inspecting him. "Are you thinking the same thing I am?" Henry asked under his breath.

"Probably. She knows exactly who's watching and listening."

"Uh-huh, and it's not us she's performing for."

"That's okay, Henry. There's nothing either one of us could do about it, anyway." John tipped his cup up to drink the last bit and waved over at Ariel, pointing to his cup. Ariel came back with the coffeepot and a handful of little plastic containers. She filled both cups. Henry started opening and pouring. John waited until Henry was done and had taken his first sip. "Heard you had some sign trouble."

"Yeah, and it was scrambled around again this morning. But it's not that bad." Henry yawned. "Sorry. I haven't been sleeping well lately. That sign business is more a bother than anything else. Myrtle's had a field day. I think she drives by each morning just to see if she has some material for her Wednesday column."

"Sounds like somebody in town has more time on his hands than he needs. You got any ideas who's doing it?"

"Nothing I could prove."

"Maybe Myrtle's doing it to give herself something to write about," John quipped.

"Right. I can see that seventy-year-old woman sneaking around changing sign letters. Anyway, she's been writing her column for fifty years and hasn't been at a loss for what to say yet. There's always some sort of gossip."

"You mean news, don't you?"

Henry snorted. "News? Right." One more sip. "That's enough about the sign. What's going on with you?"

"Same ole same ole. I've been trying to figure out why I can't get a full roster of volunteers for the 24-hour prayer vigil. The prayer chapel is supposed to have someone there around the clock. We didn't used to have a problem, but people don't seem to be so committed to the difficult times anymore."

"Difficult times?"

"Yeah. People sign up for the convenient times. The times that fit around their work hours. That means daytime mostly. I've got two women who fill in the five to six o'clock slot each morning. We're set up till midnight each night. But nobody wants to commit between midnight and five a.m."

"Can you blame them?"

"It's not a matter of blame, Henry. It's just that the prayer chapel used to be an integral part of the church, and now it seems more like an afterthought."

Henry looked across the table at his square-faced friend. They'd met soon after John was assigned to St. Theresa's. Maybe it was just because they were the two religious leaders of the community, but they had a lot of similar viewpoints, and just enough differences to make conversations enjoyable. Henry picked up his coffee cup. He thought about the hours he'd spent recently pacing the floor in the wee hours. "Would you take a heretic?"

"What are you talking about?"

"Would you take a non-Catholic as a prayer volunteer?"

"I suppose so. Why?"

"I told you I haven't been able to sleep lately. Maybe a nice stroll down to St. Theresa's and an hour or so of prayer would be good for me."

"You're kidding."

"No, I'm serious. Sign me up for the two o'clock time slot. I'll try it for a week and see how it works."

"Thanks, Henry. You're on the roster."

"Do me a favor. Don't write my name down where folks can see it."

"You ashamed of going to a Catholic church?"

"No. I just don't want people trying to second-guess what's going on."

"Small town news?"

Henry heard the irony in his friend's voice. "You got it." He wrinkled his forehead. "Is the door locked? Do I need a key?"

"Are you kidding? This is Martinsville. Nothing ever happens here."

"Except the sign," Henry reminded him.

Ariel flounced up to their table with the coffeepot in hand. "You two doing okay?"

Henry pushed his cup toward her. "We're fine, Ariel. Need a refill, though."

MELISSA AND I WALKED DOWN the street to Miss Mary's, and Melissa registered for tap dance lessons. Of course, we'd eaten our pie before we left the Delicious.

When we were through at Miss Mary's, Melissa turned right to head back to *Azalea House* and I turned left so I could pick up some leeks on the way home. This felt like a good weekend for soup. The grocery store was crowded with the usual Saturday throng, and I found myself looking at each woman in there, wondering if she was a potential tap dance classmate. Judy Smith was so busy with all her artwork, I knew she didn't take classes of any sort. My mother-in-law, however, was bending over the produce display.

"Rebecca Jo?" I asked her without preliminaries, "any chance you'd want to take up tap dancing?"

"And good afternoon to you, too, dear," she said, as she slipped a juicy-looking tomato into a bag. "Now that the niceties are out of the way, are you out of your mind? What would I do at my age with tap dancing?"

"You're only as old as you think you are," I said with a decidedly sanctimonious tone, which I tried to cover up.

She heard it, anyway. "That's a bunch of baloney, and you know it. I get out of breath walking up the hill." She reached up to adjust the neckline of her lavender house dress. "How would I ever last through a dance class?"

Good question. I had a brief vision of her passing out on the floor of Miss Mary's, with all the rest of us hovering around her, fanning her with the instruction books.

After a few more comments, lovingly said of course, many of which related to my being out of touch with reality, she went toward the bread display, and I reached for a fat bunch of leeks. While I was stuffing them in a bag—those bags are never long enough for leeks—Esther Anderson walked up. Esther was the second of my Three Petunias. She volunteered at the library on Wednesdays and Saturdays. What would I ever do without those three women? They were such a help, and Esther was particularly good with the children, which is why her being there on Saturdays was perfect.

It took me a long time to realize that I wasn't very good with children. Oh, I loved my own, and my grandkids. But I found myself running out of patience with the herds that invaded the library every Saturday. Well, not *herds* precisely, but more than I cared to deal with at one time. Maybe that was it. I was a one-on-one person where children were concerned. I felt overwhelmed by *groups* of them.

Esther must be about Rebecca Jo's age, I thought. Maybe a tad younger. "Esther?"

"Yes, sweetie?"

"Is there any chance you'd be interested in taking tap dance lessons at Miss Mary's on Tuesday evenings?"

It took her just a moment to process what I'd asked before she burst into a cackle. "Me? In one of those leotard things? Biscuit, have you lost your mind?"

Why was everyone so worried about my mind? I just wanted enough students in the class to make it happen. "It might be a lot of fun," I offered rather lamely.

"Would you be supplying the oxygen tank? Goodness gracious, Biscuit. Thank you for asking, but I'm seventy-three. I do think I need to pass on this one." She was still chuckling gently as she turned around and scooped up a heavily-veined cantaloupe.

I took my leeks and headed toward the front. Sadie, the third of my Petunias, was in line, too. What was this, a library convention? I nodded hello when she turned around and looked up at me with her sweet smile. I helped her unload her cart onto the check-out counter. Ida rang up the purchases and chatted pleasantly. I watched Sadie, noting her stature (short), her shape (rather tubby), her hair (gray, gray, gray), her age (older than the other two Petunias by quite a few years), her general state of dress (yellow, of course—she always wore yellow), her shoes (tennis shoes, coming untied, as usual). She wouldn't want to take tap dance lessons, so I didn't even bother to ask.

Ida, now. Ida was a different matter altogether. She was about my age. Once Sadie left and Ida was ringing up my leeks, I mentioned that I was going to take tap lessons starting in a week or so.

Ida's eyes went slightly out of focus and she put a hand rather dramatically over her heart. "Remember Gene Kelly twirling that umbrella around?" Her voice was dreamy and wistful.

"Tuesday nights at 7:30."

"Sign me up. It'll be my fortieth birthday present. I'll tell Ralph to sign the check because he never knows what to get me."

Yes! Only three to go.

THAT EVENING, IDA CALLED ME as I was clearing the dinner dishes off the table. "My sister's come over from Enders to stay with me and Ralph for part of the summer. I just talked to her, and she wants to take the class, too. Think there's enough room?"

Me, Melissa, Ida, her sister. Four. "I'm sure we can fit her in," I said. Then I relented and told Ida we were still two short.

"Why don't you ask Annie McGill?" she suggested. Annie was the young and healthy and extremely quiet young woman who ran *Heal Thyself,* the herb store on the corner of First and Magnolia. She also was a talented quilter. I wondered if she was too serious to do something as zany as tap dancing, but it was worth a try. So I called her. She said yes.

Yes!

TWELVE

Diane Marie's journal—Sunday, May 26th
*...I wonder how many other women are trapped the way
I feel I am? Men can get away, at the office, on business
trips, things like that. But I can't get away unless I make
a big deal of it. Or lie about it. Where did I lose myself?
Where did I go wrong? I asked him why he has such an
erratic schedule. He wouldn't say. I've heard couples say
they grow apart the longer they're married, but I've always been on the periphery of his life. Always. He acts
like he cares, but he never tells me anything. I made my
bed. I hate that cliché, but it seems so apt. I made it, but
do I have to lie in it forever?*

BOB AND I HAD BEEN renting the house on Beechnut Lane from
Elizabeth Hoskins since April, with an option to buy. The understanding was that as soon as we got back from our honeymoon, we would close on the house. But then our honeymoon
turned into a disaster, with Bob in the hospital most of the time.
And once we returned to Martinsville, he took a few weeks to
get back on his feet. We didn't want to put the house purchase
off any longer.

I called Elizabeth at the Happy Days Retirement Villa in
Hastings. Ghastly name, but at least I didn't have to live there.
And hoped I never would. After the required how-you-doing-
I'm-fine-how-about-you and such, we got down to business.

"Just call the lawyers," she told me.

"Well, I really wanted to know a little bit more before I talk
to them."

"Like what?"

"Oh, things like is the fence right on the property line or inside it? If I share the fence with Mr. Olsen next door, won't I need to ask him about anything I plant there?"

"Good gracious, Biscuit, I wouldn't know that."

I couldn't see why not. "Elizabeth, didn't you and Perry ever talk about all this before he passed away?"

"Why would I do that? He was the man. He handled it all." While I managed to refrain from grinding my teeth, I'm afraid I did clench them a bit. "Did the lawyers tell you what was involved with this sale?"

"Oh, I'm sure they did, but I didn't pay any attention. I just signed where they said to sign. Call them, Biscuit. They can answer all your questions."

There was only one law firm in Keagan County. Bushy, Bagot and Green, LLC. Not enough people, I supposed, to support more than that. Anyway, nobody had ever sued anybody around here that I knew of. I tended to leaf through phone books whenever I visited other places. Pages and pages of lawyers. Good grief! Whatever happened to talking it over with your neighbors? Of course, talking it over with Elizabeth got me nowhere.

So I called the lawyers. Lo and behold, Mr. Bagot himself answered. "Our receptionist is having a baby," he told me, "and the file clerk is at lunch, so here I am."

He was the one handling Perry Hoskins' estate for Elizabeth. "No," he said after I told him about my conversation with Elizabeth. "No, I didn't think she was listening, but we reviewed every detail."

"I'm sure you did. It's just that Bob and I feel a little funny. The price for the house is so low. We were worried that there might be some catch."

Mr. Bagot cleared his throat. "There's no catch, Mrs. Sheffield."

"McKee," I corrected him. "I kept my maiden name."

Another throat sound. "Yes. Of course. I assure you there is no catch. You and Mr. Sheffield did indeed get quite a good deal. Quite. Would you like to set up a time for us to meet? I can go over all the details with you then."

"We're ready to close as soon as we can, as long as we get our questions answered. Bob said he'd be available most any morning this week. I'd prefer either Tuesday or Thursday because of my work schedule."

"How about Thursday, then, at 10:00 a.m.? We can review all the criteria for the sale, and then set a date for the closing within two to three weeks. Does that sound reasonable?"

"Yes," I told him. "We'll see you on Thursday."

"BOB," I SAID LATER that evening, "something fishy's going on. Mr. Bagot sounded very guarded."

"Of course he did. He's a lawyer. Lawyers are *born* sounding guarded."

I looked at the way he hunched over his coffee cup. Tank sat at his feet, but Bob didn't seem to notice the kitten. That wasn't like him. He'd usually at least pat a furry head that showed up near his knees. "Did you have a grumpy day?" I asked him as Marmalade jumped up on my lap and wormed her ears under my hand.

Yes he did. He told us to get out of his way when we both greeted him at the door.

He rubbed his chin, so I knew he had a problem. He did that only when he couldn't quite figure out what to say.

"Something's going on with Barkley in Atlanta. I don't know what it is, but it doesn't feel right. I'm going to need to make a site visit soon."

Bob and his brother, Barkley, owned a construction company, building high-end, one-of-a-kind homes. Barkley ran the day-to-day operations, Bob was the silent partner. He'd put up most of the money to start the business years ago, money he'd inherited from his grandmother. For years they'd made a substantial profit, but over the past few months, the income had been dropping steadily.

"Is the company getting overstretched with the Olympics coming up?" I asked him.

What is an olympic?

"That could be part of the problem, I suppose. There's been such a building boom there getting ready for the Games…"

Games? I like games. My feather toy is right over here.

"…we should have money coming out our ears…"

That would look funny.

"…but the business is teetering right on the edge. We're not quite losing money, but we're not making any. I looked at the books about three months ago. Now I want to really go over them."

Aren't we going to play with the feather?

"Do you have any idea what it might be?"

He looked at Marmalade and raised one eyebrow. "What are you yowling about?" She quieted as I stroked her head. "I wonder," he went on, "if one of our subcontractors is taking advantage somehow. I can't quite put my finger on it. You know how something can just feel a little bit *off*?"

"How long will it take you, and when do you need to leave?"

"A couple of days at least. I'm thinking of leaving tomorrow."

"But our appointment with Mr. Bagot is Thursday."

"Can you handle it by yourself?"

I will be here with you.

"Of course I can handle it, Bob, but I want it to be a joint effort."

He reached across the little table and took my hand. He ran his fingers across my wedding ring, and smiled. "Biscuit, anything we do from now on and for the rest of our lives is truly a joint effort. But this Thursday I need to be in Atlanta, and you need to be at Mr. Bagot's office."

Oh, well, when he put it that way…

Tuesday, May 28

MELISSA STIRRED SOME soymilk hazelnut creamer into her coffee with the ornate silver spoon she always used. It had a windmill design on the handle. "Did I ever tell you about this spoon?" she asked.

"No, but I have wondered," I admitted. "It's kind of, well, touristy, which doesn't seem like you."

She laughed. "When I was eleven, my parents took me on one of those whirlwind tours of Europe. You know the kind. *See seven countries in eight glorious days.* All we saw was the inside of a bus and a bunch of scenery whizzing by. Oh, and the Louvre in forty-five minutes flat."

"You've got to be kidding. You could spend weeks in the Louvre and never even make a dent."

"Right. Tell that to the tour organizers. Here's the *Mona Lisa,* here's the *Winged Victory,* that's a Raphael, there's a Rembrandt. Back on the bus, everyone."

"What does that have to do with the windmill spoon?"

"Well," she said, drawing that syllable out for about three beats, "all I wanted to do, really, was go to Holland and see the windmills. I'd studied about them in fourth grade and they sounded simply wonderful, and so exciting to see those big paddles turning around. The tour brochure said that the Netherlands was the last country on the itinerary, so every time my parents asked me if I wanted a souvenir from France or Germany or wherever, I said no. I was waiting for Holland. Turns out that seeing the Netherlands was nothing more than a trip to a diamond dealer in Amsterdam. The next day we were in the London airport, waiting for our return flight to be called. I wandered into a little gift shop and found this spoon. I figured it was my only chance to see a windmill, so I bought it with the money I'd saved."

"Melissa, that's a sad story. Why did you ever keep the thing? I would have thrown it out a long time ago."

She rubbed her fingerprints off the narrow handle. "I think I saved it to remind myself not to hope too much."

"Nonsense, Melissa. What it really teaches you is to pick a better tour company. Or stay away from tours and set your own itinerary."

She sighed as she rotated her coffee cup slowly. "I've never had the courage to travel by myself."

"Oh." I knew what I was going to get her as a late birthday present—a couple of books on women traveling the world. "Well," I said, "maybe someday you'll change your mind." Especially after she read those books.

"Not a chance," she said. Sighing, she lifted her coffee cup and said, "Okay, now tell me something horrible that happened to you when you were a kid, so I won't feel like the only one."

It didn't take me long to think of an embarrassing story. "When I was ten, I told my mom that I'd cook dinner, and I wanted to do the *whole* thing…make a list, buy the groceries, prepare the meal. Of course, I wanted Glaze to do the cleanup afterward, but she was only five at the time, so maybe that was expecting too much. Anyway, I decided on pea soup as the main course. I looked up my mom's recipe card, and it said to soak a cup of peas for a while and then cook them, adding this and that. I got all the ingredients together. Had to walk to the store to buy the peas." I paused to sip my coffee. Melissa made great coffee; even I thought so, and I was a committed tea-drinker. Of course, the hazelnut creamer helped considerably.

"Go on," she prompted. "You bought the peas."

"Yes, ma'am, I bought peas, and brought them home. I emptied them into some water…"

"…You didn't rinse them first?"

"Quit getting ahead of me. I soaked them in water like the recipe said to, and added everything on the list and cooked the heck out of it. Then I served it."

"Yeah? What's so horrible about that?"

"My dad sort of stirred his spoon around in his bowl for a few seconds and he said, 'looks a little thin, Bisque honey. Maybe you need a better cookbook.' And then…" I couldn't help it. I started laughing.

"What's so funny?" Melissa insisted.

"Mom spoke up then and said, 'How big a bag of peas did you buy, Biscuit?' And I said, '*Bag?* You mean *can,* don't you?' You see, the recipe just said a cup of peas, so I went to the aisle that had canned vegetables and bought the biggest can of peas

I could find. I didn't know I was supposed to use a package of *dried* peas. No wonder it was like eating bumpy water."

"I'm surprised you ever cooked again."

"Guess it could have gone either way," I said as I stood up. Time to go home and start dinner. Maybe a nice big pot of soup...

THIRTEEN

Thursday, May 30

REBECCA JO SHEFFIELD walked around the corner from her living room and saw her daughter-in-law through the window on the front door. Diane Marie knocked again, louder this time. Rebecca Jo felt only a brief moment of irritation. She took longer to get out of her chair now than she used to. Time was when she could hop up on a moment's notice. Now, she felt a lot older and a great deal stiffer than *everybody*. Well, that kind of thinking wouldn't get her anywhere. Put up with the way things are and quit complaining about it, she told herself as she opened the door.

Diane Marie looked fairly washed out. She had a suitcase beside her on the porch. Rebecca Jo had always thought her daughter-in-law would leave Barkley some day, but somehow she hadn't thought it would be this soon. Good thing she aired out the spare bedroom a couple of days ago. She motioned the young woman inside and closed the door behind her. "So," she said, "has my son been acting like a fool?"

"Oh, Mama Sheffield," Diane Marie blurted out, and stepped into Rebecca Jo's open arms.

THE DRIVE TO GARNER CREEK to meet with the lawyer that Thursday was uneventful. Little did I guess what was in store for me.

"Ms. McKee...? *Ahem*..." Mr. Bagot must have had something wrong with his throat. He was still clearing it frequently. The table where we sat could have easily accommodated a dozen people. He was at the end. I sat to his left. I wondered how often twelve people gathered here at one time. Why does lawyer furniture always have to be so big and impressive? Looked like overkill to me. If all the ghosts of lawyers past who had sat at this table were gathered around it right now, whose side would they be on? The law firm of Bushy, Bagot and Green was a fixture in Garner Creek. They had been around for decades. There was a sign in the reception room that said so. This Mr. Bagot was the son of the original Bagot. Or maybe he was the grandson. I'd have to ask him…

"Ms. McKee? Did you understand what I was saying?"

"Oh, I'm sorry Mr. Bagot, my mind wandered for a moment. I was thinking about how many people must have sat at this table over the last fifty or sixty years."

"Well, not too many, I'm afraid. Mr. Green insisted that we buy this table last month. It was delivered late yesterday afternoon. So you and I are the first ones to sit here." He did another one of his little *ahem* sounds, and ducked his head a bit. His front teeth stuck out just a tad. With his wide face and his pleasant bushy moustache, he looked like a rather cordial groundhog. "Shall we start a tradition?" he said.

I had to smile. "Yes, Mr. Bagot. I think this is a fine beginning for your table." I picked up my purse from the floor and plopped it on the chair next to me. I'd stuffed in a notepad just before I left the house. "Bob and I have a list of questions."

"Suppose you, *ahem,* read them to me, and we'll see if I have the answers."

I opened my notepad. "One. What are the exact dimensions of the lot?"

"We have that information for you here in the file. I'll go over it with you, and of course you will receive a copy of the legal description and all the pertinent papers at the closing."

"Okay. Two—is the ownership of the fence shared with Mr. Olsen and the Montgomery's?"

"Shared?" he asked. "What…*ahem*…are you talking about?"

"I want to know if Bob and I will own the fence completely, or if we have to get permission before we alter it."

"Permission? From whom?"

"From the other owners."

"The other owners?" he said.

What was with this echo act? Didn't the man comprehend English? "Bob and I were talking about putting a gate in the fence at the back of the yard, or maybe taking some of the fence down, so we can get to the little stream that runs across the common area in the center of the block."

"Common area?"

"Mr. Bagot, maybe you don't know Martinsville very well." I turned my notebook to a fresh page and started drawing a diagram to help my explanation. "Bob explained to me that some of the blocks in town—" as I talked I drew a big square "—have houses around the outside of them." I added four little house squares inside the big block. "See? There's usually a house on each corner..." I filled in four more house squares so there were three squares on each side of the big block. That left a blank area in the middle. "...and there's what they call a common area in the middle of each block." I pointed at the blank spot in the center in case he was missing the idea.

"Most of the families have gotten together to maintain a play area for the children there. Some families garden in the center. Some have just planted lots of trees. Some put up benches.

"It takes an amazing amount of cooperation, but Bob said it works very well. Each common area has just sort of evolved as the town grew." Mr. Bagot was looking more and more bewildered. "Does this make sense to you, Mr. Bagot? Can you see what I'm saying?"

"It...*ahem*...makes perfect sense, Ms. McKee. I'm quite familiar with the way Martinsville was plotted. What I don't understand is why you are asking this."

"I just told you. Our block is unusual in that it has a stream that passes through the center of it. The block above ours has a tiny lake, more like a pond, that appears to be spring fed. It's on Maggie Pontiac's property, and there's an outlet that forms our stream. It passes through a culvert under Third Street—" I pointed to the spot on my map "—and runs downhill through the middle of the block. You see, there aren't any houses on the bottom side of our block. All we have are Mr. Olsen on this corner—" I made a big X "—and this house on the other corner belongs to Brighton and Ellen Montgomery." Another X. "Then here's our house—well, Elizabeth's house." A third X filled in 213 Beechnut Lane, next to Mr. Olsen's X on my little map. While I was at it, I erased all the other house squares, since there weren't any other houses on our block. "There's a small bridge right here—" I sketched in a few lines "—where Second Street runs across the stream."

"Yes," he said. "I know that."

I love maps. I added a second bridge at First Street, then plotted the course of the little stream. "And it runs this way, and passes between the grocery store and the beauty shop. Then it goes under First Street and empties into the Metoochie right near the town dock."

"Yes," he said again. "I understand."

I looked down at the squiggles and squares and streets I'd been drawing. What was so complicated about my question?

Mr. Bagot was quiet for a moment. I looked up from my paper. He shook his head, cleared his throat and said, "Ms. McKee, didn't Elizabeth Hoskins tell you what was involved with this sale?"

"Involved? No. She came in the library one day and asked if Bob and I wanted to buy her house. I told her I hadn't known it was for sale. All she and I ever talked about was books and gardening...."

As a matter of fact, we'd talked quite a bit about gardening. I remembered the day I walked her around the grounds of the old Millicent mansion that was now the library, and I showed her where I wanted to put in flower beds and a butterfly garden and bird feeders. We talked about tucking host plants here and there so the butterflies could lay their eggs on plants the caterpillars could eat once they'd hatched. She was delighted when I described the benches I wanted to place into little flowered reading nooks.

That day she agreed right then and there to donate all her gardening books to the library. When I went to her house to pick up the first load of boxes stuffed full of books, she showed me around her yard. I loved it right from the start, and told her how impressed I was with what she'd done. She had used native plants mostly, and we found out that we both liked the botanical names of plants. The Latin flowed as we walked around and talked gardening. It was a few days after that when she stopped by the library and said, "I heard that you and Bob are looking for a house."

"…and then," I told Mr. Bagot, "she said she'd sell us the house for this amount, and I asked her—I think I was joking about it at the time, but not really because the price was so low—I asked her if the land was included, and she said yes. Then we signed the lease-to-buy papers that you drew up." His face was getting more and more groundhog-ish. I was getting more and more worried. "What am I missing here?"

"She didn't say anything to you about the rent money?"

"Rent money?" Oh, for crying out loud. No wonder the house price was so low. All she was selling us was the house without any land? That was ridiculous. I wouldn't buy a house if the land didn't go along with it. But we'd already signed the rent-to-purchase papers. Maybe we could get out of it. I didn't want to get out of it. I loved that house and I wanted to stay there. But I wanted the land, too. I knew this was too good to be true.

"*Ahem*…Ms. McKee? You don't know about the rent?"

"We have to rent the land the house sits on? Mr. Bagot, I think that's the most asinine arrangement I've ever heard of." He held up a hand, but I kept right on going. "Who in their right mind would agree to such a thing, and why on earth didn't you make that plain to us before we signed those stupid papers? I knew I should have gotten a realtor!"

"Excuse me, Ms. McKee. I think we need to have a little talk here." He smiled, showing his teeth, and he looked even more like a groundhog. "Would you like a cup of coffee?"

"Coffee? You're offering me coffee when you've just told me

we won't even own the land our house is on? What makes you think coffee would make this easier to digest?"

One of the other lawyers poked his pointy head around the doorway. I suppose my voice was rising somewhat in pitch and volume. And I suppose I was pounding a bit on that ridiculous table.

"We're all right, George." Mr. Bagot waved a hand in dismissal. "Ms. McKee is about to receive a shock. I thought she might like some coffee. She thinks I'm out of my...*ahem*...out of my mind."

Why was he laughing about this?

Of course, after he told me, I agreed that a cup of coffee might be a very good idea, indeed. I wished he'd offered me a slug of brandy in it.

I WAS HAVING a hard time figuring out the implications of all this. Halfway through the cup of coffee, I shook my head. "Mr. Bagot, let me be sure I have this straight, because I'm going to have to explain it to Bob." A thought struck me. "Why didn't Bob know all this to begin with? He's something of a town historian."

"This arrangement has been handed down quietly through the generations since the late 1700's. I'm sure few people in Martinsville know about it." He smiled his groundhog grin. "Go ahead, Ms. McKee."

"Now, as I understand it, when we buy the house, we'll also own the entire block."

"That is correct."

"And the Montgomery's and Mr. Olsen will pay us rent each year?"

"Yes, they will. Each pays you the equivalent of the cost of one sheep. It's become the custom to update the dollar figure every five years, based on the economy at the time. Our expert figures out the value of the wool and meat, as well."

I had a horrible vision of slaughter, until I remembered we were talking about a hypothetical sheep. "So, because this block belonged to Mr. Hastings originally... Is he the one who founded the town of Hastings?" I digressed.

"His...*ahem*...his second son moved up the valley and that farm eventually became Hastings."

"Oh. So Mr. Hastings rented out these two other plots on his block, under the condition that they always stay within the family that was renting them. Is that right?"

"Exactly."

"And some long-gone forebear of Mr. Olsen rented that corner lot. Ditto, Brighton Montgomery's ancestor on the other corner."

"Actually, it was Ellen Montgomery's ancestor who signed the original lease."

"That means that if Mr. Olsen or Ellen and Brighton ever want to sell their houses, they can't?"

"This is where the legal niceties get a bit involved, Ms. McKee. They own their houses. They simply do not own the land on which those houses sit. You and your husband own that. Or you will once the closing has happened."

"So they could sell the house, but not the land?"

"Not precisely." Mr. Bagot ducked his head. I couldn't tell whether he was delighted to be imparting this information or slightly embarrassed about the complications it would probably—inevitably—cause some day. "They can pass the ownership of their houses on to their direct descendants, but if there is no direct descendant to inherit, the land and any buildings on it revert back to the original Hastings estate."

"But doesn't that mean Elizabeth Hoskins can't sell us the lot?"

"No. There was no restriction on Mr. Hastings' part in this, nor on *his* descendants. His first son inherited upon his death, and ownership has continued in the family to this day, but there is nothing legal that says that has to be the case. When Martinsville was founded, there were six blocks that began with such a proviso. Three of them passed out of the original families' possession, and the rental plots were sold outright. This block, though," he said, pointing to my squiggled map, "always managed to stay within the Hastings family, although a number of times the land passed to a daughter when there was no son to inherit. Hence the name change. But Perry Hoskins, through his mother, was in the direct line of descent from Robert Hastings. Perry and Elizabeth have a son, but he signed a waiver. He will not get the house."

That sounded financially irresponsible to me, but if he took after his mother, he probably had no idea what was involved. "Shouldn't he be given another chance?" I halfway asked, hoping the answer would be no.

The cozy groundhog in front of me turned lawyer-ish. "No," he said. "No, there are documents that preclude that."

It was pretty obvious from his tone that he wasn't going to tell me what those documents said. Maybe the son had been disowned. Elizabeth had never spoken of him. My mind came back to a more immediate question. "Who did the Olsens and Ellen Montgomery come from?"

"Daughters of the original Mr. Hastings. I suppose he wanted to keep them close to home."

I started giggling, much to the amusement of Mr. Bagot. He let me go on for a while before he asked if I would let him in on the joke.

"It's nothing much. I just feel like we're such a part of this huge sweep of history, I should start churning my own butter and wearing a mobcap, and maybe Bob could wear a frock coat or a lace jabot. Like Williamsburg."

"I would enjoy seeing you talk your husband into that idea, Ms. McKee." It sounded like he had a story behind his words. "I remember Bobby Sheffield from when he was fourteen years old. Ask him some time to tell you the entire story."

Try as I might, he wouldn't say anything more.

I gathered my papers, shook his hand and left. As I walked toward my car, it hit me that someday we'd have Ariel Montgomery as a neighbor, paying us a sheep a year. Oh, dear. What a thought.

AFTER THE MEETING with Mr. Bagot, I felt in need of some nourishment and a nice cup of hot tea, so I headed for the Creek

Diner. On the way, I passed by Mable's Dress Shop and figured I might as well stop in.

The bell over the door jingled merrily as I stepped inside, and the auburn-haired woman behind the counter looked up, smiling. "Hey there, Biscuit," she said.

"Hey, Sarah. What's new?"

"Do you mean here in the store?"

"No, I meant with you, but you can show me new stuff here, too."

She grinned. "I'm all signed up to start college classes during the summer session."

"Congratulations! That was quick."

"Well, it was mostly a matter of making up my mind that I really wanted to do it. I'll go to evening and weekend classes for a couple of years and then, when I graduate, I'll head on somewhere for a masters degree. Counseling." She grinned. "I'm going to do it!"

"Good for you." I hadn't known Sarah for long, but I liked her enthusiasm.

"Come on back here. I want you to see the new section we've just put in."

The sign over one of the back counters proclaimed *His 'n' Hers.* I raised my eyebrows. Sarah picked up two matching polo shirts in a soft green. "One for him. One for you," she said. "We carry only short-sleeved sets. That way we don't have to handle so many different sizes." Amazingly, the first set she picked up just happened to be the right sizes for Bob and me. Not amazing. She was good at sales, and equally good at guessing sizes.

"Okay. I'll take them. If you get some blue ones in later, let me know."

"Will do."

"Do you have any men's shirts in white?" I asked.

"No. You'll have to go down the street to Nate's for that."

I paid for the green shirts and stopped in at Nate's to pick up a new white shirt for Bob's uniform. Then I had to drop by the bank to cash a check. Used their ATM machine instead. Wish we had one of those in Martinsville. Finally—it was about time!—I went to the diner and had a well-deserved lunch, with chocolate cake for dessert.

I COULD BARELY CONTAIN MYSELF. It was so hard for me to believe that Bob hadn't had a clue about the land and rent arrangement. I hoped he wasn't going to be late getting home. I would tell him about it over dinner. Or maybe right after. Or maybe just before. Or maybe the minute he walked in the door.

When he walked in, though, he kept me from saying anything right away by the simple expedient of kissing me thoroughly. I love being newly married. I knew it would slow down a bit with time, but right then all the hugs and kisses felt so right and so warm and so wonderful. "Are you ever going to forget to kiss me when you walk in the door?" I asked him.

"Probably," he said with a grin. "But not today."

"I have something exciting to tell you."

The phone started ringing. "Great," he said. "How about some coffee first, though?" He was closer to the phone, so he stepped into the living room and answered it. I've seen some couples who seem to have an unwritten agreement that only one of them will answer the phone. My Uncle Mark and Auntie Blue—her name was Beulah, but nobody called her that—were like that. He'd be sitting right next to the phone, and if it rang, she had to come in from another room, reach across him and pick it up. That made no sense to me.

The phone call seemed to be for Bob, so I wasn't paying any particular attention, until I realized it was his mother on the line. She hated phones, so of course I wondered what was up.

"When did she get here?" Bob asked. "...And she's planning to stay...? Mom, *she* should be the one to call him...? Of course I want what's best, but getting in the middle of Diane Marie and Barkley is not for the best."

By this time I was actively trying to hear Rebecca Jo's voice. I stopped short of picking up the kitchen phone, but I was tempted. When Bob hung up, I was prancing with curiosity. "What was all that about?"

Bob rubbed his jaw with his left hand and ran his right hand through his hair until it stood on end. Something must have been very wrong to get him looking that disheveled. "Diane Marie's left Barkley. She showed up on Mom's doorstep this morning with a suitcase. Mom wants me to call Barkley. I told her no."

Before I could jump in with my opinion, he went on. "I won't get pulled into this. How do I know what Diane Marie's thinking?" He stopped talking and had another go at his hair.

"Why did your mother want *you* to call him?"

He nodded his head like one of those bobble toys. "She said if she talked to him, she'd tell him precisely what she thought of him, and she figured it would be better if somebody more diplomatic did the job."

"But you told her no?"

"Yeah. Diane Marie is the one who needs to call Barkley. She'll never do it if we jump in and do it for her."

"Think this is temporary or permanent?"

"How would I know?" He reached out and brushed my cheek. "I'm going over to try to settle everything down. Mom's sounding dangerously strung out." With her blood pressure, that wasn't a good thing. He pulled his keys out of his pocket. "I'll be back soon—I promise."

So much for telling him we were going to own the whole block. Oh, well, little details like that could wait.

My gratitude list for Thursday, May 30th
1. A stable marriage
2. Bob's level-headedness
3. Mr. Bagot
4. This great news!
5. Gratitude itself

my gratitude list for today
the bird feeder
chicken
the wide porch
cool water
ear-scratching

FOURTEEN

Friday, May 31

THE SULTRY SUMMER afternoon was well-advanced when Father John Ames strode over to the table in the corner of his office at St. Theresa's rectory. He picked up the book he'd been reading last night and tried again to get interested in it. This was not turning out to be his best day. *The Apologies of the Saints* was as boring as… Father Ames paused before even thinking the h-word. Not that he was theologically uncertain about the simile, or its appropriateness in this particular circumstance, but thirty-seven years of a mother like Diane Marie Houston Ames gave him pause every time he deviated from her rocklike certitudes about what was proper for him to say, to do, even to think.

The slender red book was something he supposed he ought to get on with reading, since the Bishop had written it. The Bishop who would soon be making a duty call on the little parish of St. Theresa's in Martinsville, where Father Ames had served with moderate success for two years. The small town in northeast Georgia was something of a refuge for him. It had gotten him 125 miles away from Atlanta where his bull-headed mother, short but pushy, reigned over her husband, her neighborhood, her church friends and, before he escaped, over her son, the priest. The whole time he lived in Atlanta he had to spend each and every Sunday luncheon at her table, plus Wednesday evenings and Fridays for brunch.

Father Ames sat down on the dark-grained cherry-wood chair. Nothing in this room matched. Different woods, different styles, different patterns. His comfortable desk chair was covered in a green plaid; the one he was sitting on had a floral print seat with big green leaves. The guest chair, on the far side of the desk, had blue and gold stripes on the cushion. Father Ames loved this room. Compared to his mother's elegant magazine-cover house, this old building and this room in particular was rumpled, a bit tattered and wondrously comfortable. His mother's furniture, by contrast, indeed her entire house, was the most expensive money could buy. His father seemed to have plenty of that. The family's electrical supply company had grown at an astronomical rate over the past twenty years or so. Father Ames could remember his childhood, when Mother had answered phones and dispatched trucks. Now she spent her days lording it over the rest of her upstart friends. Father Ames was fairly sure she didn't understand old money. The fact that she would never be accepted in old Atlanta society was a premise she apparently refused to consider. Month after month, year after year, her invitations had been politely declined, and the stately old house, purchased from the last scion of an old aristocratic family, had sat awaiting the teas and balls and soirees that Mother was always ranting about.

Not one to be daunted by any snub, be it abrupt or ever so polite, Mother had gone about creating her own version of Society. Dressed in the long flowing robes she adored, always in peacock-bright colors, she had peopled the old house with all the other would-be's she could scrape up. She held her balls, for which she bullied her husband into wearing a tuxedo. She showcased pianists and sopranos and ardent poets at afternoon teas that the outer fringes of Atlanta Society now longed to be invited to.

Father Ames ran his hand along the spare lines of the small lamp-lit table where he sat. Given a choice between his mismatched office and the peacock elegance of his mother's house, he knew that he would choose this simple room in this dark-walled rectory at St. Theresa's. This old Georgian house, built next to the church in the 1800's, had simple lines and too many small rooms. It was hard to heat in the winter and hard to cool in the summer, but he loved it. He had come to love this little town. It wasn't just that Martinsville wasn't anywhere near his mother. It was, however, an added benefit that she didn't drive. He cringed just thinking about frequent motherly visits. As it was, she invaded Martinsville too often. Two or three times a year. It never ceased to amaze him how such a small woman could offend so many people in so little time. She had the knack of what Father Ames called the bone-mot. Never a *good* word. Only a bone-headed termagant would say the things she said.

Mother always got his sister to drive her up from the city. Nobody seemed to know what to make of Madeleine. He and his sister had been good friends when they were youngsters, but now he hardly knew her. She hung about in Mother's shadow. Thirty-some-odd years old and still living at home. She ran Mother's house and apologized to the people Mother had offended. Madeleine was very good at apologizing. She'd had lots of practice.

When he was assigned to St. Theresa's two years ago, Mother had volunteered to come along and keep him company for the first few weeks. He was sure his new parishioners would have revolted, so he had declined her offer. Like a rhinoceros, she generally seemed to get her way. But that time, miraculously and uncharacteristically, she had honored his request. The last time she came, she breezed into the rectory and got him to move the furniture around. For your own good, she said. Only after she left and he'd had a few hours, and a stiff drink, had he realized that he didn't want the sofa over there or the lounger over here. So he had to get up and rearrange it all again. The alternative would have been to live with it awhile and see if he could get used to it, but he knew he'd bump his shin on the coffee table when he got up in the middle of the night when he couldn't sleep and wanted a drink of water.

He laid the Bishop's book aside—he hadn't been reading it anyway—and picked up his mother's latest letter. She had written a homily for him to deliver the next Sunday. She'd written ninety-seven of the damn things so far, delivered by mail almost every Thursday since he'd come to Martinsville.

Dear Mother Rhinoceros, he wrote in his dreams every Thursday night, *your latest, highly offensive missive arrived. Once again I will gleefully rip it to shreds and burn the tattered pieces in the fireplace of my quiet little motherless sanctuary. Quit bothering me with your outdated platitudes about sin and damnation. Quit assuming that I don't have an ounce of sense. Quit thinking I can't live without you. I'm doing it quite well. Thank God for small favors.*

And he signed it in his dream, *Your son, the priest, Father John Houston Ames.*

Every Friday he tore up her letter and then sat down to write a real note, a duty letter, thanking her for her thoughtfulness. She was in the senior citizen category now, and sometimes talked about how frail she was. Hell, she was going to live forever. At fifty-nine, she was about as fragile as an iron skillet. The only thing on earth she was afraid of was having her gray roots show. Honor thy father and thy mother, the Bible said, that thy days may be long upon the earth. The sign at the Old Church had reminded him. Ha! With a mother like that, his days were already an eternity. Or had been until he'd left Atlanta. God help him if she ever showed up on his doorstep asking him to take her in. He wondered idly if a priest could get away with matricide. Rhinocerocide. Probably not. With a sigh, he tossed her letter onto his desk and picked up the Bishop's book again.

It *was* as boring as hell, no buts about it, so he was relieved to be interrupted by a tentative-sounding knock on his front door.

"Father? Could I talk with you?"

She was slight of build, with a narrow face and long-lashed doe eyes. Her head kept turning, as if she were a moth in flight, trying to determine the source of the elusive smells upon which her very life depended.

"Yes," he said. He opened his door wider and pointed her toward his office, the first door on the right off the hallway. She scurried in. Like a mouse, he thought. A deer, a moth and a mouse, all bundled up in one blond-headed package. He watched her slide sideways—like a crab—into the striped chair he indicated, and he gave her a moment to catch her breath as he sank onto his green plaid.

"What can I do for you, my child?" he intoned, feeling, as he always did, a bit silly using those words. It was safer, though, for all concerned, to establish right away that he was a priest first and foremost. He did take his counseling duties seriously, and had found that often it was simply a matter of listening. So many people didn't have anyone to listen to them, and Father Ames had found thus far in his ecclesiastical career, that most often they already had the answers somewhere deep inside them. It took a listening heart to give them the space to find those answers.

"I'm Catholic, Father. I used to attend Mass here sometimes when I was growing up. It was a long way to get here, so we didn't come as often as we should have." She paused. "I married outside the church. Are you still willing to talk to me?"

"Of course I am. I'm Father Ames. Now, do tell me your name. I don't think I've seen you around town."

"I'm just visiting here," she told him. "My name is Diane Marie, but I'd rather not mention my last name, if that's okay with you."

Father Ames had to shift gears. Diane Marie was his mother's name. This was not his mother in front of him. This was a perfectly personable young woman who needed his help. She happened to have light blond hair, about the same shade as his mother's. This was not, repeat, not his mother. He took a large breath, and exhaled rather noisily. "Tell me, Diane Marie, how can I help you?"

"Father, I think my husband is trying to kill me."

She said it in such a matter-of-fact way that Father Ames had to shift gears yet again. "Kill you?" he said. "Why do you think that?"

"Well, he's stopped beating me lately." Her backbone was perfectly straight, and she perched on the edge of the chair as if she might take flight at any moment, like the moth he had already seen in her.

"Isn't that a good thing?" he asked.

"Good thing?"

"That he's not beating you?"

"No, Father. Well, I mean, yes. I don't like being hit, but at least I know where it's coming from, and I can sort of feel it building up, so it's not such a surprise when it happens, and I can kind of get ready for it, if you know what I mean."

No, thought Father Ames, he did not know what she meant. How could anyone choose to get ready to take a beating? Then he remembered his mother and the wide brown wooden spoon she always used when she hit him. He remembered exactly what it was like to feel that powerlessness of being little and of having angered his mother. He could remember 'girding his loins' so to speak, getting ready for the punishment that was to come. But this woman wasn't a child, and her husband presumably had vowed to love, honor and cherish her. Where did physical abuse fit into that vow?

"But this is different," she continued, not seeming to have noticed that the priest had checked out for a moment or two.

"In what way?" He was treading on unfamiliar ground here. There hadn't been anything about murder in his seminary courses.

"My car has started having problems. With the brakes. And the seat belt."

Was he supposed to understand this? "How does this relate to your accusation?"

"The day before I came here to visit Ida...I mean my sister...I told my husband I was feeling really tired and I was going to take a nap. He said he'd be out working on the lawn mower. Well, a little while later I got up to go to the bathroom. When I looked out the window, there was my husband underneath my car. I watched him for a while. I couldn't tell what he was doing, so I went out to see what the problem was. When I walked out the door, he started scrambling to get out from under there. I asked him what was wrong and he said nothing was wrong. He'd just dropped a nut from the lawn mower and it rolled under my car and he had to get it. I said something like *oh,* and he said what's that supposed to mean, and I said I just wondered if something was wrong with my car. He told me no, nothing's wrong with your car. Your car's in great shape." She paused, and Father Ames watched her eyes roam around his small office, taking in the oak bookshelves, the little maple writing table by the window, the gray metal desk that filled most of the center of the room, the piles of paper that were waiting to be sorted, answered, dealt with. His mother's latest letter was on one of those piles waiting to be torn up, but this Diane Marie didn't know that.

"Yes?" Father Ames prompted.

"You see, he knew I was leaving the next day to come here."

"So he was checking your car to be sure it was in good working order?"

"No, Father, he wasn't. And why did he say all that about dropping a nut from the lawn mower? He didn't want me to know what he'd been doing."

"What *was* he doing?"

"Well, I found out. You see, the next morning I couldn't get my seat belt fastened. It was jammed and my husband had already left on a business trip. I got more and more worried. So I stopped at a garage just outside of town and asked the mechanic to fix the seat belt and then to check the car really really carefully. I told him that I'd caught some teenage boys under my car and I thought they might have done some damage, and I didn't want to drive on to Martinsville until I was sure it was okay."

"Did he believe you?"

"Apparently so. He looked it over. It took him a long time. And then he told me he hoped I had the names of those boys because they could have really hurt me. There was a slit in the brake line. He said he wouldn't have found it unless he'd been looking for some mischief. That's what he said, some mischief."

"Was it a big slit? Could it have caused a wreck?"

"That's just it, Father. It wasn't a big slit. A big slit would have leaked the brake fluid out in my driveway, and I wouldn't have been able to drive this far. It was a teeny little slit, made with a sharp knife. The hose had to heat up from the warmth of the engine before it would start leaking. The mechanic figured the brakes would have held until I got onto these windy, twisty roads around here."

"You don't live here in the Upper Valley, right?"

"Right." She leaned forward, and her voice dropped to a whisper. "Father, I think he messed up the seat belt and put that slit in the brake line. You know what the roads are like. I could have gone off one of the bridges into the river, and it would all be over."

Why couldn't the Bishop have written something useful, like how to counsel this young woman, instead of writing about those stuffy old saints? How could they possibly help deal with a car as a potential murder weapon? He would have to take her seriously. He wondered if reporting it to the police would be a good idea. No, that would be breaking her confidentiality. Of course, this wasn't the confessional. He wondered briefly what his mother would say to this young Diane Marie. No. He knew precisely what his mother would say. *You made your bed; now lie in it.* Some comfort, that.

"Why do you think he might want to kill you?"

"I think something's going on. I don't know what it is, but I've been asking him questions lately about these business trips of his, and he's gotten so defensive about it. I wondered if he's having an affair or something."

"Did you ask him about it?"

"No. Not directly. I kind of hinted at it."

Father Ames waited for her to say more, but she stopped and lowered her head. "That doesn't seem like a reason for murder," he said as gently as he could.

"Well, if he doesn't want to kill me about that, he's going to want to when he finds out I'm pregnant."

"You're pregnant?"

"Yes, and he doesn't want a baby."

Father Ames took another deep breath as he searched for what to say. This conversation was like riding a roller coaster. "Why do you think he doesn't want the baby?"

"We've been married fourteen years, and he always made me take…precautions. He didn't want squalling brats around. That's what he told me."

"Did you agree to this before you married him?"

"I didn't know then what I know now. He was so sweet before we got married. He promised me so many things that just never happened after I married him."

Father Ames wondered if he should use the term "reeling you in," but he decided she already knew what that husband of hers had done fourteen years ago. "It is true," he said, "that a man who abuses his wife cannot be trusted to stop that abuse just because she is pregnant. It is also true that abusive men often mistreat their own children as well as their wives. But do you truly think he's planning to kill you, or are you just taking your fears for the safety of yourself and the baby and magnifying them?"

"I wish I could talk him into wanting the baby, but I don't think he will."

"Is this…" Father Ames paused. "Is this baby your husband's child?"

"Yes," she said with finality. "Yes, Father. I've been a good wife." Her voice dropped so he had to lean forward to hear her. "Lots of help that's been to me. I almost wish I'd played around. At least I could have had some fun." She shook her head. "I can't believe I just said that. I'm sorry, Father."

"God knows the wishes of our hearts, Diane Marie, and we priests have heard most of those wishes in one form or another. I think I am beyond being shocked by anything I hear." He shifted to a more upright position. The chair had a definite list to the right. "Have you gone to the police?" he asked her.

She folded her arms across her narrow chest. "I'm supposed to tell them I'm scared because my husband isn't beating me anymore?"

"You could tell them what you've told me."

"But there's no proof, Father." She shook her head. "There's nothing I can point to and say, this is it, this is a clue. In a town our size, it wouldn't take him long to figure out I went to the cops, and how do I know what he'd do then?"

Where was the right phrase? Where was the key to this woman's unhappy kingdom? "Why are you here in Martinsville?" he asked her.

"My husband was going out of town for a couple of weeks, so I wrote my sister and asked her to let me stay with her. I'm planning to stay as long as I can get away with it."

"Does she know you're pregnant?"

"No. I haven't told her yet."

"Does your husband know that you're staying here with your sister?"

"I told him she was really sick and needed me."

Father Ames looked at Diane Marie who was not meeting his eyes. "Is she sick?"

The answer was quiet. "No."

"Does she know you came to talk with me?"

"No. She needed to pick up a book that was on hold at the library. She knows I spend a lot of time just walking around town and up on the ridges, so I told her I'd pick up the book on my way back from a walk, but I came here first and then I'll get the book and she won't know."

"Doesn't she know about your troubles with your husband?"

"Good Lord, no, Father! I tried to write to her about it once, but I didn't send the letter. I threw it away. She's got one of those perfect marriages, with a perfect husband and a perfect house and a perfect car. She'd never understand, and she'd probably think it was my fault, anyway."

She looked, he thought, as if that so-called logic of hers made sense. He'd read that women usually share their troubles with other women. Why not in this case? "Diane Marie? Is that the issue here? Do you agree with your sister? Do you think it *is* your fault somehow?" He watched as her face crumpled and her body slumped on the chair, her back no longer rigid.

"My mother and my sister both said not to marry him, so I ran away. I eloped… They were right, it turned out, but I was too ashamed to admit it. And now…I did this on purpose…. I wanted this baby."

WHEN FATHER AMES opened his front door for the second time that day, he wasn't prepared for what looked and sounded like an instant replay.

"Father?" said the blond-haired woman who stood, like a bird poised for flight, on his front step. "Could I talk with you?"

She was slight of build, much like the last woman, but this face was not so narrow, and the eyes were slanted upward, as if trying to lift away from her nose. Cat eyes. She glanced behind her. "Please let me come in, Father."

"Yes," he said. "Of course." He pushed the door back and pointed her in the right direction. She sailed in and perched on the chair in front of his desk, chewing away at a large chunk of her lower lip. His phone rang, and she jumped. "I'll let the message machine pick that one up," he said. Her mouth contracted into a steady tic. A squirrel, he thought. This one was a bird, a cat and a squirrel. He was getting rather good at this.

"I'm Catholic, Father, but I didn't marry in the church. Will you still talk to me?"

"Of course I will. I'm Father Ames, in case you don't know. I don't think I've seen you around town," he said for the second time that day.

"I don't live here anymore. My name is Diane Marie." She took a deep breath. "Diane Marie," she repeated. "I was born a Hastings, but I'd rather not mention my married name."

If he were a gambling man, Father Ames thought, and thank God he wasn't, he would never have bet that two short slender blonde women bearing his mother's name would show up on his doorstep in one afternoon. It was like greasing the wheels for an avalanche, he thought, not even minding that he was mixing his metaphors. Good gracious Lord, he thought, if his mother showed up it would be more than he could bear.

Father Ames felt he needed to take a very big breath. He should have taken yoga lessons. He'd heard that would help. "What can I do for you, my child?"

Why was he not surprised when she said, "I think my husband's trying to kill me, Father."

This story, though, had nothing to do with cars. Far from it. This Diane Marie had stumbled across a ledger shoved into the back of a drawer in her husband's desk when she was looking for some paper. Then she'd heard him come in, so she pushed the ledger back, but it wasn't exactly the way she'd found it. And now she knew that he knew that she'd found the ledger, even if she didn't know what it was about.

"You were looking for some paper?"

"Yes, I couldn't find any right off hand and I thought I'd just rummage a bit in his desk. I just needed it for a list. It didn't have to be a big piece of paper. I suppose I could have walked over to the kitchen but the office was closer, and there wasn't any paper on top of the desk…"

When Father Ames was a teenager he'd lied just like that once, and the teacher he was lying to, Sister Marie, had raised one eyebrow. That made John add a few more juicy, convincing details, and the eyebrow went even higher. "John," she finally told him, "the more you embellish, the less I believe you."

So Father John Ames looked straight at this cat-eyed Diane Marie and raised one of his eyebrows. It worked. When he'd heard enough embellishing, he gently interrupted her and asked, "Now would you like to tell me the real reason you were looking in his desk?"

She burst into tears. He passed her a box of tissues, and she told him the real story.

ONCE SHE LEFT, he turned back to his desk and pushed the blinking button on his phone. "Good afternoon, Father John!" it said.

He hated it when she called him that. "Don't call me *Father,* Mother," he said back to the phone.

"I was just thinking that it's been such a long while…"

"Not nearly long enough."

"…since I visited you. Your sister, Madeleine…"

He had only one sister… "I know her name, Mother," he instructed the phone.

"…said she would drive me up there tomorrow morning. That way we can stay with you…"

"Oh, great."

"…and attend your Mass."

"It's not *my* Mass, Mother. It's God's Mass. It's the people's Mass."

"Then after we have Sunday luncheon…"

"Let me guess, we can have a lovely visit."

"…we can have a *lovely* visit. I wish my sister, Martha, were here to come along with us…."

"Oh, sure, let's do have a crowd."

"…but she can't, of course. Your sister, Madeleine, and I can stay for at least one week."

"What do you mean *at least?*"

"It's time we had a good long visit. We'll pack enough for two or three weeks just in case."

"Two weeks? Three weeks!"

"Good-bye, Father."

"Don't call me *Father,* Mother," he said again.

"Did I bring this on myself?" he asked the now-silent phone. "I go to confession. I pray all the right prayers. I pay attention when I perform the Mass. I am caring and thoughtful with my parishioners. I'm even reading the Bishop's crappy book. And what do I get? What do I get?" he repeated. "What I get is *two* Diane Marie's in one day, with their two murderous husbands, and then what else do I get? I get two unwelcome guests, my battle-ax Diane Marie mother and my completely unfathomable sister, and they're going to stay an eternity."

He turned away from the phone. Why hadn't he become a

monk? He could have lived happily in one small room. "Why me, God?" he asked aloud. "Why me?"

This was not the Father's best day.

Saturday, June 1

I WAS GETTING A BIT depressed about this dance class. Three days till the start of lessons, and we still had only five people. I unlocked the library door just as Sadie parked her yellow Chevy in front and trundled up the walk.

I know a lot of people in town treated Sadie as something of a joke. For one thing, she always wore yellow. Nobody knew why. And her driving was atrocious. But in the year that she'd volunteered at the library, I'd come to like her very much. I suppose I'd been predisposed in her favor because of a newspaper article in the *Keagan County Record* six or seven years ago, when Hubbard Martin, the chair of the town council, wanted to cut down more than a dozen of the biggest, oldest trees in town. Their roots had broken up the sidewalks. The paper ran a photo of Sadie holding on to the biggest oak on Juniper Street, right in front of City Hall. Her arms wrapped as far around it as she could reach, and there stood Hubbard, unable to do a thing about it. Sadie won. The trees still stood, and I admired her spunk.

"Good morning, dearie," she called out as she started up the front steps, patting the foot of the stone lion on her right. She paused on the third step and took a deep breath. "Oh, dear," she said, "this is ridiculous. I get so out of breath. I can't imagine why. I'm only eighty-one."

"Just take your time, Sadie," I told her. "We're not in any kind of hurry."

She smiled her sweet smile up at me and climbed the rest of the way to the door. "Tell me," she said as she walked through the door I was holding open, "other than youth, what's your prescription for staying in such good shape?"

"Well, I walk a lot. I do my own yard work. I climb all these stairs here in the library. And I'm starting tap dance lessons next Tuesday."

"Tap dance? What fun. Like that lovely Ginger Rogers?" Sadie's eyes went all soft and dreamy.

"That's right, but I think it'll be a while before I look anything like her when I dance."

"Oh, dearie, that's not the point." She set her yellow purse down on the rolltop desk. "The point is you're doing something you want to do. I'm sure it's something you've wanted for a long time. Am I right?"

"Yes, you are. I dreamed about tap dancing when I was a little girl, but nobody offered lessons around here."

Sadie reached up to adjust the yellow scarf she'd wound around her gray hair. "I can remember when *Singin' in the Rain* came out. I must have seen it a dozen times. That was when Ralph Peterson's father ran the Chief Movie Theater, long before Carl Armitage bought it from him. John Peterson took pity on me after about the seventh time, and said he wasn't going to charge me anymore, so I just waltzed in and watched the show anytime I could."

"The umbrella scene?" I asked her. "Was that your favorite?"

"No, dearie, I loved it when Debbie and Donald and Gene danced up and down those stairs and right across the sofa. That looked like so much fun. When did you say the lessons are?"

"Tuesday nights, from 7:30 to 9:00 p.m."

"Dear me, that's bedtime, but I think I can manage."

Was I hearing what I thought I was hearing?

Yes!

FIFTEEN

Diane Marie's journal—Sunday, June 2nd
...I'm so glad I've planned a long visit here in Martinsville.
This is giving me a chance to take a breath, to practice
being away from him. We've been married so long now
that it's hard for me to imagine how it would be if I were
on my own. Do I even know how to do that? Am I too old
to start over again? I just wish I'd been able to talk to him
before I left. Will I go back?

Monday, June 3

ON THE WAY HOME from the library I detoured down to the grocery store. I couldn't seem to remember everything on my list at one time. This was my third trip to the store in less than a week. Thank goodness it was only a matter of a few blocks.

As I reached the front door, I could see Madeleine Ames wrestling with a shopping cart as she extracted it from the long line of empties. Must not have been too busy today, I thought. By the time I picked up some molasses and a big package of toilet paper, Madeleine had rolled her cart up to the checkout line. The only things in it, I noticed as I got in line behind her, were two tins of smoked oysters and a canned ham. Her mother, who was wearing a dark skirt and a neon green blouse, had preceded the cart into the line.

"Once again," she was saying to Ida, "once again," she repeated, "I have been unable to find the absolutely essential items I need. You were out of my favorite brand of caviar. Why can't you be more careful about what you order?"

Picky, picky, I thought. She had oysters, and she was complaining about caviar?

Ida reached for the ham. "That's a shame, Mrs. Ames. I wouldn't want you to go without. Would you like me to suggest an alternative?" From the acid dripping through her tone, Ida was probably ready to suggest a powerful laxative or antifreeze.

"No," Diane Marie said as she shook her perfectly-coiffed head, "I doubt you could help me, anyway. But next time you send in an order, why don't you get yourself some extra-heavy-duty conditioner? It'll help that thin, lanky hair of yours."

I saw Madeleine's shoulders stiffen. The color drained from Ida's face and then bounced back as two bright red spots on her cheeks. She couldn't conceal the look of absolute loathing she threw at Diane Marie who had already turned to leave and missed the look completely.

Madeleine paid the bill, picked up the bags and said, "I'm so sorry, Mrs. Peterson."

"I'm sure you are, Miss Ames," Ida said with surprising equanimity. "The next time she wants groceries, why don't you either shop by yourself or find an excuse to drive her up to Garner Creek?"

Tuesday, June 4

THE REST OF US WERE already there, putting on our tap shoes, when Ida walked into the room, followed by a pale woman whose big brown eyes had a rather haunted look. "Hey, everybody, this is my sister, Diane Marie." Diane Marie, I thought, that's the same name as Barkley's wife. Interesting coincidence. And Father Ames's overbearing mother was named Diane Marie, too. I could feel my hands beginning to clench. Ida must have found the coincidence even more disturbing than I did after what Diane Marie Ames had said to her yesterday. Relax yourself, Biscuit. Thank goodness the old bat wasn't in this class!

Ida motioned her sister forward. "This is Biscuit," Ida said pointing to me, "and this here is Sadie..." She went around the room with the introductions. Diane Marie smiled at us all and looked like she was trying to remember who was who. The new one to a group always had the hardest time. I remembered my friend in Braetonburg who grew up in an Air Force family. Every school she attended it was always like this. She had to learn everybody else's name. Sometimes, she said, her family moved again before she even had her one little classroom memorized.

Miss Mary walked in. Once we all had our shoes on, she asked us to spread out into a line. "Now, I know this may seem a little corny," she said as we stood there, each of us trying to make as little noise as possible with our new tap shoes, "but when I call your name, I want you to make some noise with your shoes. It's called a *sound-off*."

This was bizarre, I thought.

"The idea of tap dancing is to make noise, right? Rhythmic noise, controlled noise. But it's generally pretty loud."

There were murmurs of agreement from all of us.

"Okay, let's go! Alphabetical order." She looked at her list. I was a B, so I took a breath, ready to go first. "Sadie!" she called out. Oh, she must have meant last names. Sadie Masters hadn't had time to buy tap shoes or a leotard, so she was wearing a yellow sweat suit and a pair of loafers. She did a quiet little tap-tap and then clapped her hands together in sheer delight.

"Wonderful! Now, Annie!" Annie McGill flipped her long braid over her shoulder, grinned wickedly and drummed her feet really loudly, one-two-three-four-five-six-seven-eight.

"That was great! Biscuit, you're next!" I gave a silly imitation of Fred Astaire, as if I had a top hat on my head and a cane in my hands. Tappity-ka-tappity-tap-tappity-ka-tap. It was less than the rhythm I'd intended, but it was fun.

"Fantastic!" She looked at her list. "Diane Marie? Your turn!"

She drummed out a little ditty that sounded more like tap than anything we'd produced so far. We all applauded. "Have you done this before?" Miss Mary asked her.

"When I was in grade school," Diane Marie admitted. "The

gym teacher was a dancer, and she made all of us do a dance unit each year. In fifth grade, it was tap."

"Great! Ida, you went to the same school as your sister. Your turn to sparkle!"

"My sparkle's going to be a fizzle," Ida grumped. "I was out of grade school before she did the tap unit." She did a limp stomp-stomp and then stood there.

Miss Mary didn't miss a beat. "That's the best stomp we've heard so far! Do it again for us!" So Ida stomped again, and laughed, and was over it.

"Melissa!" Miss Mary cried. Was she going to keep up this kind of enthusiasm all night long? "You're in the spotlight!" Melissa waved her arms around and did a rat-a-tat-tat that sounded like a snare drum. I think she surprised herself. Of course, we all applauded again.

Miss Mary set her clipboard aside. "I'm glad you're all here," she said. "I want you to know that tap dance has only a limited number of steps." I thought about Gene and Debbie. Nonsense. "You don't believe me, do you?" She must have been reading my mind. "You all look like you think I'm kidding." Or lying.

"The difference between amateurs—you—and professionals—the folks in the movies—is that they can do those limited number of moves very very fast, and in a lot of different combinations. So our job over the next number of months is going to be to learn some of the basic tap dance moves, and then we'll combine them into simple routines. It'll be a lot of fun." She turned to face the big mirrored wall. "Watch me as I do a *shuffle*." She put her hands on her hips, lifted her right knee a few inches, and then her foot shot out and back, scraping the floor twice. "Now you do it with me. Shuf-fle, shuf-fle, shuf-fle, stamp." She surprised us on the stamp. We were all still shuffling.

Halfway through the class, after we'd learned to do a *ball-change,* we took a ridiculously short breather during which Miss Mary told us about the recital we'd be performing in at the end of the school year. "We'll learn a couple of simple routines. Don't worry," she crooned, "you'll do fine."

There were murmurs of disbelief, but she kept going. "In

January or so, you can each start making up a little routine that
we'll work into our second recital number."

"What fun!" Annie said.

"Oh, dear," Sadie whispered. I heard her only because I was
standing right next to her.

"Not on your life!" That came from Ida. "I don't make up
dance steps," she declared.

"Oh, you'll do just fine," Miss Mary assured her.

"No, I won't do just fine," Ida said. "I've never been good at
making things up. I don't know how to do that. That's what I'm
paying *you* for."

Miss Mary looked at her. We all held our breath. "I'll help
you with it," she said.

There was a collective sigh, and we went back to shuffling
and stamping and such for another forty-five minutes. And boy,
did we have fun.

"Wow! That was great," Annie practically bellowed. I'd never
seen her so effervescent. Usually her quiet temperament matched
her demure long dresses and seemed to contradict her fiery red
hair. Now she flung her waist-length braid, as thick around as
my wrist, back over the shoulder of her rust-colored leotard and
let out a "Whoopee!" that would have been heard for blocks if
we'd been outside.

Even Sadie seemed caught up in the general congratulatory
mood of the dressing room. She had changed her sweats for a
soft yellow cotton tent dress. Her gray-blond hair was tousled
around her head any which way. "I don't feel a day over seventy-
five," she proclaimed with a grin. Sadie had held up quite well,
even though she did have to sit down for a few minutes two or
three times during the class. Miss Mary had placed a chair in a
corner of the studio, probably realizing that an 81-year-old stu-
dent might need just a few rest periods. Sadie reached over and
patted my arm. "I'm so glad you told me about this, Biscuit. It's
the first new thing I've done in years."

"Oh, for goodness' sake, Sadie," Ida put in as she readjusted the combs that were holding her straight, fine-textured brown hair off her narrow face, "no it is not. You started the Martinsville Ladies Book Reading Society five years ago, you took harmonica lessons for a while and you signed up as a library volunteer last year. You're the one who told *me* that if you stop doing new things, you get real old, real fast."

"That's true dear. But I hardly expected tap dance lessons to be on my menu of new things."

Ida's sister sat quietly while the rest of us chatted and milled around her. She was taking an inordinately long time to unlace her tap shoes.

We'd done it! We'd survived the first class. That called for a celebration. I had a feeling some muscles in my calves would be complaining tomorrow, but in the meantime, I felt like an exclamation point.

I looked over to where Melissa was combing back her damp hair. We were all pretty damp, come to think of it. "Do you want to come by for a cup of late tea?" I asked her.

"I have a better idea—why don't we all head up to *Azalea House?* My guests took off this morning and managed to leave behind some of the coffee cake I baked last night. Of course, tea's always available."

"Make mine iced," Ida said, as she tried out a *shuffle-ball-change,* the first 'routine' we'd learned this evening.

Sadie smiled. "That sounds like a lovely idea, Melissa dear. Does anyone want to ride with me?"

"I will," Diane Marie said from her chair. I saw Melissa's eyes widen. The thought of anyone volunteering to ride with Sadie was astonishing, but Diane Marie was fairly new to town, so she'd probably never seen Sadie on the road. To the best of anyone's knowledge, Sadie had never caused an accident. She'd come awfully close, though, on more occasions than anyone could count.

Ida must have heard something odd in her sister's tone of voice. "Are you feeling okay?" She walked across the room and knelt beside the chair. Diane Marie looked pretty washed out.

"I'll be just fine." Brushing her sister's hand lightly away, Diane Marie stood up and smiled. It looked a bit forced to me, but then again, I didn't know her well. "I guess I'm a little tired from the exertion, and the idea of a ride sounds good."

Sadie swooped right in and took hold of Diane Marie's arm. "Sometimes I think I'm the only person in this town who likes to drive. Everybody always seems to want to walk everywhere. You just come with me and we'll beat them all there. We might even eat up all the coffee cake before they join us." Of course, people in Martinsville never lock their doors, so it was quite possible that Sadie's threat might have been carried out.

We all left the studio together, calling our thanks and our good-nights back over our shoulders to Miss Mary as we pushed open the large glass door.

SADIE WAS PARKED right across the street at the foot of Oak Street. We watched as she and Diane Marie climbed in the car. Sadie was so short, she had to sit on a deep cushion so she could see over the dashboard. Years ago she had special pedal extensions installed so she could reach the gas and brakes. Of course, Sadie didn't believe in turning around, so she backed away from the curb and headed in the general direction of Ralph and Ida's grocery store where we assumed she would turn left. Those of us on foot turned to our right. One long block and we passed the corner health shop where Annie lived on the second floor. As we turned up Magnolia Way, Ida giggled.

"What?" we all three asked more or less at the same time.

"Anyone care to take bets on how soon Sadie's going to get to *Azalea House?*"

"Now, Ida, that's not kind," I said with just a tiny touch of holier-than-thou in my voice.

Annie may have agreed with me in principle, but she was still too geared up from the dancing to admit it. "You're right, Ida," she said. "I bet we'll all be on our second piece of coffee cake before she gets there."

Melissa was walking in front of us on the narrow sidewalk.

She turned and held up a hand. "There's not that much coffee cake left. One piece each. She'll have to hurry if she wants her share."

"All right," Ida relented. "We'll save them each a piece."

Melissa's bed-and-breakfast was just one block up from First Street, on the corner of Second Street and Magnolia Way. We walked the rest of the way in a general attitude of merriment and self-congratulations.

Holding open the front door for us, Melissa asked, "What do you think about having to learn a couple of dances for the re-cital next spring? I was surprised when Miss Mary told us that was a requirement."

"Heck, as long as all we have to do is a *shuffle-ball-change*," Ida said, "we should do just fine."

I remembered how backward my feet felt as I tried to keep up with the step. "That's right," I said, "and we'll have almost eleven months to practice it." I hoped that was long enough.

As WE SAT AROUND the big table in Melissa's roomy kitchen, Ida clinked her glass for attention. "I've been wondering," she said, "where does everybody like to go when they need to get away from it all for a little while?"

"Tahiti?" Annie said.

"No, I'm not talking a long vacation. I'm talking about your favorite spot for settling your mind. I know we all have places like that, and I want to know where they are."

"Where's yours?" Annie asked.

"The big rocks in the Metoochie," Ida said. She would have said more, but I held up my hand.

"Wait a minute. I see Sadie's Chevy coming down the street."

"*Down* the street?" Ida said, turning around in her chair and looking out the big window. "What's she doing coming from that direction?"

I took a slurp of Melissa's ginger-peach tea. "Let's wait until she gets here and ask her."

Sadie was still in high spirits as she walked into the big

kitchen. She looked at the green-and-white-checked tablecloth almost obliterated by our plates and forks and glasses and napkins. "I do hope," she said, "you saved the senior member of the dance company a piece of cake."

Ida, who had known Sadie longer than any of the rest of us, asked what we were all wondering. "Why on earth did it take you this long to drive three blocks?"

"These streets are entirely too crooked for any decent driving," Sadie said, "and you know it. That's probably why you all walk everywhere. You're too afraid to drive." She pulled herself up to her full height, which couldn't have been over five-one, and stared us down. We all knew that Sadie generally refused to make any turn that was less than ninety-degrees. That let out most of the corners in this little hillside town, where the streets followed a logic of their own, based somewhat on topography and somewhat on the old walking trails that the early settlers had worn into the earth.

"Let me guess," Ida said into the silence that followed Sadie's pronouncement. "You drove to Pine Street and then up to Third Street and then back to Magnolia from there, right?"

Diane Marie had been hovering in the background during this entire conversation. "I think," she ventured, "we went farther than Third Street before we turned. There was that big cliff on the far side of the road."

Ida sprang from her seat and waved Sadie into an empty chair. "Come take a load off your feet, darling," she said. "You made it all the way to Fifth Street. You must be exhausted from all that driving."

Sadie took the seat with exaggerated dignity, and Diane Marie slipped into the chair next to her. "Since I am the queen bee here," Sadie pronounced, "I'd like my dessert now, if you youngsters haven't eaten it all." The tap dancing must have gone to her head.

Melissa, ever the peacemaker, spoke up as she placed a slice of coffee cake in front of the queen bee. "Sadie, before you got here, we were talking about our favorite get-away-from-it-all spots. Where is yours?"

"Probably her car," Annie hooted. Annie was definitely in rare form tonight. Who would have believed it of that quiet woman I thought I knew well? Maybe tap dancing changed one's personality.

"Well now, dear, I'd need to think about that," Sadie said. "Tell me where all of you go, and then I'll tell you my place."

There was silence for a moment. "Don't everybody tell me at once," Sadie added.

I spoke up. "I alternate between my porch swing with Marmalade on my lap and the little sitting room I have upstairs. With Marmalade on my lap. And then there's the garden."

"With Marmalade on your lap?" Annie asked.

"That's three places," Ida objected, ungrammatically and vociferously.

"So what?" I said. "We can have three getaways. It depends on what mood I'm in. Tell her yours, Ida."

Ida took the iced tea pitcher from Melissa and sent it around the circle again. I was going to have to visit the bathroom before I tried to walk home.

"I like to walk down to those big boulders at the bottom of the pool," Ida said. "I love to climb out on them and sit there and listen to the Metoochie gurgle and bounce as it funnels into the gorge."

"Too bad we've had all this rain recently," I told her. "Those rocks are pretty well flooded now with the river as high as it is."

"That's okay," she said. "They'll still be there after the water level goes down, and they're predicting another dry spell. No more rain for weeks, they said." She turned to her left. "Your turn, Annie."

"If Biscuit got to say three places, I get to say at least two. One of them is the Delicious at lunchtime!" There were cheers and raised glasses and calls of *amen to that.* Annie laughed and pushed her thick braid back over her shoulder. "But the real answer is that I walk up into the high meadow. There's that grove of river birches. Sometimes if I sit on the stone outcropping quietly enough, I see deer." She took a long swallow of iced tea. "I was so glad that Carl didn't hurt the meadow when he took to farming."

"He would have if he'd been able to get to it," Ida said.

I wondered about the reason for the acid in her tone. She was referring to Carl Armitage. In a town this size, his gas station wasn't very busy, and he kept the Chief Theater open only three nights a week. A few years ago he bought a huge swath of upland that stretched back from the top of the cliffs to the one road in that part of the county. He cleared the field and planted it in kenaf, an annual crop that grew really fast. It was never invasive, like kudzu, but you'd think it might be from watching it grow by leaps and bounds. It was used for making paper. According to Carl, it was a much more efficient resource than using wood pulp from trees.

There was a steep hill and a big outcropping of rock, though, that bordered the north end of the kenaf field and protected Annie's favorite meadow. Thank goodness. I hoped Carl never thought about dynamite.

Annie looked to her left where Melissa now sat at the head of the table. "Your turn."

"Oh, I just like to sit out on the bench under my Japanese maple tree, preferably with a good book. How about you, Diane Marie? Have you been here long enough to find a favorite spot yet?"

Diane Marie still looked a bit pale. "Sure." She smiled. "I like to walk past Annie's meadow and up the path along the top of the cliff. There are some good places there to sit. I dangle my legs over the edge and drink in the view." She took the glass Melissa handed her. "I like being able to see a long way." Her voice was so wistful, I wondered if there was a story behind it. Oh, heck, there was always a story where women were concerned.

"Sister!" Ida said. "Didn't anyone ever tell you that was dangerous? Those edges could give way, or you could slip."

"Oh, Ida, I'm careful." She looked around the table. "My

other favorite place is that cute little bench in back of the library, tucked away all privatelike."

"Biscuit put it in," Sadie said, nodding in my direction.

"I know," Diane Marie said as she looked at me. "Thank you. I appreciate it."

Made my heart feel good to see the way her long-lashed eyes lit up. She looked kind of like a deer.

Ida waved her iced tea toward Sadie. "You can't avoid it any longer, Sadie. Fess up. What's your favorite spot to get away?"

Sadie patted at her lap, smoothing the soft yellow fabric. "I guess I'd have to say the cemetery." There were a few raised eyebrows on that one. Annie looked like she was going to say something smart, but thought better of it. "It's almost the only place in town that never changes." Annie muttered something under her breath about "every new grave" but we all ignored her. Sadie went on without stopping. "I love walking up to the top of it and sitting on that little bench beside my family's plot. It's so peaceful there. I somehow feel better about Eustace and Mama and Daddy being there. Little Samuel, too, of course. The dogwood tree leans out over the plot and seems to protect it."

I know Sadie didn't mean to break up the party. But it was a little hard to keep the hilarity going after she spoke. We finished our tea, cleared off the plates and forks, and left, spreading out in three different directions.

TANK WAS SITTING IN the front hall, looking at the front door when I walked in, and Bob was waiting up for me, reading. What a dear.

After I detoured to the bathroom, I sat and did some knitting while he finished his chapter. As I knit the little green booties I was making for Sally's baby-to-come, my third grandchild, I kept tapping my feet, practicing the *shuffle-ball-change*. Bob looked up a couple of times and rolled his eyes. I knew he thought the tap dancing was kind of silly, but I was loving it.

I couldn't imagine having a man in our tap dance class. There sure are a lot of differences between men and women. These bootie colors, for instance. I picked green because Sally didn't know yet whether it was a boy or a girl. So green seemed safe. But I never liked the idea of dressing little girls in pink and little boys in blue. I read once that pink calms boys and blue calms girls, so all the pink/blue stuff is backward. For years we must have been driving all our little girl babies nuts by dressing them in pink. Maybe everything I made my grandkids from now on would be green. That's the world's most neutral color. Even more so than white or beige. Look at all the green trees, green grass, green shrubs. Perfect background color. Unless you lived in a desert.

I kept knitting, and my mind kept wandering. There was a lot backward where males and females were concerned. I read once that falcons are the females of the species. There was no such thing as a male falcon. The males were called tercels. Somebody ought to tell the football people that, I thought. No, maybe not. It was too late to change anything, and it might have led to a bunch of hard feelings. Men were so sensitive, and I wasn't sure that all the people who manufactured ball caps and sweatshirts and coffee mugs would want to change their logos. "Bob," I asked, as he put his bookmark in the book and set it on the coffee table, "Did you know that falcons are all female?"

"I am once again not quite sure what you're talking about," he said—he says that a lot—and he glanced at the sports section of the *Record* that was lying next to his book. There was a picture of a beefy athlete on the front page. "I wouldn't mention that outside this house if I were you. Certainly not if you visit the city."

"But it's just a scientific fact. Don't you ever wonder what else we mess up?"

"Try Santa Claus," he said.

"What?"

"Santa Claus thinks all his reindeer are males, but male reindeer don't have antlers in the winter—only the females do."

"Really? I didn't know that."

"So, we're even. I didn't know about the falcons. *Now* can we go to bed?"

Hmm. Not a bad idea. Some of these differences were worth exploring.

SIXTEEN

Wednesday, June 5

THE NEXT DAY my tap dance legs hollered at me when I tried to get out of bed. This is good exercise, I told myself. It would get better. It better hurry. I did so much walking around town, up and down these streets, to say nothing of the stairs in the library. You'd think my legs would be immune to tap-fatigue. I guess it was just a different set of muscles.

Once I got up and started moving around, it wasn't quite so bad. Marmalade and I even made it to the library on time. Wednesday mornings were busy. That was when Esther had her story time for the preschool kids. I usually spent the time cataloging...

You hide out up there.

...while Sadie handled the checkout desk. But that day I needed to plan the spacing for the new gardening section. I was standing in the Beige Room with my tape measure in hand when Ida's sister, Diane Marie, walked up. "Do you need any help?" she asked me.

Yes, she does. I do not have thumbs.

"Bless your little pea-picking heart, I sure do." I handed her one end of the tape. "Hold this right here, and I'll be in your debt forever." I was still feeling a little dramatic from the previous night.

She laughed at me and took the tape. Over the next hour and a half, she helped me plot the entire layout. We had only so many shelves in the storeroom, and it took us a while to figure out how we could get the maximum number of shelves into the room (which I still had to paint green) and yet leave enough room for people to move around. I had a general idea of what I wanted to do in there, but I'd forgotten that some of the shelves had to go against a wall so we could attach them at the top.

You do not want anything to fall on me.

Luckily, some of them were sturdy enough to be free-standing. It was a lot to figure out. I was amazed at how well she and I worked together. We laughed and joked, too. By the end of the morning I had a new friend. I invited her upstairs to the big third-floor office for a cup of tea and some doughnuts. There was a miniscule kitchen up there that we had turned into a break room.

"Just think," she said as our footsteps echoed up the long flight of hardwood stairs, "by next dance season we'll be tapping our way up here."

"Wouldn't that be fun? But I'll be lucky just to remember how to do one little routine for the recital."

"I hope I can still dance then," she said.

I pointed her into the first room on the left. The door was open, and Marmalade preceded us. "What do you mean?"

"Oh, nothing. I just hope my legs hold out."

"Me, too." I pulled out an assortment of tea bags. "Licorice root? Chamomile? Ginger? Green tea? Cinnamon spice? Lemon?"

"That's quite a collection."

"I like tea, can't you tell?"

She laughed. "I never would have guessed."

ONCE THE TEA WAS BREWED to our satisfaction, we nibbled on doughnuts. So much for lunch. Of course, if I'd remembered to pack my lunch I wouldn't have had that problem. "Ida tells me you live in Enders?" I said.

"That's right. I grew up there, moved away for a while after I got married, but then we moved into Kelvin's dad's house last year when he…"

She let her sentence trail off to nothing. It sounded like Kelvin's dad had died. I was going to express sympathy, but Diane Marie's tone had been too dry, too devoid of feeling, so I held my peace. "My sister-in-law," I said, "grew up in Enders, too. The funny thing is that her name is Diane Marie, just like yours."

She did a quiet version of a double take. "Not Diane Marie Hastings?"

"Uh-huh. Did you know her? She's Diane Marie Sheffield now. Bob's brother's wife. I haven't gotten to know her very well, since she's hardly ever here. They live in Atlanta."

"I'll be doggoned," Diane Marie said. "We went to grade school together. I always wondered what happened to her."

"Well," I said, "you'll have a chance to find out because she's visiting here now, staying with Bob's mom, her mother-in-law."

She laughed, and I raised my eyebrows, wondering what the joke was.

"I wonder if she remembers?" Diane Marie said. "Once when we were in fourth grade, Miss Brezek, our teacher, was sick or something and there was a substitute. She wanted to learn our names, so she asked us to stand up when she got to our name on the roll call. She was using just first names. When she got to 'Diane' we both stood up. She looked at her card—all the names were on little three-by-five cards—and said, 'I meant Diane Marie.' When we told her we were both Diane Marie, she said, 'I'll have to call you by your last initial, then. Which one of you is Diane Marie H?' She didn't know we both were—I was born a Hartley. By this time, everybody in the class was giggling. I guess for fourth-graders it was pretty funny."

"I think it's pretty funny, too," I told her, "and I'm forty-nine."

THE TIME GOT AWAY from us. We sat there and chatted for almost an hour, and I marveled at the way women could connect. She told me she was planning to stay all summer. "Won't your husband mind?" I asked her.

"Oh, he travels a lot. I can always go back on weekends when he's home."

Marmalade jumped up on the table between us. The interruption was just enough to call me back to the fact that this was a Wednesday, and I was supposedly at work. "Oh, my gosh,

Diane Marie. I can't believe I've spent all this time up here when I should be downstairs working." We both grabbed mugs and plates. "It sure has been fun, though."

"Maybe I could come help out some more."

"Would you, really? There's still so much busywork to be done, with all the cataloging. We could sure use a willing set of hands."

"How about tomorrow?" she asked.

"We're closed tomorrow, but I'm planning to be here painting. Want to help with that?"

AND THAT WAS HOW I got the new gardening room painted green and all the shelves arranged in just a few days. Diane Marie and I worked all day Thursday. Painting wasn't that much of a chore if you could share it with a friend. That evening I called Roger and asked if he'd bring a couple of his buddies the next afternoon to move the shelves in for us. Why he hung around with high school kids so much was beyond me, but it sure was helpful when school was out and I needed some muscle.

My gratitude list for Thursday, June 6th
1. Diane Marie—Ida's sister, that is. The other one will never ever ever show up on my gratitude list. So there!
2. The fun of practicing my tap dance lesson
3. The "new" Green Room
4. Marmy, who was watching the butterflies outside the window this morning
5. Leftover chicken soup when I'm too tired to cook

my gratitude list for today
naps
butterflies
my feather toy
chicken
the upstairs to hide in when Widelap puts on those noisy
shoes

SEVENTEEN

Friday, June 7

THE MORNING SUNLIGHT had moved up almost above the reach of the porch overhang, so there was only a slight slant of sun coming in through the east windows of the kitchen. I punched down on the bread dough a couple more times, separated it into several loaves and plopped them into the bread pans, turning each of the loaves a couple of times to coat them with oil. That done, I washed off my hands, put the pans on a big cookie sheet, covered them with a damp towel and placed the whole thing on top of the fridge where it could stay warm while the bread rose for an hour or so. I loved making bread.

Marmy seemed to be waiting for me to finish, because as soon as I set the bread in place, she started meowing. I thought at first she wanted me to let her out the back door, but she was "herding" me toward the front. Out of curiosity, I walked into the big foyer and watched as she marched up to the front door. Okay, why not? I opened the door for her, but she paused a moment and looked back over her shoulder. Much to my surprise, Tank had followed us out of the kitchen. Most cats that I've known tended to sidle up to other cats if they were on friendly terms. Then they would go through a little routine of touching noses or ducking their heads. Not Tank, though. He walked straight up to Marmalade's side and, almost as if she'd told him to "fall in," he walked with her out the door.

Tank? Out the door? This was the cat that had refused to go outside from the moment we'd brought him home a month ago. The closest he ever came to outside was when he sat at the front door to announce the arrival of someone. He was always right. That's why I called him my greeter-cat. Now, however, he was walking outside with Marmy.

It is time for him to go to work.

I watched them march down the sidewalk. They turned left at the same time, like Esther Williams' crew in a water ballet. I had to find out where they were headed. The bread could take care of itself. I wasn't due at the library for another couple of hours. Bob was already at the station. So I followed the cats. Luckily they didn't take any shortcuts under hedges or through fences. No. They walked along like an elderly couple taking a morning stroll.

Marmalade went to the end of the block where an enormous maple shaded the intersection. She turned right, and Tank crossed the street with her. As they continued along the sidewalk, I followed at a discreet distance. I was sure Marmalade was aware of me, but she never turned around to look. At Juniper, they actually looked to the right and then the left before stepping off the curb. Across the street, up onto the sidewalk again. Past the town park. No stopping to sniff any calling cards from other animals. Their tails were both held aloft, like furled umbrellas toted by tour guides.

As they approached Dogwood Street, I could see Tom Parkman ahead, hefting a suitcase out to his car. He was driving to Philadelphia to see my sister. I hoped that would work out well. I hoped they'd get married, but maybe I was rushing things a bit.

He glanced up, did a double take at the cats as they walked past him, saw me and waved. As I got closer, he called out, "What is this? A morning constitutional?"

I am walking him to his first day at work. He does not know the way there.

"I'm not sure," I said. "They left the house looking like they were on a definite errand, and I had to follow."

"Boy, do they have you trained!"

"You're right about that." The cats kept walking, but I paused long enough to ask Tom if he'd found the mint jelly I left on his porch yesterday. He'd already packed it, he said. I watched the feline duo turn to their right up the pathway to Doc's house. Dr. Nathan Young had his offices downstairs. He lived upstairs. I couldn't look at his building without remembering how he helped Marmy when she was so badly injured a couple of months ago.

Both cats walked right up to the door, with me following right behind. Marmalade surprised me by stretching up onto the screen door and yowling, as if she were asking to be let in. A rather surprised-looking Polly Lattimore came to the door. She looked at the cats, then glanced up and saw me. "Hey, Biscuit," she said. "What's all this about?"

Here is your new staff member.

"Darned if I know. Both cats left the house this morning and walked straight here."

"Is something wrong? Are they hurt?" Her nurse's instincts were showing.

I was simply showing him the way here.

"I don't think so. It's more like they want to visit."

"Well," she said, swinging the screen door open, "that's fine with me. We don't have any patients here yet. I'm glad I got here early, so I wouldn't miss this show. Doc's still upstairs." She looked down at the cats. "Would the two of you like to come in?"

Marmalade actually nodded, or so it seemed to me. Polly must have noticed it, too, because she giggled and motioned me to come on in also. Marmalade stepped past Polly into the waiting room, sat down on the edge of the big green rug, and folded her tail around her feet. Tank, though, walked straight through the waiting room and curved around behind Polly's counter. He did a quick tour of that area. Then he walked up and down the hallway with the examining rooms, like a general inspecting the barracks. Polly and I just stood there and watched. There didn't seem to be anything else to do.

He will be happy now. Please open the door so I can leave him to his work.

Tom must have wondered what was happening because the door behind us opened and he stuck his head in. "What's going on?" he asked as Marmalade darted past him out the door and down the sidewalk. I expected Tank to follow, but Tank had stopped his inspection and was stationed at the doorway into the examining-room area. He lifted one paw and licked at it.

Polly and I both laughed. "We don't have a clue, Tom," I said. "Both cats waltzed in, and now Marmalade's left and Tank is still here."

Just then Dr. Nathan walked through the door that hid the stairway to his "home space" upstairs. This seemed to be the morning for double takes. "And just who do we have here?" he asked.

"This is Tank," I told him. "He seemed to want to come visit you and Polly this morning."

"Are you my first patient of the day?" Nathan asked me.

"No, I just followed Tank here."

"Wait a minute. Are you telling me this cat came here on his own?"

Tom was still standing in the doorway. "Not exactly," he said, as he stepped into the waiting room. "It looked to me like Marmalade brought him here. Do you think she's trying to get rid of him?"

Nathan knelt down next to Tank. Tank, who had never wanted to get into my lap or Bob's, crept up onto Nathan's knee and nuzzled his head against Nathan's chin. I could hear his purr from where I stood.

Tom hooted. "I think you're being adopted, Nathan. Whether you like it or not."

The door behind us opened and Sharon Armitage walked in, leading one of her daughters who was looking decidedly peaked and had wet tracks from tears on her flushed cheeks. Tom and I were blocking her view of the doctor and the cat. "Polly?" Sharon said. "It looks like you're mighty busy, but does Doc have time to look at Cynthia? She's running a fever and her throat's pretty sore."

Tank stepped down from Doc's knee, threaded his way purposefully—or so it looked to me—between Tom and me, and walked directly to little Cynthia. He stood up and placed his front paws on her leg. She smiled through her tears and bent down to pat his head.

Doc's voice from behind me said, "I think we have ourselves an office cat."

TWO HOURS LATER, after I'd delivered some cat food and our spare litter box to Doc's office, I looked out the library window as Margaret Casperson, one of the town characters, pulled up to the curb in her bright yellow Duesenberg, the one she inherited when she was a little girl. Margaret, like Sadie, tended to drive everywhere rather than walk, but in her case it was because her feet hurt her most of the time. She was about the wealthiest person in town, from what I'd heard, but, other than the Duesenberg, you'd never know it.

Last week she called me from one of the estate sales she loves to go to, and asked if I'd be interested in some old books. Of course I said yes, without any idea what they were. Now my curiosity, as much as a feeling that I should help her, propelled me out to the antique car. As I walked down the stairs, I reached out automatically to pat the foot of one of the stone lions Margaret had given me as a wedding present—another one of her estate sale finds. Some of the men in town got together while Bob and I were on our honeymoon near Savannah to install the lions next to the library stairs on a couple of concrete pedestals, which put their paws right within patting range. I loved it. After a few years of being patted by everybody coming or going, my lions were going to have shiny smooth patches on their crenellated paws.

"What treasures do we have here?" I asked as Margaret stepped out of the elegant car. She was hardly elegant herself. More the homey type. A few years younger than I was, but always seemed older.

"Hey there, Biscuit." She greeted me with the usual Georgia phrase. "I think you're going to like these." She opened the back door, and I saw that she'd covered the lovely needle-pointed seats with an old blanket on which were piled at least a dozen boxes. "I got them up in Surreytown," she said, referring to the town at the upper end of the valley beyond Russell Gap. She pulled open the flaps on one of the boxes and stepped back so I could look. "There was an old house being sold off, and I took one look at these and said to myself, 'Biscuit needs these.'"

She was right. Even a quick glance told me that these were lovely old books in good condition. I rummaged around a bit and smiled. "Margaret, you found me some old diaries, too!"

She was grinning in delight. "Sure did! There's a little of everything in there. Notebooks, diaries, novels, old school books, some cookbooks. Everything the family had in the way of books. I bought it all."

"Well, bless you indeed. Let me go get us some help." I grabbed the top box. "You wait right here. I'll be back in a second."

Rebecca Jo and Sadie were the volunteers today since it was Friday. I didn't want either of them carting heavy boxes up to the third floor office, but I'd seen Cory Welsh head into the library a few minutes ago, eyeing Margaret's old masterpiece of a car as he walked past us. He'd be happy to oblige.

I found him in the history section on the second floor. "Cory, would you be willing to bring in some boxes of books from the Duesenberg out front?" That was all I had to say.

"The Duesey?" He flung his head back to get the shank of straight blond hair out of his eyes. He always looked like an Afghan hound with his hair parted naturally right down the middle of his head. He plopped down the book he'd been reading and loped over to the stairs. I glanced down. What was a book on car repair doing in the history section?

By the time I walked downstairs, Cory was trudging in the front door. "Take them up to the third floor office if you will, Cory. Just put them in the middle somewhere. I'll be upstairs in a minute. I'll go grab another box first."

"Don't you do that, Ms. McKee. I'll bring all of them in."

A miracle of a young man, I thought, until it occurred to me that this would give him more time to clamber around in a 1933 Model J Duesenberg Town Car.

EIGHTEEN

Saturday, June 8

THE TAP DANCING was a good idea for more reasons than the exercise and the fun of it. I was beginning to feel a real bond with the women in the class. For the past year, since I moved to Martinsville, I had talked to Ida Peterson each time I saw her in their grocery store or on the street. Simple things. "How are you doing today? Looks like you're pretty busy." And she'd say something like, "Well, people do have to eat." And of course, we had chatted a bit about the old, old diaries she had generously donated to the library last year.

Since we started taking the dance lessons together, though, we'd found more time and more reasons to have real conversations. Like we were doing now. She had stopped by to show me a dance catalog. I put down my trowel. "Come up on the porch and have some iced tea. I need a reason to stop this transplanting. I was hauling books around all afternoon and I'm pooped."

Marmalade accompanied us up the steps. Once we were installed in the rocking chairs with our tea in hand, she opened the catalog to page seven and handed it to me. "I'm planning to order those tap shoes with the bows on them. What do you think?"

I thought they looked hideous. Something straight out of the fifties. Or maybe the forties. Why on earth was a catalog even carrying them? "I..." Oh, heck, I couldn't lie worth beans. "Ida, they look kind of dated."

"Of course they do! Biscuit, where have you been? These styles are coming back in vogue."

Oh…I didn't like them in the fifties, though, and I still didn't like them. Maybe they'd grow on me, like a fashion fungus. "I don't know, Ida. I guess I'm not too fashionable that way." In fact, my daughter, Sally, told me once that if I ever made a million dollars, she wanted me to throw out my entire wardrobe and let her select a new one for me. But I liked my comfy old turtlenecks and jeans and sandals, and my muumuu. Wished women in the south would wear those all the time. Did they make long-sleeved muumuus for winter?

I wear fur.

"Biscuit? Are you with me?"

"Sorry, Ida, I was wool-gathering, just thinking about how I have no real fashion sense at all. So maybe I'm the wrong person to ask about the shoes."

"That's okay. I may wait to order them until I find out what we need for the dance recital. No sense in having too many pairs of tap shoes lying around."

"It's not like you could wear them in the grocery store."

"Good lord, Ralph would think I'd gone out of my mind. But every once in a while, I do look at that shiny linoleum in the produce aisle and I wonder if I could do a buffalo straight down the lane."

The buffalo was one of the fun steps we were learning. I was fine with it as long as I didn't have to do anything with my arms. I could think about my feet. Or I could think about my arms. But not both at the same time. Maybe I was thinking too much.

"Diane Marie is really enjoying the class," I said as a way of changing the subject.

"Oh, she's enjoying the *class* all right," Ida said.

"You make it sound like there's something wrong."

Ida nodded. "There is, but I don't know what."

Ask her.

"Have you asked her?"

"She's always been secretive about so many things, ever since she was a little girl. But I think it has to do with Kelvin."

"Kelvin?" I asked.

"Her husband. I hate the guy." She pushed her gossamer-fine hair back away from her eyes. "He's an absolute zero of a man, if you ask me."

"What do you mean?"

"I just can't stand him. My mother and I tried to talk Diane Marie out of marrying him, but she went ahead, anyway. In fact, they eloped, and we didn't see her for more than a year. She said he was so nice to her after Bill fell and died."

"Bill?"

"Yeah. He and Kelvin always hung around together, from the time they were little kids. Way back when, Diane Marie dated Kelvin a couple of times, but then she got to know Bill better, and—well—we all adored Bill. He was a really sweet guy. Oh, he was a little wild, the way so many young guys are, and he had a corny sense of humor, but my mom and I liked him a lot. He was a good kid, if you know what I mean. We were delighted when they got engaged. Diane Marie and Bill, I mean." Her voice trailed off and she was quiet for a moment.

"What happened?"

"He fell off a cliff. It's the other end of our cliff here, where it overlooks Enders. It killed him right off. Guess he shouldn't have been trying to climb it."

Almost all the towns along the Metoochie were backed by a huge cliff. In some places in the Upper Valley it was fifty or sixty feet high. But in the Lower Valley in Enders, the cliff was more like eighty feet straight up. Who in his right mind would try to climb that? "How sad for Diane Marie," I said.

"Right. But Kelvin was right there to console her, and pretty soon she was engaged to *him*."

"What's wrong with him?"

"He wears sunglasses a lot, so he's got a white line that runs from his eyes to the top of his ears. Sort of like the markings on a rattlesnake." She paused and added, "He's got one of those artificial tans, too. I don't know if it comes out of a can or if he goes to a tanning salon when he's on his business trips, but it's as counterfeit as they come, and poor Diane Marie's as pale as a white mushroom."

"Ida, if he has a white line back to his ears, it means it's a real tan."

"It looks fake."

"Lots of people have fake tans. But that doesn't make them bad people."

"Oh, it's not just that. The man never blinks."

"What?" I looked down at Marmalade in my lap. Cats didn't blink, but they were designed that way. People had to blink, though. It lubricated their eyeballs.

"You heard me. He never blinks."

"How can anybody not blink?"

"I don't know, but he doesn't." She thought a moment, and I could almost see her calling his image into her mind. "His eyes kind of balloon out from his face…"

Hyperthyroid, I thought.

"…and he reminds me of a cobra. I can imagine him swaying to and fro, spreading his hood and striking before I can run." She stopped and shook her head, like she was trying to erase the picture. "I think he has Diane Marie hypnotized by those creepy eyes of his. Even when he's acting nice to her, I have the feeling he's doing it just so he'll look good to other people."

I didn't know what to say to that. "You mentioned business trips. What does he do for a living?"

"Good question. Nobody knows for sure."

"Hasn't Diane Marie told you?"

"Nope. She doesn't know. I asked her and she said he's started doing some sort of consulting, but she's not sure about the details. Ever since they moved to Enders, he'll work from his home office for a few weeks, and then he takes off for a day or two, or a week. Once he was gone three weeks." She brushed that wayward strand of hair away from her eyes again. "I think she's relieved when he's gone."

Come to think of it, she hadn't talked about him at all in the library when we were measuring and painting and arranging. "Does she have any other family in Enders?"

"No. Our parents are dead. Last year, Kelvin's father was sent to prison. Kelvin moved back into his dad's house, the one that Bill's family used to live in."

"The Bill that died?"

"Yeah. After he died, his parents sort of gave up. They sold the house to Kelvin's dad. He lived there until last year when he went to jail. With his dad in jail, though, Kelvin sold his house in Surreytown. He and Diane Marie moved back to Enders."

I thought about the family dynamics. Diane Marie was living in a house her father-in-law lived in until he went to prison. I wondered what his crime was. In addition to that, it was the house her fiancé lived in when he died. And now she lived there with her frequently absent husband. Sounded creepy to me. About as creepy as reptilian eyes. Yuch!

"I'm pretty sure Diane Marie wants to leave Kelvin. But I think she's afraid of him. Of what he'd do if she left."

"Did she say why?"

"She didn't say anything about this. It's all guesswork on my part." Ida set the dance catalog on the porch railing where it promptly slid off into the iris patch I'd just planted. "Whoops! Sorry."

"Not to worry." They were some of my Grandma Martelson's irises that I'd brought over from the old house in Braetonburg. "They're tough plants," I told her.

"The woman looked like a walking skeleton when she got here last week, but she's started gaining weight," she continued. "One minute she's tired—"

"And the next she's helping me paint the library," I added.

"Yeah. One day she's happy as can be, the next day she starts if she hears a sudden noise. I've heard her crying at night—the walls aren't that thick. But, Biscuit, she won't open up to me. I should think she'd know she can trust me, but she just won't say anything about what's wrong. What can I do?"

I thought about my own sister who I knew was having a hard

time processing her feelings for Tom Parkman. Why couldn't relationships be straightforward and honest and nurturing? Why couldn't people just simply care for each other and get their crazy hang-ups out of the way? Why couldn't people play nice? "I don't know, Ida. I guess just be there for her in case she decides she wants to confide in someone."

"You know, it's funny. She's as pale as can be, but at the same time her complexion has cleared up and looks kind of glowy. She's tired, but then she does great at dance class. You don't think…"

Hmm. Maybe so. "You could be right," I said.

"She's pregnant," we both said at the same time.

"Why don't you talk to her tonight?" I said. "Don't ask her if she is. Tell her you know she is, and see what she says."

Ida's eyes lit up. "I'd love to have a little niece or nephew."

"Why don't you find out for sure before you start knitting booties?" I said.

"Silly! Nobody knits booties anymore."

I thought about my green yarn project in the living room. "Want some more iced tea, Ida?" I asked.

NINETEEN

Monday, June 10

THE PHONE ON Father Ames's desk was loud enough for him to hear it outside his front door. He hurried inside and grabbed it on the third ring, before the answering machine took over. "St. Theresa's Rectory. Father Ames speaking."

"Johnny? It's your dad here."

"Morning, Dad. How you doing?"

"Fine. You?"

"Fine."

"Is your mother there?"

"I don't think she's up yet. Madeleine went out for a walk right after Mass, and I don't see any sign of movement from upstairs."

"Have her call me when she gets up, would you?"

"Sure, Dad...Dad?"

"Yeah?"

"You sound upset. Are you okay?"

"Just have your mother call me, Johnny."

"Sure, Dad."

After he hung up, he heard the toilet flush. Mother was awake.

When she came down for breakfast, he gave her the message. She nodded. "I'll take care of it later." After toast and coffee, she went upstairs to return her husband's call.

Father Ames finished his breakfast of oatmeal and eggs scrambled with cheese. How could anyone survive on toast and coffee to start the day? He ate a big meal after Mass every morning.

As soon as Madeleine came back from her walk, Mother came

downstairs and told her, in a rather peremptory tone—her only tone, Father Ames reflected—that they were going shopping up in Garner Creek. Madeleine looked over at her brother. He could almost see the question in her eyes. Didn't Mother ever *ask?* They both knew the answer to that question.

AROUND MIDNIGHT LAST NIGHT, Marmalade walked across my forehead. When I tried to ignore her, she turned around and patted my left eyelid with her little paw. I could tell she was keeping her claws tucked in, but there was just the hint of sharpness. I needed to trim her toenails soon or she'd be catching them on the carpet. Or on my eyeballs. I turned over, and she nuzzled the back of my neck with her cold nose and then licked me with her raspy tongue. Oh, well, I was awake. Wide awake. So I slipped out of bed and wandered into my sitting room, but I didn't feel like sitting. Ice cream? No. Tea? No. A stroll outside in the moonlight? No. I didn't really feel like that, either. But I had to admit I loved the feeling of moonlight on my face. Too bad our bedroom was on the north side of the house. I picked up Marmalade and padded toward the sewing area on the front side of the house. My slippers flapped gently against the carpet as I crossed the room and leaned against the window frame. I could see the tiny crescent of moon high above the trees off to my left. My gaze shifted down to the front yard where I was thinking about putting another flower bed. That much less grass to mow.

I saw a movement by the curb. I pulled back in case the person—it *was* a person, I could see that now—in case he looked up. He was crouched in among the *Hemerocallis,* the daylilies that surrounded the mailbox. I couldn't see exactly what he was doing, but I knew, of course, that I had finally caught Roger getting ready to paint the mailbox. As quietly as I could, I crept back into the bedroom and jostled Bob. "Wake up. Roger's painting the mailbox. Do you want to see?"

I'll say this for Bob. He woke up fast. "Mailbox? Let's go get him!"

"No. No, let's not. Let's just watch him and see how long it takes him. I kind of enjoy this."

"You woke me up to tell me to leave him alone and let him get away with it?"

"Sorry. Go back to sleep."

"Woman, you are amazing. Let's go look at least."

We tiptoed back to the front window and peeked out, expecting to see him slapping on a quick coat of paint. Instead, he was still kneeling by the post. "What's he doing?" Bob asked me. As if I knew.

"I don't have a clue, but this doesn't look like the ordinary paint job he usually does."

We stood there and watched Roger for another five minutes or so. Every so often we'd see a tiny flash, as if he'd turned on a minute flashlight. Bob finally yawned. So did I. "This is about as exciting as watching bread rise," I told him. We left Roger to his antics and went back to bed.

THE NEXT MORNING Marmalade and I hurried outside to check out the new color. The mailbox was still lavender, but there was a green vine painted around the post, curling its way right up onto the mailbox. It was beautiful. I ran back in the house. "Bob, come see the mailbox. You won't believe this!"

"What did he do this time?"

"Come see."

Bob took one look and started scratching his chin. "Looks good," he said, and he nodded vaguely at Ariel Montgomery who was walking down the hill. He turned back to me. "Needs some flowers on it or something. Wonder if I should put in a special order?"

I nodded at Ariel, too, and wondered idly where she was headed. If she'd been going to work at the Delicious, she'd have walked straight down Pine Street. I didn't want to be a nosy old busybody, though—well, not *too* nosy. I looked back at the mailbox. "Just don't let him paint over it," I said. "I like this one. It finally shows some real talent."

A FEW HOURS LATER, I decided that I would walk the long way to work each morning. Instead of heading down to Second and right toward the library, I figured it would get my legs in better shape for tap dancing if I walked up to Third Street and circled down through the town park. Not that much farther, perhaps, but every little bit would help. At 10:15 a.m. I walked past the Old Church where I saw Roger working on his sign. Okay, so maybe part of the reason I was walking the long way around to work had nothing to do with tap dancing muscles. Roger put up the new sign every Monday. Maybe I had wanted to see him.

"Congratulations, Roger," I called out to him.

"Thanks, Ms. McKee," he said. "What for?"

"Oh, I just think you're becoming quite an artist."

He looked at the sign. "Thanks. I just finished with it. See?" I looked at his sign.

CH__CH ISN'T CHURCH
UNLESS U R IN IT

"That's very nice, Roger, but I wasn't talking about the sign. I meant the mailbox."

He looked rather startled. We'd never talked about the mailbox. Bob was always the one who got him to go back and repair the paint job, but I'd never mentioned it to him. "What about it?" he asked.

Oh, so that was the way he wanted to play this. Okay. "Nothing, Roger. I just think you're doing a good job on it this time."

"This time?"

"We saw you last night. The first time we've ever caught you in the act."

"I didn't do anything last night, Ms. McKee."

"All right, Roger. I won't mention it. But we like the result, and you don't have to paint over it this time, unless you want to add some flowers to it." I looked around for Marmalade. She was sniffing the bottom of the sign. "Come on, Marmy. We'll be late if we don't hurry."

REVEREND HENRY PURSEY PARTED the blinds and peeked out his study window. He could see Roger taking off last week's sign and putting up the new one. As he watched, the librarian walked past and exchanged a few words with Roger. He waited until she and her cat moved on. He knew he wasn't going to enjoy this conversation, but felt he needed to pursue it, so he let the blinds crinkle back into place, took a deep breath and walked to the door.

"Roger," he said as he approached the young man who was still watching Biscuit McKee's receding back, "thank you for being so prompt about getting the sign changed each week."

Roger turned and smiled. "Wait a minute. What are you doing here? I thought Monday was your day off."

"It is. It is. I had a little something I needed to clear up, so I stopped by." He wasn't sure how to continue. "I was sorry to see there was another mishap with your sign last week." Mishap. That was the wrong word. Someone had changed ALL ARE WELCOME HERE to COME HERE REAL WALL. Hardly a mishap. Someone had been changing the signs each week. Last week they turned TODAY'S MESSAGE—THE TEN COMMANDMENTS into TODAY'S SAGES—TENSE TOM COME HAND ME TNT. Henry was sure that Roger was doing this himself. It made sense. Roger was the one who always painted the Hoskins' mailbox. Roger wanted attention. Roger was a practical joker. He must have enjoyed having the sign vandalism written up in the *Keagan County Record*. The funny thing was that attendance at the Wednesday evening prayer service had been up, way up, since the sign fiasco started. For that matter, the Sunday services were busier now, too. Maybe instead of reprimanding Roger, he should be commending him for his advertising expertise.

Maybe, Henry thought, maybe he'd just let it slide for now. "Keep up the good work, Roger," he said, and turned back toward the church.

"Thanks, Reverend P," Roger called out. "I really enjoy doing this."

I'll bet you do, young man, Henry thought. I'll bet you do.

I WAS STOCKING UP on my favorite herbal shampoo that afternoon after I finished work. Luckily I was tucked completely out of sight when the front door of Annie's shop opened and Diane Marie Ames barged in, followed—naturally—by Madeleine. I heard her ask for three or four products, none of which Annie carried.

"There is nothing," Diane Marie announced, "*nothing* of any quality whatsoever in this town. You don't carry the vitamins I need, you don't have my brand of shampoo, you don't even stock a supply of pain relievers. No wonder I have a headache."

Annie's voice was quiet, but I could hear the intensity behind it. I stayed well out of sight. "Everything I carry is natural and organic. That is what I believe in, Mrs. Ames. Headaches are not caused by our body's lack of pain relievers. I'm sorry I'm unable to help you, but I do hope you understand the reason."

"Well, it's nice to hear someone apologize for a change," Diane Marie proclaimed. Funny, it hadn't sounded like an apology to me. Diane Marie kept going. "I've never seen such poor manners as I find around here."

"Perhaps you'd consider moving here and retraining everyone?" Annie suggested in a voice as supple as a hangman's noose.

Diane Marie must have suffered from an irony deficiency. "No, young woman. I wouldn't have time for that."

Since I was peeking between the shampoos and the conditioners, I could see her turn on her heel and march out the door. Madeleine shrugged, said "I'm so sorry," and followed her mother.

I stepped from behind the display. "Coward," Annie said to me, and then we both laughed.

TWENTY

Wednesday, June 12

DIANE MARIE PICKED up her small journal. She felt a deep affection for this little book. It held her thoughts. It held her feelings. She leafed back through the pages. Most of the early entries were generic. She must have felt all along that she couldn't trust her husband, even though she hadn't thought about it consciously. But it was easy now to see how the entries had changed once she began to hide the journal.

Individual words, phrases, jumped out at her—*hiding... trapped...lose myself...go back?* An entry from a few weeks ago seemed to sum up what she was feeling:

He's gone so much of the time. I don't like being left alone in this creepy old house. But when he's here, we never talk, anyway. It's the loneliest kind of lonely, being lonely with someone else. I have to get away for good.

SUMMER VACATION FROM school, and the library was overrun with youngsters. Thank goodness it was a Wednesday and Esther was there. How she worked magic on kids from tots to pre-teens, I'd never know. Maybe she just liked them, and they felt it. I would be eternally thankful to her for volunteering. The woman deserved a medal.

She keeps them from pulling my tail. I appreciate that.

I turned away from my survey of the children's section and looked back at my rolltop desk where Marmalade was perched with her tail wound around her toes. I pushed aside a stack of papers. Egads, I didn't want to deal with that mess, either. Maybe

I'd go upstairs and do some cataloging. "Sadie?" I asked as I passed by the checkout desk. "Are you doing okay here?"

"I'm doing great, Biscuit. We've been checking out a lot of books today."

I smiled. Another one who needed a medal. What could I do for these women? "I'm going upstairs. Holler if you need me."

"Will do." She reached out to pat Marmy, who had levitated to the edge of the desk. Sadie's mouth turned up in an impish grin between her wrinkled cheeks. "I dare you to tap dance up the stairs," she said in a stage whisper.

"Very, very funny, Sadie. Do you want us to lose all our patrons?" I leaned closer to her across the little desk. "Anyway, I danced up them last night when nobody else was here."

Is that why you were sore when you got home?

Her mouth formed a very long O. "Did you really?"

"Let's just say I tried, and I found out it's easier to watch it in a movie than it is to do it."

"Well, I say good for you for trying."

"Thanks, Sadie. I'll be upstairs." I turned around and bumped into Ariel Montgomery. Why wasn't she at work at the Delicious? "Hello, Ariel," I said. "I hope that wasn't your foot I just stepped on."

"It didn't hurt much. Only a little. You're not too fat…I mean…I mean, it's okay, Ms. McKee."

I was sixteen once. Thank goodness that was a long time ago and I didn't have to go through it again.

Ariel reached out to scratch Marmalade's head. "Hey there, kitty-kitty. You're softer than my cat…."

Of course I am softer than he is.

"…I think you're a beautiful kitty-cat."

Thank you, but my name is Marmalade.

I rather doubted that Marmy liked being called kitty-kitty. "Can I help you find anything in particular, Ariel?"

"No, I was just looking for some books about…um…about, you know."

"Yes?" I said, trying to sound helpful.

"Relationships," she said.

"Right this way." I led her to the Red Room on the second floor. "This is probably the section you want." I pointed. "What…" How did I put this delicately? "…What aspect of relationships are you researching?"

"I'm trying to understand men in general," she said.

I do not understand the black tomcat who lives with you.

"You and every female who's ever lived, honey," I said with a laugh.

For a brief moment she looked as if I might have offended her, but then she giggled. "Are there any answers in books?" she asked.

I pulled two of my favorites off the shelf. "Try these," I said, handing her John Gray's *Mars and Venus on a Date* and Deborah Tannen's superb *You Just Don't Understand.* "They should help. I've used both of them a lot."

"And you're married," she said with a wistful lilt in her voice.

"Marriage is not the answer to every question," I pointed out, hoping she wouldn't take offense at my preachiness. "If marriage isn't grounded in mutual respect and understanding, it can be a miserable prison for both parties concerned."

She looked dubious but she kept the books. "Thanks, Ms. McKee." I couldn't tell if she meant it or if she was just being polite.

I watched her walk downstairs. She wasn't twitching her hips as much as she usually did. Maybe there was hope, I thought.

SINCE BOB WASN'T GOING to be home, I kept working way past closing time, until Marmalade began pawing at my leg. Must have been dinnertime. So I went home and walked in just as the phone began to ring.

"Hello?"

"It's me."

"Hey, Bob." I set my purse down and plopped on the couch. Marmalade lay down in the middle of the room and started one of her acrobatic grooming routines. "I'm glad you called. How's it going in Atlanta?"

"If I didn't know it was June on the calendar, I'd think it was wintertime."

"Is it that bad?"

"Barkley's been about as friendly as an iceberg."

What is an iceberg?

"Maybe he's just upset about Diane Marie leaving him. She's been here—what?—two weeks now? I've seen her around town a couple of times and once over at your mother's house. I don't know her well enough to tell for sure, but she sure looked down in the dumps to me. Maybe he feels the same way."

"No. It's more than that. There's something fishy going on down here. Of course, I knew there was. That's why I'm here. But I can't figure out what it is."

My heart sank. "Does that mean you have to stay a long time?"

"No. As a matter of fact, I'll be home tomorrow. Barkley's headed to Martinsville, too. He wasn't specific, but I think he's planning to have it out with Diane Marie."

"That sounds awful."

"He'd better watch his step. I think Mom likes Diane Marie a lot more than she likes him right now."

"Bob! He's her son!"

"Yeah, and he's an idiot."

From what little I knew of Barkley, I had to admit Bob probably had a point.

Before I could voice an opinion, he went on, "He's so defensive I can barely talk to him, so I just copied all the financial files. I'm going to spend a long time at the computer when I get back."

"I don't have anything planned. I'll knit while you compute."

I will be here with you.

He sounded so down, I tried to think of something to happy him up. "When you drive up, be sure you look at the mailbox."

"Good lord, what did Roger do this time?"

"No, it looks great. Remember the green vines we watched him paint Sunday night? Well, he painted morning glories on it last night. They look alive. I discovered them after you left this morning. They're beautiful."

There was a smile in Bob's voice. "I didn't know he was such an artist."

When we hung up the phone, I sat there a few minutes, gauging my interior temperature. Barkley hadn't even driven up for our wedding, and now he was worrying my Bob. I moved him up to the top of my yuch-list, and then I got up and went to the kitchen to feed Marmalade.

Thank you.

TWENTY-ONE

Thursday, June 13

REBECCA JO SMILED gently across the breakfast table at her daughter-in-law. She felt like her heart was breaking watching Diane Marie chew at the inside of her lip like that. This whole situation was so very wrong, but it had taken Diane Marie two weeks to say anything specific. Rebecca Jo couldn't tell if she was trying to give Barkley the benefit of the doubt, or if she was plotting how to begin divorce proceedings.

Luckily, once Diane Marie settled in, she hadn't had any more of the severe nausea she'd experienced at home in Atlanta. Maybe she was right. Maybe Barkley was trying to get rid of her, although food poisoning seemed such an inappropriate way of doing it. Barkley never could cook, anyway. So maybe her nausea was just the result of his poor chef skills.

Diane Marie must have read her mind. "The more I think of it, the more I'm sure he's not really trying to kill me. I just think he wants me to leave him so he can divorce me without feeling guilty about it."

"Are you sure he's slipping something into your food?" Rebecca Jo asked.

"No. Not a hundred percent." She ran her fingers back through her hair. "I'm *not* sure. But almost every time we've eaten together for the past month, I've gotten violently ill right afterward, and it happened no matter which one of us was cooking. So, even if I don't know how he's doing it, I do believe he's been trying to make me sick."

Rebecca Jo could hear the grandfather clock ticking. "Is there a chance…" She let the question hang.

"No, Mama Sheffield. I'm not pregnant. Barkley hasn't touched me in months."

Oh, dear. That was more information than Rebecca Jo wanted.

IDA SMILED ACROSS the breakfast table at her sister. Ralph walked past the two of them and picked up his keys. "See you at the store, Ida. Bye, Diane Marie."

"Bye, Ralph. Enjoy your day." He left, and Diane Marie turned back to Ida. "Thanks for the talks we've been having. They sure are helping. You're right, I admit. I need to tell him about the baby real soon. He'll be back in a few days."

"He'll get used to the idea, hon."

"I wish I believed that. I'm just glad you're happy for me."

"What's a sister for, after all? I wish you'd told me sooner."

"I couldn't. I didn't think you'd understand."

"Not understand? Why ever not?"

"Well, your marriage is so perfect…."

Ida let out what could only be described as a snort. "Little sister, you need to understand that what you see on the outside isn't always what's going on. Of course Ralph and I have a good marriage, but…perfect? Ha! We have to work at it. All the time. We've done so much sashaying around trying to figure out where we stand, we could have invented a dance about it."

"But he's always nice to you."

Ida paused. "Yes," she said. "He *is* nice to me. I've never had to worry that he might undercut me or say anything nasty. Of course, I'm nice to him, too. I don't try to fix him." She laughed. "Well, not too much." Then her face turned serious. "I never poke fun at…well…he's reached an age where sometimes he has a little trouble—you know what I mean."

"What happens…what does he do…when it's like that?"

Ida wrinkled her eyebrows. "Do? We just laugh about it and do some hugging instead."

"And he doesn't get angry?"

"Of course not."

"Kelvin sure does." Diane Marie gathered the three plates and stood up. She turned away from her sister's direct gaze. "He's been having more trouble lately, and he usually ends up yelling at me. He says it's my fault." She turned back and looked at Ida. "I'm glad you two get along."

Ida swiped at a strand of hair that tickled her forehead. "Yes, so am I. We're nice to each other. The world would be a much better place if we'd all just be a little kinder." She reached into her pocket for a tissue. "I'm so sorry you're—"

"That's okay," Diane Marie interrupted. "Don't worry about me. I'll be fine." She took the plates over to the sink. "You go on to the store. I'll see you here at lunch. About one o'clock?"

"Yeah, I'll have time for that. Have to meet with the bank guy about the ATM machine at quarter past two." She reached up to pat her hair. "I had to cancel my two o'clock perm, but I rescheduled for next week. In the meantime, it'll just have to do, but it seems like it gets thinner every time I turn around. I need all the help I can get with it."

"It looks fine. You can go another week."

"Thanks. What are you up to this morning?"

"I'm going to read the paper, and then head up to Garner Creek. I have a little bit of shopping I need to do. That gift certificate you gave me expires tomorrow. But I'll wash up here first."

"Bless you, indeed." Ida pushed her chair back, gathered up a sweater and her purse, patted her hair one more time and headed out the door. Just before it closed behind her, she turned back. "I'm really glad you're here, Diane Marie. Not just because you're doing all the dishes, either. I'm glad we had such a good talk."

"Me, too. It feels good not to have to hide anything anymore."

Ida turned down the walkway. She was pretty sure Diane Marie wasn't telling her the whole story yet, but these discussions were a start. Yes. A good start.

MADELEINE SMILED ACROSS the breakfast table at her brother. She was enjoying the fact that Mother usually slept in. Johnny never said much during these breakfasts, but Madeleine felt a real connection with him, anyway. "I think," she said in answer to his brief question, "Mother has decided to do more terrorizing—I mean shopping—up and down First Street today."

Johnny frowned a bit at her language, or maybe he had just swallowed a bite of pancake the wrong way. She thought he might lecture her on keeping one of the commandments, but she saw his mouth turn up on one side. "Does she have any shopkeeper here who will even tolerate her presence?" he asked.

"Not really. But every once in a while she does buy, and then she buys a lot, so everybody but Mrs. Peterson at the grocery store lets her get away with it."

"What happened with Ida Peterson?"

"A week or so ago she told me to take Mother to Garner Creek to buy groceries."

"Sounds like I need to go apologize to Ida."

"Don't worry, big brother. I already did." She scooped her fork full of pancake as her brother muttered something into his coffee cup. "Sometimes," she said, "I feel like I ought to change my name to So."

"Change your name? What do you mean?"

"I'm always apologizing for Mother," she said. "My name could be So Sorry Ames." He just looked at her. "Don't you get it? Instead of saying I'm Madeleine, I could say I'm *So Sorry?*"

He didn't seem to think that was nearly as funny as Madeleine did.

They both looked upward as they heard a toilet flush above their heads. Mother was up.

Diane Marie's journal—Thursday, June 13th
9:03 a.m.... How could I have been so dense for so long? I finally know what's going on. He must have thought I'd already figured it out. That's why he's changed. How am

I going to deal with this? He can't really want me dead, can he? I'm his wife. But he's going to be so angry when I tell him I know what he's been doing. How can I protect myself?

TWENTY-TWO

IT WAS ONE-THIRTY. Rebecca Jo Sheffield rubbed the back of her left hand. That arthritis was bothering her again. Well, since Diane Marie and Barkley hadn't shown up for lunch yet, she'd just sit and enjoy a cup of tea. She hoped they were getting things worked out. He'd appeared on the front doorstep at noon, and the two of them left almost immediately. No telling when they'd be back. Maybe she could rub some horse liniment into her hands while she waited. Bill, her late husband, had introduced her to Horse Salve years ago. The bottle had a line drawing of a horse's head and the slogan *Horse Salve to Save Your Horse* in bright red letters. She didn't know whether it worked because it sounded so earnest, or whether it was because it made her laugh. Or maybe because it stank to high heaven. But it worked nonetheless.

Rebecca Jo looked at the empty chairs across the table from her. She was enjoying her daughter-in-law's visit, even if it had been unexpected. She truly liked Diane Marie. It was pretty clear her marriage to Barkley was dead. Of course, that had been obvious to Rebecca Jo for a long time. They never seemed to be on the same track. Oh, they were polite to each other in company. They said all the right things. But Rebecca Jo had been blessed with a good marriage. A long marriage. She could see the difference between what she'd had and what she saw with these two youngsters. There was no life between the two of them. She didn't think it was the age difference. Diane Marie was a lot younger than Barkley, but that in itself wasn't a problem. Rebecca Jo was sure that her daughter-in-law was holding something back, but she couldn't imagine what. All those things Diane Marie had told her about that food poisoning and such just didn't make sense. Something more was going on. She hoped Barkley wasn't having an affair. Barkley is an idiot, she thought, and looked again at the clock.

IT WAS ONE-THIRTY. Ida Peterson was running late. She hurried past her sister's car that was parked at the curb. She walked up to the back porch and into the little mud room, as they called it, and then on through the spacious kitchen. "Diane Marie," she called out. There was no answer. "Where the devil is she? I don't have all day to grab some lunch." Muttering to herself, Ida turned back and pulled out the bread and a can of tuna. She opened and drained it, chopped a stalk of celery and cut up a little green pepper, mixed in some mayo and a touch of salt. Voila! Two sandwiches. Where the heck was her sister? "Diane Marie," she called again as she walked through to the living room and glanced out on the front porch. "Diane Marie?" She walked upstairs and checked the guest room where her sister was staying. The room was tidy, except for the clothes she'd been wearing at breakfast. They were strewn across the bed, next to a plastic bag that said Mable's Dress Shop. She must have driven up to Garner Creek, but the car was back at the curb, so Diane Marie had to be home. The bag was empty, except for a receipt. Ida looked at it. "Hmm. Sale prices." Her purse was on the bedside table. That was good. She can't be far, Ida thought.

Eventually Ida went ahead and ate her sandwich, covered the other one with foil, and left it in the fridge. She had to get back to work. She had that meeting with the bank manager about putting an ATM in the grocery store. Ralph was against the idea, but Ida thought it might work out well. She slipped out the back door, and hurried past the car and down the hill.

IT WAS ONE-THIRTY. Diane Marie glanced at her husband out of the corner of her eye as they walked past the river birches. He wasn't looking at her. She took a deep breath. "I won't give you a divorce, Barkley. I don't believe in divorce. We can work this out." Without waiting for an answer, as if there *were* an answer to that, she stepped off the path and walked along the edge of the meadow until she reached the stone outcropping. There was a good place to sit up there. She didn't even look to see if he was following her.

A thin brown lizard skittered out of her way as she stepped into the small hollow where the rock was warmed by the early afternoon sun. She eased down onto a small ledge, and her husband sat down, too. Not too close to her, with his body angled away to the left. She looked at his profile. Really looked in a way she hadn't done for a long time. People who were married took each other for granted, she thought. Until something like this happened. "Okay, Barkley," she said. "Maybe you're not trying to poison me, but something is wrong. Tell me what's really going on."

"Going on?" he asked.

"Quit that! You know I saw that ledger in your desk. I don't know exactly what it meant, but I've got some ideas. I know it's not good. You've been acting differently for months now, and I went looking for some evidence. Do you have a girlfriend on the side?"

Barkley's voice was sullen. "You don't have the right to spy on me."

Diane Marie bent her head for a moment and took a deep breath. When she looked up at him, she was surprised by the look of hurt—at least it looked like hurt to her. He was the one who was cheating. What right did he have to feel hurt? "I admit," she said, "that I shouldn't have handled it that way. But I've asked you what's wrong so many times, and you've always sidestepped the answer. I knew something was going on. You were taking too many business trips and spending too many hours late at the office. Now you can't sidestep anymore. If there's another woman involved, I want to know about it. If there's something else going on... Well, I want to know about that, too."

"You won't understand," he said.

She saw that muscle in his jaw contracting. That meant he was really angry. "Try me," she countered.

ONCE THE WHOLE STORY was out, little things she'd seen and heard over the past number of months began to make sense. "You know, you're going to have to talk to Bob about this," she told him.

His head jerked up. "No, I don't. I can just stop, and he'll never notice the difference."

"Barkley, are you out of your blinkin' mind? He's already suspicious. Why do you think he's been in Atlanta twice in the past few weeks? Did you honestly think you could get away with draining that amount of money from the company on a regular basis just to supply your—" she spit out the word "—your girlfriend with an apartment and clothes and goodness knows what else…." She was appalled at the figure he had mentioned. She was furious that she'd been scrimping here and there, thinking that their construction firm was in a slump, hoping it was only temporary. This green shirt she was wearing had come from the Goodwill store, and all the while he was… She didn't want to think about it.

"Bob can afford it. He got most of the inheritance."

"I'm beginning to think your grandmother showed very good sense in giving him the most. He's obviously a…" She stopped herself before she said it, but *a better man than you* hung in the air as if she had spoken the words out loud. Diane Marie was somewhat taken aback by her own vehemence. Did she really think Bob was a better man than Barkley? Did she? She turned to look out across the little meadow at another copse of river birches in the distance. Their light spring green had long ago deepened to a summer tone. Did she?

"If you don't tell him yourself," she said, "I'm going to tell him. I think, though, that he'd be more forgiving if he heard it from you."

He jumped to his feet and grabbed her arm. "I'm your husband! You can't do that to me!"

Diane Marie was too angry to feel afraid of him. She wrenched her arm away and shouted right back. "You should have thought about that before you started writing all those checks to *A. Smith*. What's her name? Alice? Andrea?"

"Amy," he said, "and I'm going to marry her."

"Why don't you cut off her allowance for a few months and then see if she's still willing to marry you? Oh, and don't forget to tell her that if you divorce me, your alimony payments will be sky high."

Diane Marie ignored his clenched fists and deliberately stepped past him. "Tell Bob about the money you've been stealing, Barkley," she said as she climbed down the side of the outcropping. "If you don't, by God, I will." She turned and walked away without looking back.

IT WAS ONE-THIRTY. Father John set the tray down and glared at his sister. "What on earth possessed you to run off and leave her like that?" he asked.

"You don't have to live with her all the time," Madeleine barked at him. "All I want is to get out of this family." She wrapped her arms around one of the throw pillows on the couch. "Not you. I'm not talking about you." She looked up at her brother and shook her head. "One minute I was standing there listening to her, and the next minute something just snapped. She insulted me one time too many, right in front of all those women sitting around the beauty parlor, and I had to get out of there before I hit her."

"You wouldn't do that," he soothed. He held out a glass of iced tea from the tray and she unwound from the couch pillow long enough to take it and set it down on the table next to her. "Be kind," he said. "She's old," he added.

"She is *not* old. She is going to live *forever*. She's only fifty-nine. That's not even retirement age, for Pete's sake." Madeleine took off her glasses and set them beside the tea. She rubbed her eyes. Father John hoped she wasn't going to cry. "She is hale and hearty," Madeleine continued, "and full of spite. She can drop dead for all I care, and if she doesn't, I will happily throttle her if she says a single word to me when she comes in that door."

"I need to go pick her up," Father John said. He felt rather a need to get away and breathe some fresh air. He started rummaging around on the little hallway table, looking for his keys. "I've already put some sandwiches on the table. Drink your tea. We'll eat as soon as I get back."

Madeleine muttered something under her breath.

"What did you say?" he asked.

"I said, I hope you never find her."

"Madeleine, you don't mean that."

"Yes, I do! You don't know what it's like," she practically spit at him. "You're her perfect child. You're the male. You're the priest. You're the one who escaped." She threw the couch pillow at him. "If you'd be completely honest with yourself, you'd realize you hate her as much as I do."

Father John fielded the pillow, then paused with his keys in his hand. When he was five or six years old, he had dropped a green glass vase on the kitchen floor. His mother locked him in a closet. It was dark and crowded with old clothes and shoes and bags that rustled when he brushed against them. To this day the smell of mothballs made him sick to his stomach. He could still see her face when she let him out after he had finally cried himself dry. "God will never forgive you for this," she told him. "You are a bad, bad boy." Then, as if locking him in a closet hadn't been enough, she'd spanked him with the heavy wooden spoon and sent him to bed without any supper.

He took a deep breath. "You need to cool off before she gets here, or you're liable to say something you'll regret."

"Yes, sir, my brother, the wise one, the father, the priest." She threw the words at him, just as she'd thrown the pillow. "You are so full of bull, it makes me sick. I don't even know who you are. Excuse me while I go barf." She stormed out the front door before he could make sense of what she was saying, much less think of a pacifying rejoinder.

Maybe his mother didn't need him to pick her up right away. Maybe she'd stay and get her hair cut or something. Didn't that make women feel better? Maybe he'd make himself a strong cup of coffee. He walked into the little kitchen.

IT WAS ONE-THIRTY. As Diane Marie paced down Fifth Street, she tried to imagine what else she could have said to convince Kelvin. The conversation had not gone well. But she still had a chance. Maybe she shouldn't have answered Ida's phone, but it had kept on ringing and ringing. She hadn't expected Kelvin home for another three or four days. She wasn't ready.

"Hello?"

"Why aren't you home?"

"Oh, Kelvin, are you back?"

"Of course I'm back, and I'm waiting for my wife to come home. If you leave now, you can be here in time to fix dinner."

Diane Marie wanted to take a deep breath but her lungs didn't seem to be working. She reached out her free hand and touched the kitchen counter. It felt solid. It felt secure. "Kelvin, this morning I was looking at a copy of last Sunday's Atlanta newspaper."

"What does that have to do with anything?" he barked at her.

"They had an article about a whole chain of robberies at ATM's and convenience stores."

There was a pause. "So?" Even that one word sounded so harsh, Diane Marie almost chickened out.

"They had a list of all the dates and times of the robberies.... Every one of them happened when you were on your business trips."

"Baby…" His voice had shifted to what she thought of as his wheedling tone, the one he used to convince her it was her fault whenever he had to hit her. "You don't think there's a connection, now do you?"

"Yes, I do. You've never said just what you do for a job. *Consulting* doesn't mean anything. I compared the dates…" She almost said *with my journal,* but remembered in time that she'd told him she had lost it. "…with the calendar, and not a single one of those happened when you were back in Enders."

"So what?" She could hear the challenge in his voice.

It was now or never. "You have to turn yourself in," she said.

"Are you nuts?"

"I'd rather have a husband in prison than one who's running from the law."

"I'm not running. They don't have a clue who I am or where I am."

"Either you turn yourself in, or I'm calling the cops."

"You wouldn't do that."

"I won't be married to a bank robber, Kelvin."

"What's gotten into you? You don't know what you're saying. Why don't we meet somewhere and talk about this?"

"You're not going to change my mind, and I don't want to talk about it. I want you to turn yourself in."

"Meet me up top. You know, that place where we used to go to before we got hitched."

Diane twirled the phone cord around her hand several times. Maybe she could talk some reason into him. She had the baby to think about, after all. "All right, I'll be there in twenty minutes or so."

Before she left the house, she changed into the new blouse and jeans she'd just bought at Mable's. Maybe it would give her the courage to stand up to him. Maybe he would think she looked pretty and wouldn't want to hurt her. It was one thing to talk back on the phone, but quite another when he was standing there in front of her. Oh, dear God, she thought, please don't let him hit me. Maybe she should ask Ida to go with her. But Ida was still at the store. For extra courage, Diane Marie dabbed her favorite perfume on her wrists and behind her ears. Gardenia. She loved the scent.

She slipped out the front door and walked along Fifth Street toward the path at the top of Beechnut Lane. The only other person she saw was a young woman down the hill, just turning the corner onto Beechnut. The woman called out something, but Diane Marie didn't wave. She was thinking about what she was going to say to convince Kelvin to confess. She was thinking about her baby, too.

TWENTY-THREE

"Mother!" Madeleine called out to the fuzzy green-clad being at the far end of the block. Even through her myopic haze, she could see the person stop and turn, then continue walking. She doesn't even want to talk to me, Madeleine thought. Well, she wasn't going to let this pass. It was about time she had it out with that woman.

She started jogging up the hill, surprised that Mother could walk so fast. By the time Madeleine got to Fifth Street, her mother was nowhere in sight. Madeleine would never have expected her to take a walk in the woods, but she'd seen her green blouse go that way. Madeleine stepped into the shadow of the tall pine trees that stood like sentinels next to the small graveled turn-around area. The path ahead of her veered off to the left. She squared her shoulders, tried to calm her overactive heart and stepped toward the dense layer of pine needles.

The old Frost poem about two roads came to mind. I could turn back, she thought. Take the coward's road. Things would just stay the way they had always been, except that Mother would be more hateful, more spiteful. As if that were anything new. Every time Madeleine gave in to her demands, she just wanted more. Madeleine knew she could never give that woman enough to make her happy. And that's what she wanted. She wanted her daughter to fill her empty heart. Madeleine paused.

Her heart's not empty, she thought. It was full of tar and acid. Madeleine wasn't going to do it anymore. She was leaving home…home? Ha! She was leaving that fancy house. She didn't know where she'd go, but it would be someplace far from Atlanta. Someplace where she could write without hiding it.

She stepped onto the path and quickened her pace. After only a few moments, she saw her mother ahead of her, stopped in the middle of the path. "Mother!" she cried out. "Wait for me." Her mother turned toward her. Madeleine steeled herself. As she pulled closer to the figure ahead of her, she had a vague feeling that something was wrong. Mother's colors were wrong somehow. Instead of the tan pants, there was dark blue below the lime green. That wasn't right.

She heard a voice, lower pitched than her mother's. "I don't know who you think I am, but I'm definitely not your mother."

By this time Madeleine was close enough for her mother's face to come into focus. "Oh, no! I'm so sorry! I thought—you see, you're wearing her blouse."

The woman clearly thought she was crazy. "Whose blouse?" she asked.

"My mother's. I mean, my mother has a blouse just like that one, the same color." Madeleine took a deep breath. "Can we start over again?" The other woman was silent. Madeleine took that for a *yes*. She held out her hand. "My name is Madeleine. Madeleine Ames. I'm Father Ames's sister, and no, I'm not crazy. But I left my glasses at the rectory, and I'm awfully nearsighted. In that green blouse you looked like... Well, I mean I thought you were my...mother." She tried not to spit out that word, but spit it out she did.

"I see," the other woman said, although it was fairly obvious that she didn't. She took Madeleine's outstretched hand. "My name is Diane Marie."

Madeleine jerked her hand back. "If that's meant to be funny, it isn't," she said. "Is this a joke you cooked up with my brother?"

"How did you know I'd talked to your brother?"

"Because you said you were Diane Marie."

"What does that have to do with anything? Did he tell you I'd come to talk to him? That's pretty lousy. I can't believe a priest would do something like that."

"What are you talking about?" Madeleine asked her.

"What are *you* talking about?" Diane Marie retorted.

"I'm talking about this ridiculous game you're playing, saying your name is Diane Marie."

At that, the blonde woman looked genuinely confused. "My name *is* Diane Marie," she said.

"It can't be. That's my mother's name, and you're wearing her blouse."

"This is *my* blouse. I bought it in Garner Creek this morning, and I've got a sales slip at home to prove it."

Madeleine had the good grace to lower her eyes. "I'm an idiot," she said.

"Well, yes, it did seem like that for a bit," Diane Marie agreed, "but maybe I just didn't understand."

"Your name really is…?"

"Yes."

"How can there be two Diane Marie's in this little town?"

"It's worse than that. There's another one, I mean besides your mother and me. She and I grew up in the same town down the river, and I just found out she married a guy from around here. They live in Atlanta now, but she's here visiting."

"I wonder if she has a green blouse, too," Madeleine thought out loud.

"In a town this size I'm bound to run into her. When I see her, I'll ask." She smiled. "I hate to be curt, but I really do need to be going." She held out her hand for a somewhat warmer hand-shake this time. "Maybe I'll see you around."

"I promise to wear my glasses next time. And I guess I ought to tell you, I like your perfume a lot better than the one my mother wears. And," Madeleine grinned, "up close, you don't look like her at all."

"That's a relief. You made me think I was aging fast." She turned, gave a little wave and walked on up the path. Madeleine watched until the green blouse faded out of sight behind a thick hedgelike growth that filled in under the tall pine trees where the path meandered to the right. Then she turned and headed back toward the rectory.

HE WAS ON HIS second cup when he heard the door open. He looked around the corner and saw Madeleine picking up her iced tea. He didn't know what to say, so he didn't say anything, just walked back into the living room and sat down. She sank into the chair across from him and turned the glass around and around in her hands.

"I started to take a walk," she told her brother. "I thought that would cool me down a bit. You're right, Johnny. I was pretty hot under the collar. I went over toward Beechnut. I thought I'd walk out of town into the woods, up that path you showed me the last time I was here. But when I turned the corner, I could see Mother walking up ahead of me, headed toward the path. It turned out—"

"How could you even see her?" Father John pointed to her glasses, still lying on the little table where she put them earlier. "You didn't have your glasses."

"John, remember what she was wearing this morning? That horrible green shirt? I don't need glasses to see that a block away. Two blocks, even. The problem is that I finally caught up with her, and it wasn't Mother."

"What do you mean it wasn't Mother?"

"It was some other woman wearing an ugly lime-green blouse." She took a short swallow of tea and plunked the glass back down. "Yuch! The ice is all melted." She stood and turned toward the hallway. "Back in a minute. I have to go to the bathroom."

DIANE MARIE STOOD OUTSIDE the Beauty Shop. She had never been so humiliated in her entire life. She had walked several blocks down the street, looking for the car. She had no idea where Madeleine had parked it. Rather than look like she had been abandoned, she crossed over the street and stood watching those ridiculous ducks swimming around and around in the wide part of the river. Even standing still, she was silently fuming. She straightened her already ramrod straight spine and walked back across the street. There was the car, parked in front of the framing shop. She must have passed it twice already.

Luckily, the car wasn't locked. Whatever has gotten into that child, she thought. Couldn't she ever do anything right? You should never leave a car unlocked. There was no telling what might happen. Diane Marie sat herself down and reached across to lock the door on the driver's side. Disgusting, that was what this whole event was.

She wasn't sure how long she'd sat there in the car, but she finally decided Madeleine was not going to come back to get her. She unlocked her door and stepped out onto the sidewalk. One of the women who had been in the beauty shop was walking toward her. Diane Marie stared at her and the woman dropped her eyes and wiped the smile off her face. Holding tightly onto her purse, Diane Marie walked up the street.

As she turned left at the corner onto Pine Street, a black Lincoln pulled up next to her.

"Where are *you* going?" her husband asked out the window.

"What are you doing here?"

"Your vacation is over. I'm taking you home with me. Now."

"Lower your voice, Conrad. Do you want to make a scene?"

"I don't care what kind of scene I make." He pulled a wad of papers out of his shirt pocket and waved them at her. "Some *more* credit card bills came in yesterday, and you're going on a short leash starting today."

Diane Marie looked around. Two women were walking down Pine Street half a block away. She walked around the Lincoln and got in the front seat. "Take me up to the rectory, and we'll talk about it there."

"No. We will talk about it right now." He threw the papers into her lap and pulled away from the curb, only to drive half a block and stop on the other side of Pine Street. He turned off the ignition and stabbed his finger at the papers she was gathering up into a pile. "This has got to stop."

"We have plenty of money," she shot back at him, "and I deserve every bit of this."

"You're heading me toward bankruptcy, that's what you're doing." He was snarling. She drew back against the door. "I've written the bank," he went on. "I cancelled all your credit cards."

Diane Marie's face went from furious red to ashen white. "You can't do that to me!"

"Oh, yes, I can. This…is called—" he ground out each word "—an intervention. Somebody has to get through to you, and it's going to be me. I should have done this years ago. I'm mortgaged up to my eyeballs. I borrowed everything I can, and then you go out and buy…" He flailed his hand at the papers she was holding under the arms crossed over her chest. "What has gotten into you?"

She thrust her chin forward. "You owe me. I gave you so many years working in that dingy office."

"And I'm *still* working in it, trying to keep up with all your wasteful foolishness. Do you have any idea how many contractors you've alienated on this house renovation? They're pulling their business from me and going to other suppliers. Competition is fierce in this business, and you are ruining me, and then you go out and buy twelve dresses—TWELVE!—in one day. At those prices? And those phone calls to Martha."

"What's wrong with calling my sister?"

"She lives in *Tahiti,* for criminey sakes! Do you know how much your phone calls are costing me?"

"Conrad Ames, you cannot talk to me like this."

"Why not? Because I've put up with your crap for thirty-eight years? Well, this is the last straw. I'm not putting up with it anymore. You're going to change. If I have to take out the phones and put you on house arrest, that's what I'll do."

He started the car, drove to the rectory and parked in front. When he opened his door, Diane Marie just sat there, her mouth in a grim line. If Madeleine hadn't abandoned her at that beauty shop, Conrad wouldn't have found her walking—her! walking! He would have come to the rectory and he would have had to behave himself in front of Johnny. He never would have attacked her like this in front of Johnny. It was all Madeleine's fault.

Conrad opened her door. "We're going in there and you are going to pack up your things and we are going to leave."

"Madeleine will pack my things," Diane Marie snapped as she stepped from the car.

As MADELEINE STOOD UP to go to the bathroom, the front door opened. Diane Marie Houston Ames walked in, followed by her husband. She nodded at her son and turned to her daughter. "God," she said, "will never forgive you for what you did to me."

Father John watched his sister pick up the glass of warm tea and fling it in her mother's face.

"YOU TOOK YOUR sweet time getting here," he said as she emerged from the top of the woodsy path.

"I'm sorry. I didn't know exactly when you'd be here, and I…" She paused, unwilling to mention her conversation with that woman on the path. It seemed too bizarre in the first place, and yet it was a happy little interlude. Maybe she'd write about it in her journal tonight.

He didn't seem to have heard what she was saying, anyway. "You know I don't like to be kept waiting. Why do you always keep me waiting?"

"I don't always do that. I'm usually on time. I just got held up today. Anyway, you didn't say a particular time."

"Yeah, well, you used to come running anytime I called."

"Kelvin, that was a long time ago. I'm not a silly little girl anymore. I'm your wife."

"Fat lot of good it does me when you'd rather be over here, hanging around with your sister. You ought to be home with me."

"I told you she's sick. She needs me."

"Yeah? She doesn't look sick. She didn't look sick when the two of you took a walk the other night. She didn't look sick when the two of you were sitting on her front porch playing cards yesterday."

"You've been spying on me!"

"You've been lying to me!"

I will not shout, she thought. If I shout, he'll hit me. She lowered her voice. "I have the right to spend time with my sister."

"No, you don't. Your job is to be home taking care of me."

"But you've been gone."

"I'm home now, and I want you to pack up your things and get home tonight."

"No, Kelvin. I can't do that." She took a deep breath and straightened her spine. "I want you to call the police tomorrow and turn yourself in. I have a doctor's appointment here early tomorrow morning, and I'm going to go to that. After that, I'll call the police if you haven't done so already."

"Now you listen to me, and get it straight. I'm in charge here. I'm not turning myself in. You've been living just fine with the way I make money, and I'm going to keep on. I've got a good thing going, and you'll keep your mouth shut about this."

"Kelvin, I told you I'd rather have a husband in jail than one on the run. But there's another reason."

"Yeah," he growled. "You want to run my life."

"No. Please listen to me. I told you I need to see the doctor tomorrow."

"Yeah? So?"

"Kelvin, I'm pregnant." She didn't wait for an answer. "I want our baby to be proud of you. If you do your time and then get out, you can still have a good life with our little boy. I bet it'll be a boy." She looked at his golden brown eyes. Maybe the baby would have eyes that color some day. They were always blue to start out with, or so she'd heard.

She was still thinking of the baby when he hit her. Diane Marie spun to her right, but somehow kept her footing. All she could think of then was to get away. Get away. She started running blindly toward the kenaf field. The rows were wide enough apart that she could run down them.

She'd always been fast on her feet. When she was a little girl she used to love running down the hill and back up again, just for the sheer joy of it. Now she was running for her life. Running to protect herself and her baby. Her baby. She made it quite a ways into the kenaf field before her husband tackled her from behind. It knocked the wind out of her as she fell with him on top of her. Before she could think what to do, he had flipped her over onto her back. She struggled, but he had always been so much heavier than she was. She saw it coming. He hit her on the jaw. Hard.

Part III
After The Fall

TWENTY-FOUR

MY KITCHEN HAD a cozy, homey warmth and familiarity to it, but I still felt somehow disconnected. It had been only a matter of hours since I'd seen Diane Marie Ames jump off the cliff. In spite of the warm shower I'd taken, in spite of the short nap, in spite of the cup of tea my stiff hands were wrapped around, in spite of the birds scrabbling around at the feeder outside the kitchen window—in spite of all this I felt cold and disoriented. Maybe I should have asked Scott to stay with me instead of letting him drive back to his grandma's house. But I'd wanted some time to get cleaned up. I'd wanted some time to sit here and cry out the frustration, the helpless feeling of having stood by and watched someone die. Well, I hadn't been standing by, exactly. I'd been hanging onto a cliffside. I still had this vague sense of unrest, though, as if I ought to have been able to do something. Maybe it was just that, as a woman, I felt a sense of connectedness to Diane Marie simply because she was another woman. The fact that she was—that she had been—overbearing, insulting, obnoxious, dictatorial, bossy, rude…

Oh, phooey. This wasn't about what I thought of her. Surely there must be someone, somewhere, who loved the woman. I'd never met her husband. Maybe she hadn't always been like this. Whose job would it be to tell him? Would Bob have to do that? No. He'd call the police in Atlanta, and they'd send two officers to his home. Wasn't it always two who showed up? Or had I seen too many movies?

A long time later, too long for my overwrought nerves, Bob walked into our warm kitchen. He had Marmalade in his arms. I was so relieved to see her. She jumped down and came over to me, winding her back around my shins and nuzzling her head into my hand. As I picked her up, I wondered where she'd been all this time. Bob headed for the coffeepot, pulling his big blue police mug off the rack as he walked past it. He was shaking his head and chuckling as he poured the coffee.

"What's so funny?" I asked him. I was still shaky and he was laughing?

He set the cup down on the table across from me and pulled me up into a big soft bear hug. Felt lovely. Made most of the bears go away.

"How does your face feel?" he asked me. "You're getting two black eyes out of this."

"I know. It doesn't feel great, but I can stand it. What did you find out that's so funny?"

"Nathan found a suicide note at the top of the cliff," he said.

I backed up and perched my hands on my hips. "There's nothing funny about that."

"Well," he said, "not really, except that I took it to Father Ames and told him that I was very sorry I had to inform him that his mother had committed suicide by jumping off a cliff earlier this afternoon."

"How awful."

He grinned. What on earth was wrong with the man?

"He seemed a bit confused, so I showed him the note. I'd put it in a plastic bag, of course, but he could read it through the plastic. It was just one sheet of green note paper."

"What did it say?"

"It said, *I can't go on like this anymore.* It was signed *Diane Marie.*"

"Well?" This was like trying to pull teeth. "Tell me what happened."

Bob took an unnecessarily long slurp of coffee. "He told me it wasn't his mother's handwriting. Then he invited me into his living room and showed me…" he paused, set down the coffee mug and waved an arm in a cavalier flourish.

"Yes?" I prompted.

"He showed me his mother who was sitting right there, wearing a wet lime-green blouse."

"And...tan slacks?" I asked.

"How did you know that?"

"I just did. Why was her blouse wet?"

"I didn't ask. There was enough tension in that room to wind a spring on. Madeleine was on her hands and knees cleaning up a spill—looked like Mrs. Ames had dropped her tea."

"Then who's the dead woman?"

He sat down and the smile disappeared. "You're not going to like this," he said.

I felt something wrench inside my stomach. There were two other Diane Marie's in town. Bob's sister-in-law. I still didn't know her very well. If it had been her, he would have been more upset. Then there was the Diane Marie I'd come to like so much. The one I'd been tap dancing with just two nights ago.

"Ida's sister?" I asked, feeling the tears start.

He reached out and took my hands. "I'm sorry to have to tell you."

"Does Ida know yet?"

"Yes. Father Ames is the one who mentioned that if the Diane Marie in the note wasn't his mother, it might be Ida Peterson's sister. I knew it wasn't my sister-in-law... Why on earth are there three women with the same name in this town? And *two* of them with green shirts? Father Ames asked if he could go with me. Ida's Catholic, you know. I'm sorry I had to put him through that fiasco about his mother, but how could we know? The face wasn't recognizable, since she landed—"

I pulled my hands back and clapped them over my ears. "Bob! I don't need to hear this!" He looked somewhat chagrined, and rightly so. "Is Ida home now?" I asked.

He nodded. "Father Ames went back there with her from the funeral home, after Ida identified the body. She recognized the shoes and a watch she was wearing. She said the green blouse was a new one Diane Marie had just bought."

I left almost immediately to go to Ida's. I wasn't like a lot of women who always seemed to have a tuna casserole ready to take to a neighbor in distress. All I could take was myself. Ida lived up on Fifth Street, near the cliff where her sister had died. Wouldn't it have been terrible, I thought, if Scott had rung *her* doorbell when he went looking for a telephone? The poor woman would have raced up to the cliff and found her sister there dead. As it was, Sharon Armitage was the one whose phone Scott had used. She wasn't taking tap dance lessons, so she didn't know Diane Marie well, and anyway, we both thought it was a different Diane Marie all that time.

MADELEINE FOLLOWED her father out of the rectory and down the front walk to the car, carrying her mother's bulky make-up case. Her father had already made two trips, loading the big suitcases into the trunk and backseat of the Lincoln. Mother was sitting in the front seat looking straight ahead. Madeleine handed over the case and watched as her father wedged it between two of its larger cousins. *It's a good thing they have such a big car,* Madeleine thought. It was a tight fit driving up here in the first place. Why on earth did Mother need all those clothes? Madeleine had brought one small suitcase for herself, and even it wasn't packed full.

"Take care now," her father said as he turned to her and held his arms wide. "You drive safely coming home." She stepped up to get a farewell hug.

"I won't be coming home for a few days, Dad," she said.

"You won't? Why not?"

She looked back at the rectory before she answered. "It won't work anymore. When I come home, it'll be to pack up my things. I'm going to look for another place to live."

He nodded. "How will you manage?"

"I don't know, Dad. But I will not live in that house with her anymore."

Madeleine's father turned and looked at the profile of his wife. "You're right. The next few weeks aren't going to be any fun at all."

The next few months, Madeleine thought. The next few years.

He reached out and patted her on the shoulder. "Let me know what you decide," he said as he walked behind the Lincoln. "Say good-bye to Johnny for me." Opening his door, he gave a brief wave.

Madeleine backed up onto the sidewalk. As the car turned around to head downhill, she waved. Mother kept her eyes riveted on the windshield. When the car turned left onto First Street, Madeleine looked up at the sky. "I'm free," she said. "I'm not sure how I'm going to manage this, but I think I'm going to do okay."

"No," she almost heard the sky say, "you're not going to do *okay*. You're going to do *great*."

Madeleine grinned from her toes to the top of her head. Come on wrinkles! Nothing was going to stop her from smiling anymore. She turned toward the rectory. She was very sorry that woman was dead, the woman named Diane Marie. She had the feeling the two of them could have been friends. But she could not mourn someone she had spoken to for only two or three minutes. "When Johnny gets back," she said aloud, "we're going to celebrate."

IDA HAD TO CRY HERSELF out before I felt comfortable leaving her, although I knew there'd still be a lot more tears to come. I helped her make some phone calls, but mostly just sat with her and Ralph. I finally talked her into going to bed late that evening.

When I got back home, Bob and I sat down at the little round table by the bay window in the kitchen. He slathered some butter on a corn muffin. "I may be working a lot of extra hours over the next week or so," he said.

"What have you found out so far?"

"Not much. Nobody seems to know why she did it."

"Did you talk to her husband yet?"

"Haven't been able to reach him. He's not answering the phone. There's no answering machine. I even drove down there, but nobody was home. I talked to the next door neighbor down the hill from him, and she said she'd have him call me if she saw him."

"Ida told me he'd been out of town on business. That's why Diane Marie came to stay with her and Ralph."

"The neighbor said she saw him there yesterday morning."

"Does Ida know how to contact him?"

"Only the home phone number. I got the feeling there's not much love lost between the Petersons and Diane Marie's husband. I'm going to drive back to Enders in half an hour or so. He must be home by now, and I can give him the bad news. I don't want to do it by phone."

Even though we were eating, I let Marmalade get away with creeping into my lap. She kneaded my knees briefly and settled in for a snooze. I wondered where she had been for so long.

I followed the big human and watched for a long time.

As I stroked her silky orange and white fur, I felt her purring quietly. "Diane Marie was really subdued last Tuesday in tap class. I wondered if she was coming down with something, but maybe she was just trying to sort out her life. Did you know she was pregnant? Ida told me."

"No," he said. "No, I didn't know that. There'll be an autopsy, of course."

I leaned my elbows on the table and buried my face in my hands (carefully, to avoid touching my swollen nose). "Why couldn't I have seen it coming? I should have said something, or done something to help her."

"Bisque." Bob's voice was gentle and so soft I barely heard it. "Unexplained suicide is one of the nastiest actions a person can take because it always leaves the family and friends wondering. It's the ultimate guilt-inducer." His voice rose steadily. "I will not let you think that you could have prevented this. There's no value in thinking that. None at all." He reached over to place his hand on the back of my head and ran his fingers through my hair. "You can't second-guess her. Don't even try."

On one level, I knew he was right. But she had been a living, breathing, dancing woman only two days ago. Now…I was very glad that I hadn't seen them turn the body over.

My gratitude list for Thursday June 13th
1. It is so hard for me to write this list tonight. I have such a wonderful life, and I cannot understand people who are in so much despair that they can discount the hopefulness of life. There is always hope. I believe that strongly. But I do not really know what was in Diane Marie's mind. In spite of her death, I can still find things to be thankful for:
2. Life itself
3. Bob and my children and grandchildren
4. Glaze—I'm so glad I called her about this
5. Friends—especially Sharon and Ida and Nathan and Marmy, too
6. Ice packs
7. Warm showers

my gratitude list for today
Widelap
Softfoot
good reflexes
my good sense of direction
being patted gently
leftover fish
this soft bed

TWENTY-FIVE

Friday, June 14

"…AND IT COULDN'T have been just an accident."

"What makes you so sure about that?" Bob asked me as he turned away from the window.

He enjoys watching those birds at the feeder. They calm his mind.

"If she'd fallen accidentally, she would have been screaming all the way down. She never made a sound."

"She must have. Several of the folks up on Fourth Street said they heard someone screaming, but they couldn't tell where it was coming from."

It was Widelap.

"That wasn't her, Bob," I said. "That was me."

He was silent for a moment. "Then, maybe it really *was* suicide," he said.

"No, it couldn't be suicide. She wouldn't have done that."

"Why not? People get depressed sometimes."

"Maybe so, but she was taking tap dance lessons."

"What does that have to do with it."

"You don't start tap dance lessons if you're thinking of killing yourself."

"Woman, that makes no sense."

"Yes it does. Tap dancing is happy. It's something you do when you feel really good about yourself. It's not something you start if you've given up."

It is something you do if you want to make a lot of noise.

He ran his hand along his jaw. "I have to admit," he said, "I've been wondering about that suicide note."

"What about it?"

"It's not complete enough. All it says is *I can't go on this way.* The signature is right below that."

"You're right. That doesn't sound like suicide. It sounds more like someone who wants out of a job."

"Or a marriage?" Bob asked. I nodded. He stroked his jaw one more time. "I think I'm going back to talk to Kelvin this morning."

"Where was he yesterday, anyway?"

"He said he was working on his car most of the day, which was why he didn't hear the phone."

"But you drove there and he wasn't around."

"Yeah. He said he took off and went to get something to eat at the Enders Diner. We must have just missed each other." He looked at my raised eyebrows. "Of course I checked. He did go to the diner."

"So what did he say when you told him?"

"He fell apart. He kept saying he never should have let her come to visit her sister."

"Surely he doesn't blame *Ida?*" I sputtered.

Bob looked at me with a measured glance. I would make a lousy cop.

I LET MARMALADE OUT the back door late that afternoon as I heard Bob walking in the front one. Poking my head around the kitchen doorway, I smiled to see him grinning.

"Bob, how on earth can you keep finding things to laugh about while you're going through an investigation like this? This is the second time you've walked in the door chuckling."

Bob took off his wide-brimmed hat and hung it on the rack near the front door. "There's nothing at all funny about any death," he said. "But I keep running into some pretty strange people. First there was Mrs. Ames with her tea spilled down her front. Then today, after I questioned Kelvin, I talked with his

next door neighbor up the hill. Her name is, get this, Cornelia
Przybylski."

"Shuh-BILL-ski?" I parroted. "What kind of name is that?"

"It's Romanian." He spelled it for me. Twice.

"How would you ever learn to spell that in kindergarten?"

"Beats me. Put a bunch of Y's and Z's together, and I get
lost."

I thought of the word puzzle GHOTI. "Maybe people from
Romania have a hard time with English, with all *our* weird spell-
ings. I suppose it's just a matter of training."

"Yeah," he said. "Remember GHOTI?"

"I was just thinking about that." The letters sounded out *fish,*
a perfectly reasonable English word, but you had to put together
the right sounds chosen from the right words. First there was
GH the way it was sounded in the word *laugh.* And so on. It was
fun to figure out the first time. "So, what's this Cornelia person
like?"

"She looks about two hundred and thirty years old. No teeth
to speak of. Skin like the inner layer of a piece of cardboard.
Carries a pair of binoculars around her neck. They're hanging
from a bright green dog leash, the sort of thing you'd see a poo-
dle attached to."

"What are the binoculars for?"

"She said she's a bird watcher, and she *does* have one bird
feeder in her front yard. She showed me her 'bird-watching chair'
that sits right next to her front window. Mighty good view all
the way down her street since her house sits right at the top end
of it. By the end of the interview, she'd filled me in on the comings and goings of practically everybody nearby, including our
Kelvin."

"Did you find out anything of value?"

"Sure did." He chuckled. "Kelvin would rather pee in his side
yard than take the time to go inside."

"Bob! She didn't tell you that!"

"Sure did," he said again. "Said he'll be working on his car
in the driveway, and all of a sudden he ups and strolls around

to the side of his house where he thinks he's out of sight, and he lets loose a stream that shows up pretty clearly in the binoculars."

"That's awful!"

"What's awful about it? I think it's funny that she saw him."

"Bob, nobody in his right mind would pee in the yard like that."

Bob got this funny look on his face. "I don't see anything wrong with it," he said.

"It's disgusting!"

"It's normal."

"It is not!"

"It is if you're a guy."

"Oh." There didn't seem to be an answer to that. I stirred a pot, sliced some bread, added more water to the tea kettle. "Does that mean *you* pee in the yard?"

Bob opened his mouth to speak, but I cut him off. "No! Don't tell me. I don't want to know. Just don't ever do it on my flower beds. Or the vegetable garden."

"Should I climb over the back fence?" He was still chuckling. "That would kind of defeat the purpose, wouldn't it?"

This whole topic must be a man thing. Marking territory. I knew dogs did it. Sounded dumb to me, though. "Tell me more about Cornelia," I said, happy to change the subject.

Bob rubbed his jaw with his left hand and then stretched. He hadn't been getting a lot of sleep lately. "When a woman's murdered, it's always her husband or boyfriend who's the number one suspect. Even with a suicide, we check out the spouse. But our Cornelia with the un-spellable name gave him a pretty good alibi with the peeing story. Seems she got up from her usual nap and saw him peeing around quarter to three in the afternoon on June 13th, which was just shortly after Diane Marie fell off the cliff."

I thought about it. "Is she sure of the time?"

"Yeah. She said she naps every day like clockwork, and she always gets back to her bird-watching by 2:45 p.m. There's no way he could have driven the seventy miles from Enders to here, killed her a little past two and been back home by quarter to three."

"What if he drove halfway up the main road, cut over onto Carl's farm road, went across the kenaf field? That would cut the trip in half."

"Won't work, Biscuit. I considered that, but the kenaf field is almost a mile wide, and you're still talking more than 25 miles of driving. On top of that, his neighbor down the hill said his car was there all afternoon."

"Maybe it was a different day. How do they know which day it was they saw him?"

"First of all, it was only *yesterday*. But in addition to that, Mrs. Przybylski said she was surprised when he actually waved at her just before she took her nap. She said he's never done that before. And she said her daughter and granddaughter were bringing the great-grandchildren at three o'clock to celebrate the littlest one's birthday. She remembers being glad that the children weren't there yet when he started peeing. She said her great-grandson would have been watering her hydrangeas within minutes if he'd seen that. So, it gives Kelvin the perfect alibi."

I knew I was grasping at straws, but I thought I'd try. "Maybe he waded up the Metoochie?"

"That's stretching it, and you know it. But even assuming I'm willing to grant the possibility, he would have had to swim through the gorge for a mile against the current—and it's strong because the river's so high. That would mean a wet trail wherever he got out of the water. Somebody would have seen him coming through the gap or dripping up the street. He would have had to make it all the way through town and up to the cliffs. The man couldn't possibly be invisible like that." Bob looked at me over the top of his glasses. "Ida said the note was definitely her sister's handwriting. We know that Kelvin was in Enders when it happened. We haven't been able to find anybody else who had anything against her. I know you don't like this idea, but it looks like this truly was a suicide."

He was right. I didn't like that idea, but there didn't seem to be another argument. "Go upstairs and change. Dinner will be ready in about ten minutes."

Dinner was a quiet affair that evening. We both seemed to be lost in our own thoughts. Marmy came home and meowed to be let in. Other than that, there wasn't much going on. After dinner, Bob and I sat around for quite a while. I was knitting, he was looking over his notes from the investigation.

When we went to bed, Marmalade jumped up next to me. I was glad our four-poster bed was big enough for Bob and me and a cat.

I do not take up much room.

As I was stroking her soft tummy, she jerked, twisted around and stood up. Her ears went back against her head, a sure sign that she was upset. Her nose twitched. Bob was just walking out of the bathroom. He reached up and took his uniform shirt off the bottom post of the bed. "What's wrong with her?" he asked as he tossed the shirt in the general direction of the clothes hamper.

"I don't know, but her ears are back, so she's mad about something."

He slid into bed and turned off the light. "I'm too tired to deal with any problems tonight. Go to sleep, Marmalade."

TWENTY-SIX

Saturday, June 15

"THIS IS RIDICULOUS," I muttered to myself. I couldn't turn off my brain. I could hear a tape playing inside my head. It's two in the morning, I thought. 2:03 a.m. My nose still throbs. It's so swollen I have to breathe through my mouth, and my mouth is so dry now, I feel like I've been eating sand. No wonder I can't sleep. I hate tossing and turning, especially since Bob is snoring softly on my right. He doesn't really snore. It's more of a snuffle sound. Soft and almost musical. Like a bassoon with a head cold. I listened for a moment to his part of the stereophonic symphony that enveloped me. There were subterranean rumblings near my left elbow, where Marmalade had burrowed under the comforter for warmth. I'm the cheese in their snore sandwich. Why are they asleep and I'm awake?

I am awake. I am simply breathing deeply.

Every time I turned over I dumped Marmalade off my shoulder, or my hip, or my back, or wherever she'd settled in....

You are wiggling a lot. It is hard for me to sleep when you wiggle.

Why doesn't she just go sleep at the foot of the bed, like a dog...?

A dog!

...That way it would be easier for me to sleep. Oh, you're being ridiculous, Biscuit McKee. Marmy is not the reason you can't sleep. Usually you like having her furry little body keeping your knees warm. Or purring on your back. Why am I talking to myself? When I do that I feel like I'm two separate people.

Of course, at 2:03 a.m…no, now it's 2:16 a.m. Where did thirteen minutes go? Have I been easing in and out of sleep? Have I been grumping to myself all that time?

There was an electric sizzle of sheet lightning outside the window. Maybe that was what woke me up. I read once that lightning usually traveled from the earth up to the sky, not the other way around. But sheet lightning just seemed to go sideways. I wondered when the storm would hit.

It will not rain. The clouds are just talking to each other.

Usually if I wake up in the middle of the night, the snoring sounds comforting. I can almost imagine Bob's deep, calm breathing as a lullaby, and it'll put me back to sleep if I simply let myself feel the ebb and flow of that breath. That's usually. This is now. I want to clop him upside the head with a two-by-four and tell him to shut up. How dare he be asleep when I'm miserable? Maybe it would be better if I got up and made myself a cup of tea. It beats lying here thinking of murdering my husband. I'd miss him, even his snoring, if he were dead.

I am awake. I will keep you company.

Death. That's the last thing I need to be thinking about. Rats! Now I'll never get back to sleep. I don't want to picture Diane Marie's body hurtling down the cliff, but the image feels like it's burned a hole right behind my eyeballs.

I eased out of bed and pulled on my fuzzy bathrobe. Comfort clothing. Marmalade was standing on the bed watching me. I could see her in the dim light from the big windows. I wonder sometimes if she's afraid of storms. Whenever there's lightning, she always seems to be right here with me.

I protect you.

I scooped her up in my arms and buried my sore face, carefully, in the fur at the back of her neck. Her warmth felt good…

Your nose is cold.

…and I felt her purr starting up.

Instead of going downstairs for tea, I detoured into my little sitting room. The lamp had a three-way bulb, so I turned it on low and settled onto the love seat. There was a bottle of water.

Now my mouth feels a bit better. I left that *Monster Crossword Puzzle* book on the coffee table the other day. What was the clue I was working on? I turned to the page I'd marked with a paper clip. I love crossword puzzles. They get my brain to working. Here it is. *188-across. A place for dressing.* All I could think of yesterday was *salad,* but it's supposed to be a six-letter word, and it starts with a *T.* Tonight it's obvious. I filled in the capital letters. *TURKEY.* She couldn't have killed herself. You don't buy a new blouse and dress up in it if you're planning on killing yourself. Or do you?

What about this one? *144-across. Wherever, Lat.* Oh, great, I'm supposed to be able to think in Latin at this time of night. Eight letters. It starts with a *V* because *144-down* is *VARIETY.* Last letter is an *I* because *146-down* is *IRRITABLE.* That's what I feel like right now. I rolled my neck around, and that brought on a huge yawn.

You would rather be sleeping.

Maybe *145-down*...hmm...*Elizabeth and Mary.* Could that be *QUEENS?* Diane Marie looked like a queen when she was dancing. She had style, with her great big brown eyes. She looked like she owned the world when she was dancing. Funny thing is, when she wasn't dancing, she kept herself sort of hunched over, like she was scared of something. Couldn't be *QUEENS.* What would we do with a Q in the middle of a Latin word? *QUO,* maybe. Why on earth would Diane Marie have thrown herself off a cliff? Wouldn't pills have been easier? Yes, it *is QUEENS,* because there's a *U* after the *Q* because *131-down* is *POLYPHONIC ECHO.* That's a *FUGUE.* I should think she would have been screaming, and the echoes would have filled the valley. But she fell silently. Why? Why?

Place for Yeat's nine has to be that island in the poem where he plants the bean rows. What was it called...? *INNISFREE!* That's it. *176-across.* I need to build a tepee to grow pole beans on next year. I'll make it big enough that Verity Marie can play in it. She can help me plant the beans. Diane Marie would have had so much fun playing with her baby. I pulled a tissue out of the box on the coffee table. Phooey!

So *INNISFREE* picks up one *E* from *QUEENS* and one from *FUGUE*. This is going to work.

What's *114-down? Staged productions.* Six letters. Well, it's plural, so it probably ends in an *S*. Has to, anyway, because of the *S* in Yeat's island. So, I've still got *V-blank-blank-blank-QU-blank-I*. Good grief, this is ridiculous. What kind of word is that? How do they ever come up with these ideas? Why didn't Diane Marie ask for help? Why didn't she even give me a hint when we were painting the Green Room? Something like *Oh, by the way, 16-down: I'm thinking of killing myself.* How many letters would that be? Doggone her! Why didn't she talk to her sister?

Baby battery 130-down. Three letters. Oh, of course. I filled in *AAA*. Three *A's*. Three Diane Marie's. Now there are only two.

Oh! *114-down* is *OPERAS*. So now I have *VE-blank-AQU-blank-I*. My mind is fuzzy. What's *115-down*? A three-letter word for *each?* I ought to know that one. That would give me the letter between the *E* and the *A* in my Latin word. I stretched. I thought about it. I yawned again. I gave up.

I turned to the back of the book. Puzzle number 17. "Crazy Quilt" it was called. Most crossword puzzles had a regular pattern of shaded squares, but this one looked chaotic. Just like my thoughts. How can you go from tap dance to suicide in two days? That's crazier than this crossword puzzle. I'd completed most of the top part of the puzzle, so I put my hand across the whole thing and worked my way down carefully. I didn't want to see the Latin word. I wanted to figure it out. I wish I could look up clues to Diane Marie's state of mind the same way I can look up this one word. It takes a lot of work, though, to spot just a couple of letters in a crossword puzzle answer without looking at the other words around it. I was proud of myself.

I saw it. *PER*. Oh, why didn't I figure that one out? *Each*. It was so easy. I turned back and filled it in. I squinted at the result. *VERAQU-blank-I.*

"Why are you cheating?"

Bob's voice from the doorway startled me so much I dropped my pen.

"I'm not cheating," I said. "I'm looking at the answers."

"That's cheating."

I yawned once more. "It is not!"

He looked at me and raised one of his eyebrows. "If you look at the answers, how can you say it's *not* cheating?"

"Bob, this is not a tournament. I can't sleep. I'm working a crossword puzzle. It's not a big deal." I picked up the pen and stuck it behind my ear. I liked having hair long enough to hold a pen in place.

"If you need help in order to win—"

"To win is not the object."

"Of course it is," he said. "You have to fill in all the squares."

"*My* object is not to win," I repeated. "My object is to have fun. And no, I don't *have to* finish filling in anything. I choose to. For the fun of it. So if I get stuck and can't go any further, I look up one word."

"I still say you're cheating."

"Bob, why are you making such a big deal about this?"

He rubbed his jaw. I could hear the scratchy, scratch sound from where I sat. "I'm just surprised, that's all. I didn't think I'd married a cheater."

That did it! I slammed the book down on the coffee table, stormed past Bob and sailed downstairs. I thought I'd go get some ice cream, but as I stomped past the front door, I veered that direction instead. The night was its usual balmy self, despite the sheet lightning. I inhaled. Early roses, lilies and viburnum. Why did the world smell good when I felt like this?

Bob stepped through the door behind me. "Bisque?"

"Go away. I don't want to talk to you right now."

"We promised we'd never do this."

I crossed my arms over my chest. "What of it? You think I'm

a cheater, anyway, so I'm cheating on that promise. Please go away. Now."

He went. It felt like he pulled all my insides with him as he turned, but I was still in a royal huff and wasn't about to call him back.

IT NEVER DID RAIN. By the time day was starting to think about dawning, I crept into the living room and lay down on the couch, pulling my bathrobe around me. The pen I'd stuck behind my ear poked me in the neck. I felt cold inside and out. Even Marmalade, purring beside me, couldn't warm me.

When I woke up, Bob had already left for work. The afghan that had been folded on the chair in our bedroom was draped over me. I felt like crap.

TWENTY-SEVEN

I LUGGED THE OLD upright vacuum cleaner out of the laundry room and plugged it in. There was entirely too much cat hair accumulating. The carpet looked like an angora sweater, even though Tank had been gone for a week. He had as much hair as five normal cats. I hoped Nathan didn't regret adopting him.

This was not a good cat day. When I picked up the laundry hamper this morning I found Bob's new uniform shirt behind it. Marmalade had peed on it. She never does that.

It smelled of the bad person.

Luckily, it hadn't gone through onto the carpet. I even hollered at her, something I never do. She just sat there and looked at me.

It is very difficult sometimes to get you to hear me.

I hope she doesn't have a urinary tract infection....

I do not. I am perfectly healthy.

...Those are not fun for cats. With as little sleep as I'd had, I wasn't in a mood to deal with problems.

I wasn't in a mood to deal with *anything*. Watching someone jump off a cliff had disrupted *everything*. I still felt sick thinking about it. Diane Marie had been so vibrant when she was telling me that silly story about her fourth grade substitute teacher. Yet just a week later she was dead. How could things like that happen? How could her mood have shifted so quickly?

If you will listen to me, I will tell you.

I jumped when I heard a loud knock on the front door. Who knew how long I'd been standing there beside the vacuum cleaner? Well, the sweeping up could wait a bit. I abandoned the silent Hoover and walked into the foyer. Melissa was standing outside on the porch. "Why didn't you just walk on in?" I asked her as I opened the door. "That's what you usually do."

She held up two fancy gift bags with bright yellow tissue paper sticking out of the tops. "Couldn't," she said. "My hands were full."

"What's that?"

Her happy face split into a wicked grin. "Presents, of course."

Did you bring something for me?

"Why?" I asked her.

"Just because. You needed something to take your mind off the whole Diane Marie thing." She saw the look on my face. "I'm right, right?"

"Were you peeking in my window?" I asked as I led the way into the living room. "I've been standing here forever, trying to get the vacuum turned on. But I haven't had the gumption to push the button."

"I know," she said with a serious look settling over her usually impish face. "I felt that way for a long time after Jake was killed." Last year, shortly after I moved into Melissa's bed-and-breakfast, a drunk driver, an old guy from Enders, had been visiting somebody in Surreytown, up at the top end of the valley. He missed his turn in Russell Gap, and just outside of Martinsville he veered into the oncoming lane and hit Melissa's favorite nephew. The impact threw Jake and his bicycle over the guardrail and into the Metoochie River thirty feet below. The drunk kept going. He wasn't hurt. His car had a dent in the left front fender. Jake was dead at seventeen years old.

They finally got the guy for vehicular homicide. He was serving time, but that didn't make Jake's family feel any better.

His dad was Melissa's twin brother. There had been too much death in the past year. Way too much. I know we all die, but I didn't expect it from kids or from women in my tap dance class.

Melissa touched my shoulder and guided me over to the couch. "Here," she said, "open this one." She put one of the bags on my lap and set the other one down next to the harp. My dad's harp that he couldn't play anymore. I wanted to start playing it again myself. It had been months since I even touched it. Things had just been too chaotic around here, ever since I moved in.

"Biscuit?" Melissa said. "Aren't you going to look in the bag?"

"Sorry, Melissa, I was off somewhere in the clouds." I dug through the tissue paper and pulled out a book. Essays by some woman I'd never heard of. "Thanks, Melissa." I set the bag down on the floor. "Are these any good?"

"No, I picked the worst book of essays I could find so I could bore you silly." She laughed. "Of course they're good. At least, I thought they were pretty interesting. Read one—they're short."

I opened the book and riffled through the pages. I spotted the word *vacuum* and figured the topic was appropriate for the way my day was going. I settled back on the couch. "This one sounds intriguing. It's called *How to Save a Red Button*."

Melissa settled back next to me. "I haven't read that one yet. Read it out loud."

So I did, once we finished laughing at Marmy who had jumped into the bag.

Thank you. This is a good gift.

She wiggled and squirmed and waved her tail around. In the process of making herself a little nest in the bag, she managed to knock the *Keagan County Record* off the coffee table. It scattered at our feet. Then, as her tail made another sweep, I rescued the half-full cup of cold coffee that had been sitting there overnight. "When am I ever going to get this mess cleaned up? I feel like such a slob, Melissa."

She didn't miss a beat. "That's okay. I don't care what you smell like."

It's good to put things in perspective. I stuck the coffee cup by the lamp on the end table, giggled and read to both of us.

How to Save a Red Button
"Because I don't trust central vacuum systems." My interrogator certainly thought I was being less than candid,

but, you see, she probably never had an old reconditioned tank-type vac, or before that a GE canister that looked like an abbreviated version of R2D2.

And, unless *you* understand old-fashioned vacuum cleaners, you might not know how to keep your marriage together, either. It all has to do with getting rid of the dirt in our lives. When we bought our current house five years ago, the previous owner gushed, "Oh, you're just going to love the central vac. Why, it makes cleaning so much easier. Just plug in this end and whoosh, all the dirt disappears."

"Where does it go?" I asked. A logical question, I thought, since I've always believed in the principle of the conservation of matter. The dirt doesn't, after all, disappear. It's just moved somewhere else. My vac always picks up the dirt, the hair from three dogs and one cat, and the other assorted detritus dependably enough, and transfers it to a little bag at the base of the hose. Periodically I take off the bag and empty it into the garbage, which eventually ends up in the sanitary landfill, helping to create, in a matter of years, new land.

But sometimes, the tubular blue machine picks up something that doesn't deserve to be made into extra land. Not yet, at least. The fifth die from the Yahtzee game, perhaps. Or the teeny key to the black briefcase. Or once, even my wedding ring, which used to fall off my finger occasionally when I lost all that weight after my daughter was born. All I did in each case was turn off the motor, pull down the chromed lever, open the lid, dump the contents onto a plastic bag and sort through them, getting dusty, dirty and somewhat hairy in the process, but invariably finding the die, the key and—voila—the ring.

Soon after we bought this big house, though, I accidentally sucked up a button that had come loose from my red dress. I had put it on the sewing machine, meaning to sew it back on right away. Of course, it fell on the rug, and whoosh, disappeared down the tube. The only replacement button I had. I traipsed down into the cellar, opened the twenty-gallon canister and trudged upstairs into the light on the back deck with twenty packed gallons of not only my own dirt and dog hair, but that of the previous owners, as well. Cleaning the house before we moved in did not, apparently, include emptying the contents of the vacuum cleaner.

After two kids, a constant succession of hairy pets and a stint as a Red Cross volunteer, there is very little that can turn my stomach. But plowing through a vacuum cleaner filled with someone else's grimy dirt took me to the limit of my endurance. I found a badly used pair of undershorts (how did the two-and-a-half-inch tube manage to handle that?), more plastic twisty ties than I care to mention, milk-jug lids—didn't those people EVER pick up after themselves?—and a disgusting array of dirt. Not the good clean dust and dog hair that I was accustomed to, but grimy-looking grunge, and no red button. Only a little poking through my old vacuum cleaner bag would have produced the prize. But the central vac can was a veritable jungle of intertwined clumps of unmentionable mess that I couldn't bear to look at, except in indignant horror, much less pick my way through.

Every time my husband and I have a disagreement about something, he storms around for a while, and I sulk. But ultimately, after not too long a time, we dump the contents of our garbage bag and start anew. Maybe a joke gets us back to laughing together, or maybe a chance word brings on a look of apology, or maybe we just dump it out and don't talk about it too much. The point is, our emotional dust catcher isn't very big, so we don't have time to accumulate too much garbage before cleaning-out time. Any wedding rings that get lost get found again, somewhat dusty, perhaps, but quite capable of being cleaned off and brightened up.

But people with central vacuum systems in their psyche can store away a whole twenty-gallon load of upsets and resentments. And by the time they get around to purging the contents, everything's had a chance to simmer and even rot a bit. Makes for a messy routine. Makes one wonder if it's easier to buy new buttons than to try to find and save the one that was there before.

So, no, I don't believe in central vac. And never will.

I looked up at Melissa. She was grinning at me. "See?" she said. "Didn't I tell you this would help?" I smiled back, then gave her a hug. If I could choose a second sister, Melissa would be my choice. She stood up and retrieved the other package and plopped it in my lap. As I opened it, she bent over and picked up the sheets of newspaper Marmy had dumped on the floor.

"You going to wash my dishes for me, too?"

She screwed her mouth up into a tilde and kept folding papers. "Fat chance. Go ahead—open it."

I loved presents. This one was…

Another bag for me to jump into.

…a new journal, the color of the sky on a bright summer day. "I'll use it for my gratitude lists," I told her. "The current one is almost full."

Melissa glanced down at the paper that was still in her lap. "Lots to be thankful for?" she said, and then gasped.

"What's wrong? Melissa, talk to me. What's wrong?"

She pointed at the paper. I picked it up and read one of those notices that newspapers are always putting in when they make a mistake.

Correction
Diane Marie Murchison died in a fall last Thursday. Her name was incorrectly given as Diane Marie Peterson in Friday's issue. It is the policy of the *Record* to correct all errors of fact.

Murchison. Why did that sound familiar? I looked up at Melissa's face. She had paled considerably. She wasn't crying, but her lips were trembly and her eyes had scrunched up. It took me only a moment to remember that Bill Murchison was the drunk driver who killed Melissa's nephew Jake last year. I hadn't known Diane Marie was related to him. Only by marriage. He must have been her father-in-law. The one she had talked about at the library. The one I had assumed was dead. I leaned toward the end table and pulled a tissue out of the box.

"I thought I was over the hurt," Melissa said after she blew her nose.

"You loved him a lot. Of course you're not over it. You don't get over losing somebody like that, ever."

She motioned toward the tissue box. I handed her the whole thing and waited for her to wipe her eyes. "I knew I still felt bad about his death, but I wasn't prepared for the…" She pointed again at the paper. "That felt like an assault. Sometimes I think I see him running into *Azalea House,* just like he did when he was a little boy. He'd head straight for the cookie jar." Her voice fell to a whisper and each word was a poisoned dart. "I will never forgive that man for what he did."

"Melissa." I reached out and touched her hand. "Take a breath, a deep breath. You're hurting yourself more than him. You know that."

She pulled her hand away. "What he did to Jake was murder."

I felt helpless faced with her anguish, but I loved her enough to say, "That's right, but your hatred won't bring Jake back."

She shot me a look that was sheer venom, enough to stop me cold. There was a long, long moment of silence. Finally she shook her head and leaned toward me. I scooted close and gathered her into my arms and simply held her while she cried. I needed to talk to Bob really soon and get things back to normal between us. What would happen if he were hurt somehow and thought I had stopped loving him? I hated crossword puzzles.

ONCE THE TEARS DRIED UP a bit, Melissa sat up straighter and grimaced. "Do you want me to take your blouse home and wash it?" she asked.

I looked down. The inevitable results of a crying fit—drool, tears, snot—streaked across the shoulder of my shirt. "Heck, no! What are friends for?"

"Thanks," she said. "I'm glad I was here when I saw that."

My hand brushed across the little journal that was still in my lap. "Melissa? Why don't I give this back to you so you can start a gratitude list?"

"You trying to fix me, lady?"

"No. But it sure would help if you could concentrate on what's good rather than what's wrong. Especially now." I thought of my fight with Bob. I thought of Diane Marie's death. "Especially when it seems like so much is sad." I held out the little book.

"Lots to be thankful for?" she repeated.

"Yes," I said. "Yes, indeed."

We sat there for a moment just watching Marmalade who was still rustling around, pawing at the tissue paper, getting it arranged just the way she wanted it. "Try keeping the list for a couple of weeks, and see if it makes a difference."

Melissa nodded and gave a rueful grin as she reached for the sky-blue book.

Does that mean I have to give back my bag?

There was a loud meow from Marmy who had finally settled in. "See?" I said. "She agrees with me."

TWENTY-EIGHT

IT WAS NICE to have non-hairy rugs. I put the vac away and the phone rang. "Biscuit? Could you help me with something?" Ida's voice sounded tentative.

"Sure, Ida, what's up?"

"Kelvin called me yesterday and wants me to pack up all of Diane Marie's things and return them to him. He asked for her jewelry and her journal and her personal effects."

"Personal effects? That doesn't sound like anything a real person would say."

"Yeah, it sounds more like a TV show, but that's what he said. Anyway, would you be willing to help me with it? I don't think I can face it alone."

"Sure," I said. I looked over at the dirty dishes in the sink. Then I had to go to work. This was Saturday. The library was open from ten to two.

"Oh, thank you." The relief in her voice was palpable. "The door's open. Just come on in."

I didn't have the heart to tell her I meant later—much later. "Let me wash my hands off and I'll be right there. I'll drive." It was only four or five blocks, but she sounded desperate. I remembered how hard it was for my mom and me to clean out Grandma Martelson's house when she went into the nursing home. She hadn't even died, but the sorting and deciding was excruciating. This would be even harder, I should think. I called Rebecca Jo and explained to her what was going on. She said not to worry about the library. I knew I could count on her.

Ida looked ten years older when I got there. "I brought some boxes home from the grocery store to pack things in. She was here less than three weeks, but it seems like she moved half her stuff in without my realizing it."

"Do you think…" I started, and then paused. It wasn't a delicate question.

"Yes I do," she said, finishing my thought for me. "I think she was using this as a way to move out of her house without Kelvin knowing what she was doing. I even found a box stashed under the bed that was full of her favorite kitchen implements."

"The poor woman." There didn't seem to be a lot more to say than that. "Are you going to send it all back?"

"I'll send her jewelry. Her watch was broken, so I don't think he'll want it. None of the jewelry is heirloom stuff, but he probably knows every single item by heart. Maybe I'll include the watch just in case. I don't want him to accuse me of stealing it."

Surely he wouldn't do that, I thought. But I held my tongue.

"I'll pack up her clothes and such," she continued, "although I can't imagine what he'd want with them. But I haven't found a journal."

"Even if you *did*," I said, but then shut my mouth. He was her husband. Maybe if he read in her journal what a schnook she thought he was, and that she wanted to leave him, maybe he'd straighten up and fly right.

Ida just looked at me, but I could tell her thoughts had gone on to something else. "Maybe I'll call him and ask if I can send her clothes to the Goodwill store. That would save him from having to do it, and we can pack them separately just for that."

"Good idea." We walked upstairs, and I was struck by how tidy her little room was. No shoes left lying around. No socks on the floor. Nothing disarranged. Why, I wondered, if you were going to kill yourself, would you tidy up the room first? Maybe to make it easier for your sister. Nonsense! If you were truly planning suicide, the last thing you would think about was someone else's feelings. If you *really* cared, you wouldn't go through with it, because you wouldn't want to hurt them. That caring would keep you from killing yourself, wouldn't it? I needed to talk to Glaze about this.

Ida interrupted my thought process. "The day after it happened I came in here and cleaned up. I guess I was looking for a letter or something. Something to explain it. I walked around and looked at everything. She'd just bought that green blouse at Mabel's. It was on sale. She…" Ida crumpled down on the chair next to the bed. "She bought it with a gift certificate I gave her for her birthday."

There was a tissue box on the little dresser. I picked it up and sat down on the side of the bed. "Here," I said, holding it out to her. "I'm sorry."

She nodded and blew her nose. "They even got her name wrong in the obituary. They said she was Diane Marie Peterson."

"Yes. I saw the correction you put in."

"What correction?"

"There was one in the paper this morning."

She shook her head. "I never called them. I figured everybody who knew her and liked her knows what…what happened." She blew her nose again. "Everybody else can mind their stupid beeswax as far as I'm concerned."

People showed grief in a lot of different ways. Bitterness was one of them.

Once Ida composed herself a bit, we pulled the sheets off the bed. A whiff of gardenia drifted up as I took off the pillowcase. I paused, and Ida said, "I know. When I went to the funeral home to…to identify the…I could smell her perfume, even though she was dead." After a few minutes, I suggested that we start on the closet. She scurried off to get the empty boxes she'd gathered, and I began by taking things off hangers and folding them. Diane Marie certainly had brought a lot of clothes over. Goodwill would make good use of them. Assuming that Kelvin was willing to part with them. There were two soft summer dresses there with the price tags still attached. She must have bought them when she got the green blouse. I set them aside to show Ida. Maybe she could return them.

When Ida came back upstairs, she had a funny look on her face. "I called Kelvin while I was downstairs," she said. "He said it was okay to give away all the clothes, but that he wanted the jewelry and the journal."

"That makes sense," I said. "What's wrong with that?"

"I told him there wasn't a journal here, and he said, 'That's good. Just bring me the jewelry.' I should think he'd want to come pick it up himself and see where she spent her last few days."

"People deal with their grief in many different ways, Ida."

"Yeah, I guess." She didn't sound convinced. "He said to leave the package inside the back screen door if he wasn't home when I got there."

We continued and finished the packing. Ida said to give away the two new dresses, as well. She couldn't face them. "They were on sale, anyway," she said, "so they're not returnable." We piled the sheets in the laundry basket. Then we carefully wrapped up her small collection of rings and necklaces and earrings. Ida added the broken watch, sealed the envelope and put it in a brown paper bag. After she added Diane Marie's purse to the bag, she wrote "Diane Marie's Things" with a black marker. It looked so final.

"I'll drive down to Enders with you, if you want me to," I offered.

She nodded. "Could we go right now?"

"Let me call Bob and tell him where I'm going. My car's out front. I'll drive." She didn't look like she was in any shape to be behind a wheel. I called Bob. Got his voice mail. There wasn't time to tell him everything I wanted to, so I left a simple message, ending with *I love you.*

The trip to Enders was uneventful. We managed to laugh along the way about having to drive more than sixty miles each way to get to a house less than a mile down-river. We talked a lot about Diane Marie. Good memories. Ida cried some. So did I, for that matter. I would never be able to walk into the Green Room at the library without thinking of her.

WHEN WE GOT TO ENDERS, Kelvin wasn't home. I watched Ida head around to the back. I climbed out of the Buick to stretch my legs a bit. I could see the cliff looming over the back of the house. Out of curiosity, I turned to look at the house next door. The one at the top of the street. Sure enough, there was the little birdlike Cornelia (with the long last name) looking at me through binoculars. I waved and smiled. She waved back, and didn't look even slightly chagrined that I caught her spying. Maybe it was just such a way of life for her that she no longer thought it was rude. Maybe it wasn't rude. Maybe if I were frail and couldn't get around too well by myself, I'd use binoculars, too. Hmm. I wondered what I would see from the second floor windows on Beechnut Lane?

Ida came back before I was thoroughly corrupted, and we drove home without incident.

"HELLO?"

"Glaze? It's me." I hated when people said *it's me* on the phone. Why was I doing that?

You are doing that because you are unhappy.

"Hi, me."

"No, I'm serious. Do you have a minute?"

"Sure. What's up?"

"When you tried to kill yourself those times, were you really serious? Did you really truly want to die?"

"Whoa! What brought this on?"

"I don't know. I'm so angry with Diane Marie right now I could spit. I just finished helping her sister pack up all her clothes and stuff."

"That must have been hard."

Yes it was. She is crying on the inside.

"Yes. It was. Ida's a basket case. She just can't believe this happened. Neither can I. You're the only person I know of who's ever tried to commit suicide. So I thought you'd understand. I know it was a long time ago, and I know you're well past all that now, but…Glaze, I just don't get it. I don't get it, and I want to know what could have stopped her."

There was a long silence. "Sis, you know there's no answer to that. But I can tell you I thought about suicide a lot when I was really deep into my depressive episodes. I've heard some people, who ought to know better, joke about a 'bipolar moment,' as if it's something that just comes and goes. But we're not talking a minor disturbance here. Somebody has to be pretty deep into despair even to consider suicide. But because of my own experience," she went on, "I do think the difference between considering suicide and actually doing it is just a matter of degree. For me, it was thinking about Mom and Dad. Even when I took those pills, and that time I tried to jump off the roof of that hospital, I kept hoping somebody would stop me. Fortunately, they did. Thank heavens my roommate found me with the pills and took me to the emergency room. And that nurse heard me crying and saw me heading up the stairs and knew I shouldn't be there." She paused again. "I'm very grateful to her now. But, looking back, I don't think I really would have jumped. It's hard to second-guess myself after all these years. But I do know I wanted someone to stop me from hurting, and I didn't know how to stop the hurt myself. I think I was just crying out for help in the only way I could figure to do it."

I paced one more time around the living room before I asked, "So are you saying I could have done something to help Diane Marie?"

"No. I'm *not* saying that. If I had really truly honestly deep down inside wanted to kill myself, I would have found a way to do it. But I must not have been at absolute rock bottom, even though I thought at the time that I was, because something inside me made me choose to take those pills when I *knew* my roommate was on her way home. And the next time, I let that nurse hold me back from the railing because I guess I didn't really truly want to go through with it."

"So you're saying Diane Marie must have been serious about wanting out?"

"For heaven's sake, Biscuit, I don't know! But it sure would seem like that. She jumped off a sixty-foot cliff. What would you expect?" She paused, and I could hear her take in a deep breath. When she spoke, it was in a measured voice, as if she were weighing each word. "I think when someone is completely overwhelmed by such deep psychic pain that there doesn't seem to be any way out of it, there's nothing—at that moment—that you could…" She paused again, and her voice wavered. "If I'd really been at the bottom all those years ago, if I'd truly been hurting so much that I couldn't see even the smallest glimmer of hope—then, no, I don't think anything or anyone could have stopped me. I guess that's really the crux of it. Unbearable pain. Unbearable," she repeated, "coupled with complete hopelessness. The certainty that the pain can never change, never lessen, never stop. In that situation death is the only choice. Why would anyone want to keep living?"

"I'm so sorry I dumped this on you," I said. "Is this hard for you to talk about?"

"Not really. I do feel it at the pit of my stomach, Biscuit. But I survived. I got help, and now I'm okay. Even after all these years, hearing of someone killing herself makes me realize how close I came." I could hear her turn away from the phone and blow her nose. When she came back on, she said, "What I'm sorry to hear about is *your* pain. I'm really sorry this happened, but you cannot read the mind of a dead woman. You can't. And if you try, you'll never be able to trust the answers you come up with, anyway. Because they'll be nothing more than guesses."

She was right. I knew that. So I changed the subject and chatted about inconsequential things. She told me the visit with Tom had been a lot of fun, but she sounded like there was more to it than that. I didn't even question her. I couldn't deal with anything more. When I hung up the phone, I cried for a long time.

FATHER AMES ALWAYS opened letters from his mother with a few qualms. He almost never wanted to read what she wrote. But this was a package. He ripped it open without too much hesitation. Last Sunday's *Atlanta Journal Constitution* fell out. Yellow sticky notes marked the pages she wanted him to see. Why hadn't she just cut out those few articles? Too much bother, he supposed.

He carried the paper to a chair nearer the window and opened to the first sticky note. The Bishop. My gosh, he'd almost forgotten about the Bishop coming for a visit. The Bishop's picture was accompanied by a rather prosaic article about some renovations on one of the bigger metro churches.

The second section had a photo of his mother. Why on earth was she in the *AJC*? He skipped through the article, something about the Board of the Manitou Society, another one of her endless pet projects. The headline on the opposite page was more interesting. She hadn't marked it for him to read, but he read it, anyway. It was a story about thefts of construction equipment. Not just hammers and chisels. They were talking about bobcats and pallets of sheetrock and dump trucks. Who could steal a dump truck and get away with it? There was a fairly substantial reward for information leading to the capture of the perpetrator. What a strange word—perpetrator. It seemed to give a certain air of dignity to the crime. He went for his dictionary. It came from a Latin word meaning *to accomplish*. Grrr. Crime wasn't an accomplishment. Why didn't they just call the guy who did it a lousy thief? That would be nearer the truth. Perpetrator, indeed. A bunch of nonsense.

He kept looking through the section, happy to know that he was no longer a part of the city scene. There'd been a series of robberies by a masked gunman at ATM's and convenience stores scattered widely around the metro Atlanta area. That guy got around a lot. Another reward offered for the perpetrator. Thug, more likely.

The comic section was on the back page. He read that with a bit more equanimity, and rose from his chair afterward with a grin on his face and a lilt in his walk. He liked those cartoons about the cavemen. Especially the dictionary definitions. Funny.

I WAS FINALLY all cried out after my phone call to Glaze. When Bob came home, he walked in slowly. I didn't blame him for being unsure of his reception. I held my arms open, though, and he walked a little faster. After we kissed and hugged for a bit, he pulled back and raised his eyebrows at me.

"Forgive?" I said.

"Sure."

It would have felt a bit better if he'd apologized for his bull-headedness, but I decided to let it pass. "I still want to discuss what went on last night, but I think I can do it without being nasty now."

"That'll be a relief." He didn't sound like he was teasing. "What changed your mind?"

"I didn't change my mind, but we have two different defini-tions, and I want to clear that up."

"Wait a minute," he said. "If you look up the answers, you're cheating."

"No. If I'm playing against someone, trying to win, then it would be cheating to look up answers. But I was just having fun by myself."

"The object is to finish the puzzle, though. To win."

"Bob, my object is to finish the puzzle and have fun doing it, and learn some new words along the way. I wasn't compet-ing with anybody, not even with myself."

"Oh."

"You play your way, although just trying to win doesn't sound like any fun to me at all…"

"But…"

"…and I promise to keep the vacuum cleaner bag emptied out."

At that he held me back at arm's length and gave me a long, clear stare. Apparently he noticed that I was beginning to gig-gle, because he folded me up in one of his wondrous hugs, still being careful not to bump my nose, and said, "Woman, once again you have confused me completely." He nuzzled his chin against my hair. "But I don't think that matters very much."

We had a late dinner that evening.

TWENTY-NINE

Monday, June 17

RALPH POURED HIMSELF another cup of coffee. Ida just sat there, doing nothing. "You okay, honey?" Ralph asked.

"Yes and no. I need to get Diane Marie's room put back into some semblance of order, but I can't face it."

"I thought you said Biscuit helped you clean it out on Saturday."

Ida shifted in her seat. The kitchen chairs needed new padding. After so many years they were squashed flat. "It's not that simple, Ralph. We got everything boxed up and organized and cleaned. But now I have to go back up there and pretend that none of this ever happened. I feel like if I put sheets back on the bed, I'll be erasing her."

"She's already gone. There's nothing you can do about it. Just get the job done and you'll feel better."

Ida glared at her husband. "Don't try to fix me, Ralph Peterson. I should have seen this coming. I should have known something was wrong. I *did* know something was wrong, but I couldn't figure out what."

He took a slurp of coffee. "If you ask me, it was pretty selfish of her to kill herself."

"I didn't ask you." She drummed her fingers on the tabletop. "How could I have helped her?"

"Are you asking me?"

"Not really. I think that's what they call an unanswerable question."

"Rhetorical."

"What?"

"It's a rhetorical question. It means you don't expect an answer."

Are all men completely dense, Ida thought, or just the one I married? "I don't need an English lesson, Ralph. I need a hug."

Ralph walked around the table and patted her on the shoulder. "Once you get those sheets back on the bed, you'll cheer up."

Ida rubbed her hands across her face, trying to iron out the worry. Her sister had jumped off a cliff, and her husband thought she would cheer up. "Sure, Ralph. I'll do that. You go on to work and I'll meet you at the store in about half an hour."

Ralph picked up his battered hat, the one he had to wear all the time now since Dr. Nathan treated those beginning skin cancers on his bald head. "I'll see you there. You cheer up now, hear?"

"Sure, Ralph. That's a good idea." She sat a while longer, looking out the window at nothing. And then she stood up. It was a start.

A BED WITHOUT SHEETS looks so forlorn, Ida thought. Like someone died. Someone had died. She couldn't keep standing there in the doorway. She ruffled her hands across the lace edging of the sheets she was holding. *I can do this,* she told herself.

She surveyed the room, halfway hoping her sister would walk through the doorway from the little bathroom. But the room stayed quiet and unpeopled. Ida took a deep breath and walked over to the bed. "As long as I'm at it," she said out loud, and her voice seemed to ring in the empty room, "I might as well turn the mattress. Haven't done that in a couple of years." Not that anybody except her sister had ever used the bed, and Diane Marie wasn't heavy enough to make anything sag. But gravity was always at work on a mattress, so she might as well do some maintenance while she had the bed unmade.

Ida set the sheets on the little bedside table, slid it away from the bed and grasped the edge of the mattress with both hands. They oughta put handles on these things, she thought. Real handles, not those little loops that would pull out of their moorings in a heartbeat. She wrestled with the mattress for a few seconds before she had it standing up on its edge beside the bed.

There was a small book lying on the light blue box springs. Its dark green cover made it stand out against the shiny fabric. She forgot about the clean sheets and didn't think about the mattress, even when it toppled over against the wall with a thump. Sitting down on the side of the bed frame, Ida reached out and touched the book. This was it. This was the missing journal. This was what her sister wrote in when she was alive. Ida picked it up and held it against her heart. "Why, Diane Marie? Why did you do it?" Her wail echoed in the empty room, but no answer came back to her unanswerable question.

FATHER AMES WALKED AROUND the side of the church toward the rectory. He was looking forward to finishing some of his paperwork. That desk was definitely turning into a pigsty. He didn't see the woman standing at the front door until she turned away and started down the walk.

"Ida?" he called out. "I'm here. Were you looking for me?" She nodded.

"Come on in, then." He reached inside the door and switched on the overhead light. As he held the door open, she stepped past him. He could see the track of tears on her cheek. After she sat down in his office, he asked, "What can I do for you?"

She uncrossed her arms and passed a small book across the desk. "Would you read this, Father? Read it and tell me what to do?"

He took the simple green notebook. It had lined pages. The kind of blank book designed to be used as a journal.

"What is it?" he asked.

"I found it under Diane Marie's mattress this morning. I've read some of it, and she talks in there about coming to see you. I didn't realize she'd done that. Her husband is very insistent about wanting the journal back, but she says in there that she told him she'd lost it. She said she could tell he'd been reading it, and she wanted to be able to write her thoughts without worrying about making him mad. So she was going to hide the journal. Then, a week or so later she came here to stay with Ralph and me. Right after she died, Kelvin told me he wanted her journal. I hadn't seen it, so I told him it wasn't with her things. Which it wasn't. It was under the mattress, and I didn't know it." Her voice wound down and she picked at the fabric of her shirt sleeve.

"Why do you want me to read it?" Father Ames asked her.

Ida reached up and pulled on her earlobe. Then she pulled on the other one. Father Ames thought of asking her why she was doing that. Maybe it was relaxing. He'd have to try it himself sometime. "I guess…" she said, "I guess a lot of it is that I don't like my brother-in-law much at all. I don't trust him. He reminds me of a snake. If she told him she lost the journal and he's asking for it now, it means he didn't believe her. I can't see anything in the journal that would justify how much he wants to get his hands on it. Could you look? Maybe you'll be able to see it."

"I can try, but I don't know if it will be of any value."

"Father, I don't want to give it to him. I never saved any of her letters. I've never been one to take pictures. I don't have anything left of Diane Marie. I want to keep her journal. I keep thinking there must be something in there that will tell me why she…why she did this awful thing."

He handed her the box of tissues. "We can't know the despair that was in her heart, Ida. When I spoke with her she didn't strike me as the kind of person who would take her own life. But we cannot always see the pain inside."

"So, will you read the journal?"

"Yes. If it will make you feel better, I will read it."

Ida stood up. "Thank you, Father." She turned and walked to the door, then looked back over her shoulder. "Let me know what you find."

He nodded as she let herself out. Then he opened the cover. *Personal Journal of Diane Marie Hartley Murchison* it said on the first page. The first entry was more like a weather report than a personal journal. The second one was a listing of house-hold chores that she was going to get done *while Kelvin's out of town. He said he'd be gone two days this time.* Then came a resume of how she'd been trying to help the elderly lady next door. Each entry was carefully dated. She even put in what time she was writing. He thumbed through the book. Sometimes she wrote early in the morning: *7:00 a.m. Kelvin just left on another of his business trips. I'm going to go back to bed for a couple of hours. I haven't been sleeping well.* Sometimes she wrote in the afternoon: *5:30 p.m. Kelvin will be home soon from the hard-ware store. I'd better get dinner on the table. He doesn't like to be kept waiting.* There didn't seem to be a pattern. Sometimes she'd write for three days in a row, then nothing for a week or so.

One particularly sad entry said *I tried writing to my sister today, but it made no sense. I wanted to tell her things I can't seem to say on the phone. Nobody sees the real me, not even her. There is an undercurrent of anger in this old house. I can't even begin to say what I want to say. So I threw the letter away. I'll just have to keep going, one day at a time, but I don't know how long I can stand this.*

He found the entry Ida had mentioned. *9:05 a.m. From now on I need to start hiding this journal. I left it on my dressing table*... The poor woman. Father Ames let the journal settle onto his lap. He ran his wide hands through his dark brown hair, clos-ing each of his fists around a shank of hair. He'd found that when he tightened his grip this way, he could pull some of the tension out of his head and neck. There probably was a physical reason why it worked, but the reason didn't concern him. He just knew it worked. Of course, he never did it when anyone was watch-ing. They would have thought he was tearing his hair out. In this case, today, they wouldn't be far wrong. Diane Marie had come to him for counseling, for help, and now she was dead. What could he have said that might have made a difference?

The journal was going to have to wait for a few minutes at least, until he could pull himself together. What could he do?

His eyes fell on the newspaper his mother had sent him. That was it. He could put some order into the mess on his desk. He started to toss the newspaper, but saw a photo that looked interesting. Maybe he'd just put the paper on this pile of things to read. He set it down on top of the Bishop's book, and ran his hands through his hair again. Aha! His mother's letter. He picked it up, crumpled it and with a cry of "Slam Dunk!" he heaved it in the wastepaper basket. Two points! There. He felt better already.

Then he picked up the journal again and went right back to feeling useless. Helpless. Ineffective. What kind of priest was he if he couldn't help a young woman in obvious distress?

THIRTY

HENRY SHUT OFF the quiet alarm clock before it woke up his wife. Thank the Lord she was a heavy sleeper. When their daughter was young, Irene used to hop up every time she heard a squeak, but as Holly had grown, Irene went back to sleeping straight through the night. Henry's recent nocturnal ramblings through the house never disturbed her. When he told her he'd signed up to go pray at two o'clock each morning, all she said was "be sure you take your key so I don't have to get up to let you back in."

Still he was grateful his alarm clock made a tiny little *ding* instead of those horrible loud *brannngggg* sounds. He hated having his ears flogged. In fact, he'd pretty much taught himself to wake up without any alarm. But then one of his parishioners had given him this lovely little clock with its respectful tone—funny to talk about a clock being respectful, he thought. Well, he'd have to get up if he was going to make it down to St. Theresa's in time. Not that anybody would be checking up on him, but he wanted to honor his commitment.

Commitment. Maybe that was what he needed to talk about in an upcoming sermon. There were so many people nowadays saying that it was okay to try something and if it didn't work out, go on to something else. That was fine for Mexican food or skateboarding. But so many people applied it to things like marriage. Wasn't the idea to stay and work things out? Shouldn't that be the focus? Of course, there were times when a marriage was all lopsided. He'd had enough counseling sessions with various parishioners to see that clearly. Sometimes it wasn't going to work out. But how did you know for sure? When to stay, when to cut your losses and split up? If he couldn't even make up his own mind about the right or wrong of it, how was he supposed to counsel couples? That was a lousy sermon topic.

He swung his feet over the side of the bed and touched down on the cold wooden floor. Doggone it. They needed to get a big fat rug in here. Especially if he was going to keep getting up in the middle of the night. This early American decorating was for the birds if it gave him cold feet. But it kept Irene happy. The decorating, not his cold feet. She went for all those patchwork quilts and that heavy maple sideboard and the cobbler bench coffee table thing he always stubbed his toes on. That was what he was talking about. He didn't like early American decor. But he loved Irene. So he put up with the furniture and the quilts and the floors. The cold feet, too. Maybe he should just get some slippers. Hated the things. But they had their uses.

He threw on his black sweatpants and a white knit shirt. The summer nights weren't too chilly, but the chapel, he'd learned, tended to be on the cool side. Sitting there without moving much for an hour—sometimes he stayed two hours—well, he got to feeling cold. Maybe he'd throw on his old navy blue sweatshirt instead. Didn't need to dress up for God, he thought. He made the switch, pulled on his dark brown soft-soled loafers, and eased out of the bedroom.

The night air had that Georgia softness to it that he enjoyed so much. He still remembered his midwestern upbringing. Didn't regret even once moving here where there wasn't any snow to speak of. Georgia fitted his mood. He headed down Juniper, glancing to his right to admire what little he could make out of the simple lines of the Old Church. What a dark night, he thought. Should have brought a flashlight. Maybe we could put in some outside lighting around the church, the way St. Theresa's did a couple of years ago. To make it look more welcoming. At the very least they could light up the sign. He had decided not to list the upcoming sermon topics on the sign anymore. This way he could change his mind mid-week if he wanted to. Instead, he was having Roger put an inspirational message there. This week it was A DEAD END IS MERELY A GOOD PLACE

TO TURN AROUND. He looked farther down the block to the corner where the sign stood and saw a shadowy someone moving next to it. Henry stopped, wondering what he ought to do. This was his chance to catch Roger. Did he even want to do that? Would attendance slow down if the sign wasn't being tampered with each week? There was no way he could get past without being seen, unless he turned around quietly and backtracked. He could go across Fourth Street to Pine and down that way.

What was he thinking? Was he actually considering letting Roger get away with this? What happened to integrity? What happened to right and wrong? What happened to…oh, good grief! This was hardly an earth-shaking event. It was just a silly young man fiddling around with a sign that he had to fix himself every week. Why not let him have his fun?

On the other hand, it was about time Roger learned that he didn't need to play stupid tricks just to get attention. It was time for Roger to grow up, and by golly, Henry thought, I'm the one who needs to do something about this. He started easing his way down the street, glad that he'd chosen quiet shoes. The figure had moved around to the other side of the sign and was hidden from Henry's view. He moved closer, pausing every few steps to give his heart a chance to slow down. This was the most fun he'd had in ages, he thought as a grin spread across his face. He hunched down a bit and crept closer until he was within a few yards of the sign. Did he call out to him now? Should he creep up on him and scare him spitless? That sure would be fun. Oh grow up, Henry, he admonished himself.

He couldn't help himself. He crept onto the grass. He could hear the letters snapping into place. One step at a time, he advanced slowly until he could reach out and touch the back of the sign. He struggled with himself one more time and then gave in to temptation. He lowered his voice to a God-like tone and boomed, "What art thou doing?"

There was a screech from the other side, and Roger's dark-clad figure tried to dash past him. But Henry was ready—

and darned proud of himself, too. He jumped out and grabbed Roger's arm. Roger spun around and fell, and the pale light from the thin moon illumined his face. It wasn't Roger. "Ariel? Ariel Montgomery? What—" Henry stuttered "—what are *you* doing here?"

"IRENE, WAKE UP," Henry urged as he shook his wife's shoulder. "Wake up, Irene. I need your help." Irene didn't want to wake up. That was pretty clear to Henry. But this was a desperate need. "Come on, Irene." He retrieved one of her slippers, the one he'd bumped under the bed a moment ago. Picking up her chenille bathrobe, he shook her shoulder, gently, one more time, and she surfaced from under the coverlet.

"What's wrong?" she asked, not even bothering to suppress a big yawn.

"Ariel Montgomery is downstairs, and I need you to come down there with me."

Irene looked at the long earnest face of her husband. "What on earth is Ariel doing here—" she glanced over at the clock "—at two in the morning?"

Two? Oh, shoot! He was late for his stint at the chapel. "We'll figure it out together, okay?" He held out her robe.

"Henry Pursey, you're going to be the death of me some day," Irene grumbled.

"Would you rather have me sitting in the kitchen with an attractive young woman in the middle of the night while you're up here asleep?"

She tied her robe firmly around her ample waist. "Glad you woke me up, Henry. I love doing chaperone duty."

"Thank you, honey," he said. He pushed her slippers close to her feet.

"Call her folks, Henry, and tell them she's okay. She is okay, isn't she? She's not hurt?"

"She's fine."

"Then just tell them we'll bring her home when we're through here. That way they won't worry. Well, they'll worry, anyway. But be sure you tell them she's not hurt, and then join us in the kitchen."

WALKING THE WINDING half block from the church, all he'd gotten out of Ariel was that she was sorry, so sorry, and please don't tell her parents, and she didn't mean to hurt anybody. Now, as he walked into the kitchen after calling Brighton and Ellen, who would be waiting for their daughter's return, Irene was bustling around making hot chocolate.

Henry watched Ariel as she glanced at the block letter she still held in her hand. She put it down on the big round table next to her, and then sat there looking thoroughly dejected. None of her usual perkiness. Thank goodness. Henry didn't think he was up to perky this time of night. Irene set down the mugs of hot chocolate, one for each of them. Henry didn't particularly like hot chocolate, but as Irene placed his mug in front of him, she gave him what he always thought of as *the look*. "Drink it and behave yourself, Henry." She might as well have said it aloud. So he nursed his hot mug and watched in wonder as Irene interrogated Ariel. It was the gentlest piece of grilling Henry had ever imagined. How did women do it? Within minutes, they knew what she had done, and why. It didn't make a blamed bit of sense to Henry. Why try to attract Roger's attention by messing up his signs and repainting that mailbox?

"He doesn't even know I exist," was the way she'd put it to Irene, with a quiver in her voice.

"Well, he certainly will know now." Irene spoke to the top of Ariel's head as it bent over the chocolate. "You do realize you ought to apologize to him?"

Ariel's head whipped up. "I can't do that!" she wailed. "He'll think I'm an idiot!"

The word vibrated in the silence of the kitchen. Irene cocked her head to one side. "And just how did you think you were going to get out of this?" she asked in a tone that somehow combined compassion with steel. Henry was amazed.

"I thought I could kind of, you know, tell him I felt sorry that somebody was messing up his signs. I thought it would be a good way to get him to talk to me, without being obvious about it."

Why not just say hello to him? Henry thought. Irene lifted an eyebrow at him and he closed his mouth.

"Ariel, did it ever occur to you that you could simply say hello to him each time he comes in the deli, and see what develops?"

"But I always say something when he comes in. All the time, but he doesn't pay me any attention! It's like I don't even exist."

"Hmm." Irene nodded. "How old are you, Ariel?" she asked. Henry knew darn well she knew exactly how old Ariel was. She had one of those minds that kept track of every parishioner's birthday. All those little details that slipped through Henry's mind like dandelion fuzz on the wind.

Ariel clenched her teeth. "I'm sixteen," she said. It wasn't quite disrespectful, but it came real close.

"And how old is Roger?"

Ariel shook her head, but Irene persisted. "Ariel, how old is Roger?"

Henry had to strain to hear the girl. "Twenty-two last November fourth."

Irene let the silence settle around them. She patted the rim of her mug, then ran her finger around it. "So, you're sixteen," she said as she circled the rim a second time, "and he's twenty-two." Another circle. "That means that when you were born, he was in first grade." Once more around the rim. "By the time you got into high school, he was turning twenty." Around the finger went another time before it stopped.

"I'm not too young for him! I'm not. I'm a lot more mature than just my age."

Irene glanced over at the M that sat next to Ariel's left hand. "Mature. An M-word." Irene sipped her chocolate and then just looked at Ariel. Henry couldn't stand it. This was nerve-wracking. They were only six years apart. Henry was *nine* years older than Irene. Didn't she remember that? He shifted in his seat, got *the look* and settled down.

"Mrs. Pursey, I know Roger and I are meant for each other."

Irene's voice was gentle. "How do you know that?"

Ariel turned her head away. "I can feel it every time I see him. Even when he's not around, it's like there's this…this connection."

"Connection." Irene looked across the table at her husband, then shifted her gaze back to the young girl. "Ariel, look at me. I mean it. Stop looking at the stove, and look at me. If you want to be treated as a mature young woman, then you're going to have to start acting that way. Among other things, that means making eye contact even if you're hearing something from an older woman that you don't want to hear."

Ariel started chewing on her fingernail. Her index finger. Henry noticed with some surprise that all her nails looked pretty ragged. Why hadn't he ever seen that before?

"Yes, ma'am," she said. At least some of her manners were back in place, he thought. He glanced over at his wife. This was like watching a ping-pong game.

"Henry." Startled, he waited for instructions. "You might want to leave the room. If you stay, you're going to learn something you might not want to hear."

I wouldn't miss this for the world, he thought. But all he did was shake his head. Irene turned back to Ariel.

"If you and Roger are made for each other," she said, "I guarantee you there is nothing…nothing," she emphasized, "that can keep you apart…"

Ariel's face lit up.

"…except your age difference," Irene said, and Ariel wilted. Henry had tried planting a garden once, and found out he couldn't get the timing right. He thought Ariel looked like his poor lettuce in the broiling summer sun. "When I was a little bitty thing," Irene went on, "I was on the school playground one day, and I slipped off the monkey bars and fell onto the gravel. Skinned my knee pretty badly. Of course, I cried." She sipped some more chocolate.

What did this have to do with anything? Henry wondered.

"We lived in a small town in the midwest, and back then the school had all the grades. The high school kids went to classes in one end of the building, and the grade school was in a different wing. As I was lying there crying, a boy rushed out of the high school wing and came running over to me. He asked me if I was hurt, which was pretty obvious since there was a lot of blood. Anyway, he picked me up and carried me to the principal's office. I don't know what had happened to the teacher on playground duty that day, but it's just as well she didn't see me. Because I looked at that boy who must have been…oh, about fifteen or so at the time…and I said to myself, 'I'm going to marry you some day.'"

Irene's eyes were on Ariel during this whole narrative. She didn't look over at Henry even once.

"So what happened?" Ariel asked.

"Oh, nothing much. The boy went back to his class. I think he got into some trouble for running out like that. The principal patched me up. We didn't have school nurses in those days."

"No, I meant about…*him*."

"Ariel, I doubt he thought a second thing about it. I was six years old. Then, when I was sixteen—" she reached over and picked up the M "—he was in graduate school. Several years later, he went to the seminary." She put the letter back down and picked up her mug. She cradled it in her hands. Henry noticed how long her fingers were. When had he stopped looking at them?

"And…?" Ariel prompted.

"And when he came back after he graduated, I married him."

The look of disbelief that Ariel shot at her minister took him aback. "Reverend P? Was he ever that romantic?" she said and then clamped her mouth shut. "I can't believe I said that," she muttered.

Irene leveled a stare at her. "Most of the time it wasn't romance, Ariel. Most of it was just me growing up one month at a time." She looked over at her husband and smiled. "If Roger's ever going to get interested in you, Ariel, he'll do it, don't you worry." She wasn't looking at Ariel when she said it. The Reverend Henry C. Pursey blushed.

"Now." Irene stood up. "Help me wash these cups." She paused. "Henry," she said, "you've got a job to do, even if you're late. You go on and I'll take care of this end. Ariel and I are going to go put the sign back the way it was, and then I'm going to walk her home. I'll see you when you get back." She smiled, and Henry blushed again. Luckily, Ariel was busy picking up mugs.

THIRTY-ONE

Tuesday, June 18

I WATCHED MY HUSBAND rummage through his side of the closet. We had talked about moving that end wall over so we'd have more room for a big closet. I hoped the wall wasn't holding up the floor of the attic. It probably was. One more reason for me to move my clothes into my sitting room closet and leave the wall the way it was.

"What are you looking for?" I asked him.

"That green shirt you bought me."

"The *his and her* shirts?"

"All I want is the *his* one."

"Very funny. But you're working today. Don't you need a white shirt?"

"Not a chance. I'm headed up to the county courthouse to research some records, and their air conditioning isn't working. The last thing I want to do is wear my uniform."

"They still don't have it fixed?" I'd read about the problem in *The Record* last week.

"Not yet." He finally located the shirt. As he was slipping it over his head, he asked, "What are you up to today?"

I yawned and stretched. "I'm going to the library to do some stuff I can't do when there are people tromping through the place." Of course, not that many people tromped through all the time, but I'd been pleasantly surprised at how our clientele had increased over the past few months. The biggest demand was for romance novels, but at least people were reading. "Will you be home for lunch?"

"Probably not," he said. "Why don't you wear your green shirt, too, and I'll take you to dinner at CT's? Then we can be a matched set."

"Sounds good, except I haven't completely gotten the stains off the back of it yet."

"Stains?"

"Yeah, some blood. When Diane Marie died."

"Too bad. We could have made quite an entrance at CT's."

I laughed, straightened his collar a bit and went downstairs to start breakfast.

THE LIBRARY PHONE RANG for the fourth or fifth time, but I left it to the answering machine. You'd think everyone in town would know by now that the library is open only on Monday, Wednesday, Friday and Saturday. They might not know the precise hours of operation, but for heaven's sake, three-and-a-half days a week was pretty easy to remember. I was rearranging the reference section on the main floor. The shelves never seemed to be the height to take care of some of those oversize books. I was going to have to take all the books off the second shelf and lower that shelf a notch or two, just so I could fit in the new atlases. Oh, phooey! Then I'd have to lower the third shelf, too, because the encyclopedias just barely fit the way they were. I sure wished Diane Marie could be here to help me. Diane Marie. Doggone it. Now I needed a tissue.

Someday—some wonderful day I was going to get real library shelves in here instead of this makeshift lot of leftovers. And she wouldn't be here to see the finished result. Luckily, since the library was closed, I didn't have to deal with the possibility of people seeing me cry. Or of them tripping over the stacks of books I was piling on the floor.

Finally, I had the two shelves moved into their new positions and was starting to replace the books. I lifted three of them from the farthest stack. I should have taken them off in reverse order. Then it would have been easier to put them back quickly.

Every time I bent over, my nose throbbed. One more reminder of Diane Marie.

Someone knocked on the front door. Luckily it wasn't glass. Whoever was out there couldn't see me inside. Where did that thought come from? I was a helpful librarian. I could walk to the door and explain gently that the library was closed. There was a sign on the front door that said *Closed* and listed the hours of operation. Why would someone who couldn't read a sign want to get into a library? This country might have a thirty percent functional illiteracy rate—a shocking figure if you asked me— but here in Keagan County we had almost one-hundred percent literacy. There had been some dedicated people teaching adult reading classes up in Garner Creek for the past dozen years or so. It was working. Okay, so that meant that whoever was pounding on the door knew darn well the library was closed. If we were closed, why would they think anyone was in here? The knocking continued. Whoever it was wasn't going to give up. I set down my armful of dictionaries and thesauruses. How many other words are there for *closed,* I wondered as I walked across the hardwood floor. The library was shut. The library was unopened. The librarian was unavailable. Couldn't they read? The librarian was ticked off.... I reached the door just as another volley, louder than before, resounded through the room.

"Hold your horses!" I called out.

"Biscuit! Open the door!" It was Bob's voice.

I turned the heavy lock. "What's wrong? Are you okay?"

"Why haven't you answered the phone?" he demanded as he barged in.

I closed the door and locked it again. "Bob, I've been work-ing. The library is closed."

"What were you talking about this morning when you said something about blood?"

"Blood?"

"Yeah, the blood on your shirt."

"On my shirt?"

"Biscuit, quit sounding like an echo and answer me!"

"Quit hollering, then! What about the blood?"

I could see him clenching his teeth. "That's what I'm asking you," he said in a more subdued but rather intense tone. "Where exactly was the blood on your shirt? Didn't you say it was on the back?"

"Yeah. There was a big streak right down the back."

"Why didn't you tell me that before this?"

I didn't like his tone, so I decided to be flippant. "You never asked me."

He narrowed his eyes, and then he rolled them. "Biscuit, listen to me. This morning when you mentioned blood, I just assumed it was from breaking your nose when you slammed into the cliff. But while I was in the courthouse, I remembered you said something about it being on the back of your shirt. That wouldn't have been from your nose, unless you had your shirt on backward."

"Don't be ridiculous. Of course I didn't have it on backward."

"So, where did the blood come from?"

"It was Diane Marie's, of course."

"Bisque...dear one...listen to me! Do you remember Scott saying that it looked like she jumped out over the edge, and she didn't hit the rock until she was *below* you?"

I didn't particularly want to remember that conversation, but it was still fairly fresh in my mind. "Yes," I said. "So?"

"So, where did the blood come from?"

"Oh..."

"Right. She was injured *before* she went off the cliff. Was there a lot of blood?"

"It was a fairly wide stripe."

"Do you see what this means?"

I nodded. All of a sudden I didn't want to be here rearranging books. I wanted to be home. I wondered if Ida would have it easier now, knowing her sister hadn't committed suicide. Knowing she had been murdered. "Yes," I said. "I know what it means."

Bob left. I threw books on the shelf as quickly as I could, and fled back to Beechnut Lane.

"JOHN AMES," HE SAID to himself in the bathroom mirror as he adjusted his clerical collar, "you are definitely wasting time this morning." He knew that Diane Marie's little green journal would be waiting for him on the top of that stack on his desk, as soon as he got back from celebrating Mass. He wasn't looking forward to reading more of it. "But a promise is a commitment. If I can't keep my promises, how can I advise my parishioners about issues of integrity?"

He squinted into the old mirror above the sink. Did he need glasses? Or was it just the dim light in here? He raised an eyebrow at the shadowy Father John before him. "Young man," he told that other priest, "get to work. Now." The priest in the mirror saluted him. Good. The underling was respectful. Grinning, he walked into the hall where he bumped into his sister.

"Who were you talking to in there?" Madeleine asked. "It sounded like quite a conversation."

"How long have you been listening, Squidling?" he demanded, reverting to his pet name for her when he was, oh, about ten and she was seven or so.

"You haven't called me that in ages!"

"You haven't looked this happy in ages, maybe that's why."

She took in a deep breath and let out a big sigh. "Yeah." She tucked her arm around his elbow. "Let's go to Mass, shall we, Sharkey?"

"Don't you dare call me that in front of my congregants."

"What? You don't want them to know you were a little kid once upon a time?"

"I think they've already figured that out. But *Sharkey*...? You," he echoed her, "haven't called me that in ages."

She pulled away from him and took a good long look. "Okay," she said. "You're not much of a Sharkey anymore, anyway."

"Thank God for small favors."

Laughing, they walked out of the rectory and headed toward the church.

AN HOUR LATER, Father Ames was reading more of Diane Marie's journal. He found that he couldn't read it straight through. Knowing that this poor woman was dead, that she had taken her own life, that she had been afraid of her husband, was more than he could handle all in one session. He had, of course, talked to Bob Sheffield soon after the death and told him of Diane Marie's fears about her husband's intentions, but Bob assured him that Kelvin's alibi was airtight. That neighbor had seen him just a few minutes after Diane Marie died. Bob said he had checked with the elderly neighbor's daughter and granddaughter to confirm the times. Father Ames and Bob had talked through the possible scenarios, trying to figure out how Kelvin could have driven to Martinsville and back to Enders within that very narrow time frame. It just wasn't possible.

But *this,* Father told himself as he read the next entry, *this* was not the word of a woman who was desperate. This was a woman looking forward to life. She had made her decision to leave her husband. She may have wanted him to want the baby, but deep inside she understood that her life would have to continue without him. If she'd even considered suicide, she could not have written *this* just two days before she died:

> ...*I have felt so isolated in Enders, and I'm coming to see that Kelvin feels threatened by every friendship I've tried to have with women. But I feel so much more alive now that I've started these tap dance lessons. Just laughing with the other women feels so—healthy! I'm looking forward to lesson #2, but I do feel I need to take it a little easy. I'll ask Dr. Young about it when I meet with him on Friday. I hope it was okay to do that painting with Biscuit in the library. That wouldn't hurt Baby, would it? We kept the windows open and there was a good cross-breeze. She's someone I want to know a lot better.*
>
> *Oh, shoot! There's no way I can dance in the recital. Baby will be here in January or so. I guess I have to tell Miss Mary right away. I hope she'll let me keep dancing, anyway, for as long as I can. Will Ida let me live with her until I can figure out a way to support myself and Baby?*

Father Ames set the journal down. How could a simple diary be so intense in its impact? He shook his head trying to clear it and turned aside to the stack of papers that awaited his action. The newspaper. He glanced at the clock. Maybe just a few minutes. He picked up the back section, the interesting one. He wanted to finish that article on the ATM and convenience store thefts.

The man was slippery, that's for sure. He'd pull three or four robberies in a couple of days and then nothing for a week or two. Then four, maybe five hits. Then nothing for a while. They were sure, the article said, that all of these robberies were the work of the same man. Father John looked at the list again.

Something seemed to sound inside his head. He picked up Diane Marie's journal and began to look carefully at the entries, each dated meticulously. *Kelvin is gone...Kelvin is back...Kelvin is gone...Kelvin is back.*

Pulling a notepad out of the top desk drawer, he started jotting down a list. When he was finished, he reached for the telephone. "Bob? John Ames here. Can I drop by and talk to you for a few minutes? I think I've found something interesting."

MARMALADE WAS EATING her dinner, but I saw her pause and look toward the doorway to the front hall. She was beginning to act like Tank.

Excuse me? If he is not around to do his job, I have to do it.

Marmalade looked back at me and then preceded me out of the kitchen and sat down facing the door, curling her sleek tail around her dainty paws. She looked like a doorstop with whiskers.

I opened the door even before my son Scott bounded up onto the porch.

"Hey, Mom," he said by way of greeting. "You must have heard the car."

"No," I said. "Marmy told me you were here."

Scott reached down and tousled Marmalade's head. "That's quite a talent, little girl." Marmalade just looked at him, although she did incline her head a wee bit. I've never known such a composed cat.

I closed the door and then gave my son a long hug.

"Are you okay, Mom?" he asked.

"While I was at the library I got some disturbing news, and I'm still a little shook up. Plus my face hurts like the dickens. Let's go have some cookies so I can get my mind off it," I said.

He followed me into the kitchen and sat down at the little round table in the bay window. "What have you been up to?" I asked him.

"Oh, nothing much. I took a temporary job with that catalog company up in Russell Gap. They're growing fast and needed someone to fill in the holes for a month or two. I start next Monday."

I wondered if he was planning on moving back here permanently? Surely he wouldn't want to keep living with his grandparents. Was he looking for an apartment? How could I find out without sounding nosey?

Why not just ask him?

"So, what are your plans?" I said.

"I dunno, Mom. I'll probably just hang around the valley for a while. There's still plenty of time to get back to Alaska before winter hits in late September."

Winter. In late September. That was when the autumn asters were just getting around to blooming here, and the *Solidago* was turning golden. That was when the Japanese maples thought about turning scarlet, and the tulip poplar trees were still as green as my garden hose. They didn't turn buttercup-yellow until October or even November. I was glad I lived in Georgia. "Well," I said, "I'm sure your grandparents enjoy having you around."

"Grandma's pretty with it. I think she likes me a lot."

I call her Sunset Lady.

I reached into the jar and put a few cookies on one of the blue-ringed pottery plates this young man's with-it grandma had made for me almost two dozen years ago when I was expecting him. "Yes," I said. "She does."

He took a cookie for each hand. "What's Bob up to these days? Did he ever figure out why that lady killed herself?"

She did not kill herself.

"She didn't, Scott. That's what I've been upset about. We found out she was murdered."

"You're kidding!"

"Do you remember seeing that blood on the back of my shirt?"

He nodded as he munched.

"It meant that she was injured before she went over the cliff. Bob called a few minutes ago and said he'd looked around up in the kenaf field and found where she must have been attacked. He's pretty sure she may have still been alive when she was thrown over the side."

His jaw stopped its chewing. He began to look a little sick. "Does that mean she was there when I climbed up to set the rope? I didn't see her."

I thought about it. "The kenaf grows pretty fast, Scott. It was up a foot or two. I imagine she could have been lying flat in the field and you wouldn't have noticed."

"Does that mean…" he started, and hesitated. "Does that mean the guy who murdered her was up there, too?" He set the uneaten cookie down on the napkin I'd just handed him. "He probably heard me climbing up. We weren't being very quiet. He could have flattened himself out and I never would have seen him unless I'd been looking for him."

"You couldn't have expected to see them, Scott. If somebody really wants to hide—"

"Why not just leave the body up there? Why throw it over the cliff? Why'd he have to do that?"

"Maybe," I thought out loud, "to be sure she was dead." My hands felt sweaty all of a sudden and I wiped them on my jeans.

"So when Marmalade started howling and spitting like she

did, it was because she saw somebody lugging a dead body. That must have looked really scary to her, poor little thing."

I was not scared. I was angry.

Marmalade, who had finished her meal, hopped up into Scott's lap and he patted her purring little body absentmindedly.

I watched the two of them for a moment. "I wonder how she got up there," I said.

"Who? Marmalade?"

"Yes. One minute she was with us, and the next minute she was looking down at me over the edge of the cliff."

Scott picked up the cookie again and took a big bite. He chewed and swallowed before he said, "Maybe she went up the trail."

I did. It was the easy way.

"Trail? What trail?"

Marmalade nuzzled her head up underneath his hand and he began to rub in back of her ears. How could he not when she was so insistent? "The trail up the fissure," he said. "Don't you know about it? A little farther down the valley from where we were climbing, the cliff sort of folds back on itself and forms a flap. Kind of like this little extra fold of skin on the side of Marmalade's ears. You wouldn't see the fold in the cliff unless you were standing right next to it. In back of the flap, there's a way to walk—well, not walk exactly, it's still quite a climb. But it's easier than the kind of climbing you and I were doing. Using hands to pull yourself up here and there, you can almost walk right up, and you don't need a rope."

I had to jump up the steep parts.

"Could the murderer have been hiding on that path?"

No, the bad man was in the field.

"Maybe so." He took another cookie. I was going to have to make another batch really soon.

I warmed up to the subject. "Maybe," I said, "he used that path to get away once we were gone."

"I doubt it, Mom. Bob and Nathan were there with the body a long time after we left."

"I suppose he could have just walked down the regular path to Beechnut Street and right into town."

"Nope," he said. "Too much of a chance that he'd be seen."

"Then where was he?"

Scott's eyes got that out-of-focus look that meant he was thinking. He wet his index finger with his tongue and scooped up the final crumbs off the plate. I was glad he liked my cookies. "He could have run away across the kenaf field, but I don't think he did that. The field's a mile wide. It wouldn't offer much cover." He licked the crumbs off his finger. "Maybe he went down the other one," he said.

"What are you talking about?"

"There's another one of those folds in the cliff less than a mile down the valley. It's even more hidden than this one. I found it when I was a kid."

"What do you mean, a mile? That's impossible. The cliff curves around and cuts off the valley not fifty yards from where we were climbing."

"I didn't mean just the Upper Valley. I meant the whole Metoochie Valley. The first trail, the one Marmalade must have used, is tucked into that corner close to where we were climbing, but the other one goes from the kenaf field down into Enders. I climbed down it once, but it lets out right in somebody's fenced backyard, so I stayed away from there after that."

"Does everybody know about these trails except me?"

"I don't think so. Well, the people in the climbing club know about the first one, but I never heard anybody mention the other one. I don't think I ever told anybody about it."

"Why not?"

"I dunno. It just seemed like a good secret for a kid to have." I thought about how often Carl Armitage must have worked the land up top. "Surely Carl would have seen the trails when he was plowing," I said.

"I doubt it. They're pretty well hidden—just sort of tucked into the land. Unless you knew they were there, you'd never see them. The kenaf field doesn't come up real close to the edge."

I reached for the phone. "Bob," I said when he answered, "Scott just dropped by and I think he has some information you need to hear."

"Have him come on down," Bob told me, "but he may need to wait a while. I just got a call from Father Ames. He's on his way over."

"Well, this is pretty important, so don't keep him waiting too long."

"Sure thing."

I nodded to Scott. He stood up. "Tell Bob I'm on my way." I nodded again and relayed the message.

THIRTY-TWO

I SAT, JUST looking at the phone. Hardly a worthwhile exercise. I wondered about those trails. Surely, it wouldn't hurt to check them out. "Marmy?" I said. "Do you want to take a walk with me?"

I traded my sandals for socks and sturdy tennies, even though the path through the woods was an easy one. We strolled up Beechnut to where the pavement ended. There was a little turn-around area there, beneath some huge old pine trees. That was where the path merged with the forest floor. I loved the way the trees moderated the temperature. On a hot day the temp dropped by a good ten degrees from the pavement to the woods. I should have brought my flannel shirt, I thought. Oh, well, I wasn't going to be gone very long.

I loved walking along there. Today, though, I knew I had quite a hike ahead of me, so I didn't linger as I normally would have to inhale the forest smell and watch for small birds and lizards. I passed the big stone outcropping that overlooked the meadow and headed straight up toward the kenaf field. Marmalade was pacing along next to me. As we neared the big flat rocks that form the top of the cliff where Scott and I had been climbing that day, she pulled ahead of me, almost as if she were leading the way. Since she was already going the direction I wanted, I followed along behind her. Another fifty yards or so along the path, she veered off to her left and looked over the edge.

It was the trail. I doubt I could have found it quickly without Marmalade. I could see now how the cliff seemed to have split apart at a deep angle. It would be possible to climb down there. But that wasn't what I wanted to see. "Come on, Marmy," I said, and turned back to the path.

I wished I'd brought my sunglasses. Up here the sun seemed brighter, harsher almost, than it was down in the valley. Luckily, there was enough of a breeze to keep me from overheating. Marmy and I walked along at a fairly steady pace. The path ran out. There was practically no foot traffic up here. But this part of the upland was still mostly those flat rocks. I knew that far to my left the Metoochie ran through the long, steep-sided gorge that cuts off the Upper Valley from the lower one, but we were too far away from there to hear any river sounds. A few birds, that was all. I wasn't a good judge of distance, but after quite a ways—a mile maybe—I could see the land to my left give way abruptly to the Lower Valley. Marmalade crossed in front of me and walked toward the edge. I knew the cliff here was higher than the one in the Upper Valley. I'd seen it from the street below. But I wasn't prepared when I looked down for just how steep and how high it was.

I heard the high-pitched, happy voices of small children. There were four of them playing in the cul-de-sac. My maternal instinct made me look around until I saw a clump of three women, obviously the mothers, chatting on the side of the street. One of the children called out, "Look! Look!" and pointed up toward me. Her voice carried clearly on the updraft I could feel rising into my face. The other children shouted and waved at me. I felt like a trapeze artist must feel so high above the crowds, so I waved back with a sense of exhilaration that seemed out of proportion with that simple act.

I wondered if the children could see Marmalade, too, outlined against the bright sky. But when I looked around she wasn't near me. She had walked farther along and was again peering over the edge. I joined her, and looked, and saw the second pathway. The second split in the cliff. The second anomaly that had allowed Kelvin Murchison to kill his wife at half past two and be seen in his driveway fifteen minutes later.

"Come on, Marmalade," I said to her. "We've got work to do." She followed me as I turned and headed back toward Martinsville. I wasn't running, but I was walking fast. Fast enough that

I was somewhat out of breath by the time we got back even with the Upper Valley. When I stopped to catch a few deep breaths, Marmalade scooted off into the kenaf field. She must have found a field mouse because I could see her jumping up every so often in the way cats do when they're pouncing on prey. Or on cat toys if they're indoor cats. Each time I saw the inverted U of her back above the edge of the kenaf stalks, she was a bit farther from me. Maybe there was a whole nest of mice scattering in different directions.

Time for me to go, even if she was busy.

"Nice day for a walk, isn't it?" I whirled around, faintly embarrassed at being unaware of my surroundings. He was a fairly short man, healthily tanned, wide-shouldered, almost stocky, wearing dark pants and a white shirt. He stood just three feet from me in the middle of the path. He had on a pair of those reflective sunglasses that make it impossible to see the eyes. I hated those things. They were so disconcerting. All I could see was a distorted double reflection of myself in miniature.

"That kenaf grows fast, doesn't it," he said. It didn't sound like a question. I nodded. "Are you headed back into Martinsville?" This time it *was* a question. I nodded again. "Mind if I walk along with you?" he asked. It was a little hard to say no since there was only one path headed that way. I shrugged.

I looked back over my shoulder at the field. No sign of Marmalade, but I knew she could find her way home. I turned to my left and began walking on the path. He paused a moment, and then moved up beside me on my left. "Are you just out for the exercise?" I asked him.

"I guess you could say that," he said. We walked on in silence for a bit. He did one of those horrible gag sounds that men do and spit off to his left. Yuch. I eased farther away from him, more to the right hand side of the path. You know how everybody has a certain personal space? That area around them that needs to stay free of other people? If you liked someone, they could be a lot closer into your personal space without making you feel uncomfortable. But a stranger, particularly a strange man, needed to stay at least a couple of feet away. This man was invading my personal space. I thought about my sister, Glaze, and her ability to set really clear boundaries, something she'd learned after having had a truly creepy boyfriend for several years. What would she say to this man to keep him from crowding closer?

"Did you hear some woman committed suicide along about here last week?" he asked.

"No, she was mur…" I started to say. "I mean, yes, I did hear about that."

I glanced over at him and watched as he slipped off his sunglasses and tucked them into his shirt pocket. I noticed he had a white line in his suntan that ran back from his eyes to the top of his ears.

I moved to my right, and he eased to his right. I was being herded, just like a cow into a branding chute—that was the only word for it—toward the flat rocks near the cliff.

"You found that trail down the cliff," he said. "I was in my driveway and I saw those kids wave at you." He moved even closer and I began to back away from him. "You probably think you're pretty smart, don't you? Figuring out how I could have killed her and gotten away with it?"

That did it. That turned me from a herded cow into a panicked rabbit. I started running and he tackled me. I've never kicked another human being, but by golly I got in a few good ones before he grabbed my foot and wrenched it. I felt something tear in my knee. I was already winded from the run and from being knocked down. I thought I would black out from the pain.

He started dragging me off the path toward the edge of the cliff. I could tell I'd peed in my britches. I couldn't say anything. I couldn't scream. I've heard of the deer-in-the-headlight effect. Well, I was right in the middle of one. I felt sharp rocks digging into my back and an excruciating pain in my knee. He must have known he was hurting me, dragging me along like that, but he didn't seem to care.

I remembered Glaze spraining her ankle when she tumbled

down the stairs last month and thought *that would have been easier than this.* Then I saw his unblinking eyes gloating over me and realized he was enjoying himself.

To buy time more than anything else, I pulled my voice together and said, "Are you planning to make this a habit?"

He stopped dragging me but still held on to my foot. My whole leg was throbbing. We were awfully close to the edge. "Don't have anybody else in mind right offhand." It was bizarre. He sounded almost chatty. "She had to go over, you know. She was still alive. And so are you. I suppose I could have choked her and left her for the combines to shred, but this way I had an alibi. And it was easy to toss her over the edge. She wasn't fighting me by that time." He tightened his hold on my foot. "You'll be number three," he added, almost as an afterthought.

"Three?" I was gasping for breath. Why was I having a conversation with this maniac? "Three?" I repeated. "Then you knew she was pregnant?"

He stopped pulling. "Hadn't thought about that. In that case, you'll be number four. Only the second one here in the Upper Valley, or the third if you count the brat she had inside her, but a long time ago this guy in Enders tried to take my girl."

It took me a moment to process what he'd just said. The arrogance of this man! "They were engaged," I reminded him, which probably wasn't the smartest thing to do, since he still had both hands on my ankle. My knee throbbed.

He twisted it a little farther and I felt the blood leave my face. "She was *mine*," he snarled. "But I took care of him. They thought he fell while he was climbing."

I had to say something. I couldn't stand the pressure of his hands. I felt defiled. His fingers had slipped under the hem of my jeans. His touch on my skin was surprisingly cool. Reptilian. The thought crossed my mind that I had just insulted every nice snake I met years ago when my son took me up to the meadow on an adventure. I looked straight into Kelvin's unblinking eyes. "You wrenched my knee," I said. "Would you at least let me try to stand up, and then you can push me over the edge? It'll be much more dignified for me, and I can't possibly run away with my leg hurting the way it is."

I had no plan in mind. I thought it would be a miracle if I could even stand by myself. But I'll be darned if I was going to get dumped over the edge like a loaded garbage bag. He looked like he was considering whether to kick me or to laugh. He chose the latter. It was not a happy sound.

"You just surprised me, lady, and I kind of like surprises. It'll be a pleasure to push you over the edge, and it'll be a lot easier than trying to pick you up. You look a lot chunkier than she was." He dropped my foot, which almost made me pass out right there, and extended his hand. I ignored it. I didn't need help from him, particularly since he'd called me *chunky*. Instead, I inched myself over onto my side. I pulled my one workable knee under me.

As I knelt there on both hands and one knee, trying to keep from putting any weight on the injured one, I saw a streak of orange flying toward me. Marmalade sailed over my head and launched herself off my rear end, straight onto Kelvin's face. He started shouting obscenities, and I looked up in time to see Marmy's long back claws raking his eyes, ripping into his cheeks and his mouth. I didn't know she could move that fast. He yelled at her and swore and tried to pull her off, but she had four feet and a mouthful of teeth actively holding on, and he had only two hands. I wondered what I could do to help. I couldn't kick him—my leg just wasn't working. Despite the noise and furor above me I managed to drag myself closer to his flailing feet. He spun around, knocked into me, lost his balance and lurched over the cliff edge with Marmalade still hanging on to him and fighting for all she was worth.

I could hear someone start to scream...and scream...and scream.

It was me.

IT COULD HAVE BEEN minutes. It could have been hours later. I had no way of knowing. I crawled to the edge and looked over. Far below I saw the body. He was very obviously dead. There was a lot of blood. I could see it even from this far up. There was no sign of Marmalade. He must have landed on top of her. I killed her. I killed her. She gave her life for me. She was protecting me, and if I hadn't tripped him, she'd be alive....

If you had not tripped him, he would have thrown you off the cliff.

...I couldn't believe she was gone. Not Marmy. But she couldn't possibly have survived that fall....

Yes, I could have, but I chose to jump onto the ledge on the way down.

...I knew it was just wishful thinking, but I could almost hear her sweet little voice making that funny, gravelly meow sound of hers. It seemed to get louder...and more insistent...and more real-sounding. There was a definite yowl coming up from below. I leaned farther out over the edge.

I cannot climb up this smooth rock...

Marmy was perched on the ledge twenty feet below me, looking up as if to say, "Come get me."

...and I do not want to go down the rest of the way like he did.

"Stay right there, Marmy," I called to her. What could I do? I could try to climb down to her myself.

Do not be ridiculous.

I could crawl back into town and call Scott to bring his climbing rope.

That would take too long. Your leg is hurt badly.

How could I get help?

Try screaming.

As silly as it seemed, I figured that if I hollered long enough and loud enough, someone would hear me.

And they did.

The End
For now.

* * * * *

REQUEST YOUR FREE BOOKS!

2 FREE NOVELS
PLUS 2 FREE GIFTS!

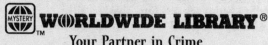

WORLDWIDE LIBRARY®
Your Partner in Crime

YES! Please send me 2 FREE novels from the Worldwide Library® series and my 2 FREE gifts (gifts are worth about $10). After receiving them, if I don't wish to receive any more books, I can return the shipping statement marked "cancel." If I don't cancel, I will receive 4 brand-new novels every month and be billed just $5.24 per book in the U.S. or $6.24 per book in Canada. That's a saving of at least 34% off the cover price. It's quite a bargain! Shipping and handling is just 50¢ per book in the U.S. and 75¢ per book in Canada.* I understand that accepting the 2 free books and gifts places me under no obligation to buy anything. I can always return a shipment and cancel at any time. Even if I never buy another book, the two free books and gifts are mine to keep forever.

414/424 WDN FEJ3

Name	(PLEASE PRINT)

Address	Apt. #

City	State/Prov.	Zip/Postal Code

Signature (if under 18, a parent or guardian must sign)

Mail to the **Reader Service**:
IN U.S.A.: P.O. Box 1867, Buffalo, NY 14240-1867
IN CANADA: P.O. Box 609, Fort Erie, Ontario L2A 5X3

Not valid for current subscribers to the Worldwide Library series.

Want to try two free books from another line?
Call 1-800-873-8635 or visit www.ReaderService.com.

* Terms and prices subject to change without notice. Prices do not include applicable taxes. Sales tax applicable in N.Y. Canadian residents will be charged applicable taxes. Offer not valid in Quebec. This offer is limited to one order per household. All orders subject to credit approval. Credit or debit balances in a customer's account(s) may be offset by any other outstanding balance owed by or to the customer. Please allow 4 to 6 weeks for delivery. Offer available while quantities last.

Your Privacy—The Reader Service is committed to protecting your privacy. Our Privacy Policy is available online at www.ReaderService.com or upon request from the Reader Service.

We make a portion of our mailing list available to reputable third parties that offer products we believe may interest you. If you prefer that we not exchange your name with third parties, or if you wish to clarify or modify your communication preferences, please visit us at www.ReaderService.com/consumerschoice or write to us at Reader Service Preference Service, P.O. Box 9062, Buffalo, NY 14269. Include your complete name and address.

WWL11B